ALSO BY CLAIRE AMARTI

The Silent Daughter
The First Wife's Secret

BOOK CLUB DISCUSSION GUIDE

To download a free Discussion Guide for this
novel, please visit claireamarti.com/welcome

AFTER SHE LEFT

CLAIRE AMARTI

LARGE   PRINT   EDITION

Chapter One

Dinah arrives on my doorstep with a massive bouquet of flowers, which actually isn't so unusual when your sister-in-law is a florist. But today, they're sympathy flowers. She's gone to trouble not to make them *seem* like sympathy flowers—they're an explosion of gold and saffron and russet, flame colors designed to raise my spirits—so I manage a smile and take them from her as she kicks off her shoes in our hallway. It's the day after Christmas and cold outside, and I'm home alone. Oliver's out working at the brewery—the new normal these days. I turn back to Dinah.

"How do you feel about mimosas? I'm drinking again."

She looks at me and I know what she's thinking: *do I take this at face value, or just start showering her with sympathy?* But one of the reasons I've come to love Dinah is that she tends to take people at their word, and she trusts them to handle what they say they can handle.

"Mimosas sound great," she says.

"Excellent."

They say you can't drown sorrows, but I'm sure as hell going to give it a go today. It's been a rough Christmas this year—Oliver and I really had our hopes up this time.

We go into the kitchen and I get the sparkling wine and orange juice from the fridge, and take down a vase from the high shelf.

"I'll take care of the drinks, you do the flowers?"

Dinah nods. It's a given that she'll do the flowers, she always says she can't bear to watch me butcher them. Apparently I lop off the stems at exactly the wrong place or something, not to mention I have no eye for arranging them and tend to just plunk them in the nearest vessel I can find. She always makes them look special.

We do our little tasks in silence though I can feel her solicitousness, the unasked *how are yous*, in the air. She sets the vase down on the kitchen island just as I top off the second mimosa. With the pale winter light streaming in, it looks like something you'd find on Instagram—the bright flowers, the sparkling gold of the mimosas, and the kitchen pristine for once. But I don't do Instagram anymore. It's too hard—all those pictures of happy women, happy moms, happy children.

Dinah picks up her mimosa and looks at me, her eyes soft. She gives me a small salute with her glass, but there's no *cheers*-ing today.

I have much to be thankful for and I know it: my health, a good home, a stable marriage, a secure job that I mostly enjoy. But there's something else I've been wanting—yearning for—for what feels like an impossibly long time now. And this time I thought, I really thought, that maybe, finally, I was going to have it.

I've more or less gotten my head around the false pregnancy thing by now but I'll just say this: it didn't *feel* false. It felt like something. Like...like a spark of sorts. Like it wasn't just me in here anymore. I could have sworn I felt someone else, the glimmer of someone else, finally here with me.

"I'm so sorry, Gillian," Dinah says. "I was rooting for you, you know that."

"I know," I say. I *do* know.

Dinah's a good friend.

She and I haven't always been close, though we've known each other since grade school. We ran in different groups back then—I thought she was trouble and she thought I was a priss—but her family went through hard times a couple of years back and I think we both started to see each other in a new light since then. And then, the fact that her on-again off-again relationship with my husband's brother finally cemented into something rock-solid was the clincher. These days Jeff and Dinah live just around the corner from Oliver and me, and I teach their daughter Josie at Birch Bend Elementary. As it happened, Dinah came into my life at exactly the right time—with most of my friends suddenly swallowed up by motherhood over the last few years, I hadn't realized how lonely I'd become—and now I can't imagine how the days would look without our friendship.

"I really believe it'll happen for you, you know," she goes on. "I'm not just saying that. You hear so many stories—people trying for ages and then, out of the blue..."

I nod. You do hear a lot of stories like that: people doing everything to get pregnant and then, the minute they stop actually trying— bingo. The ironic thing is, that actually *is* my family story. Mom and Dad had basically given up after years of trying, when suddenly in Mom's mid-thirties she had my sister Abigail and then me within a year of each other. Looking back, I probably should have taken it as a warning, the fact that Mom had so much trouble getting pregnant to begin with, but to be honest I'd always kind of taken it as a sign that these things do work out in the end. Which now that I think about it is absurd. Of course things don't always work out in the end. If I'm honest, I guess what I meant was that they would work out *for me*. How delusional is that?

"Thanks, Di," I say. "I hear you."

Maybe next month, I think to myself, trying to keep the inner voice from sounding bitter. Because *maybe next month* is what I've been saying to myself for about two years now. My sister Abigail got pregnant the month after her wedding. I just never imagined it would be like this for me.

5

"You know..." Dinah takes a sip of her drink and gives me a cautious look. "I saw this clinic that opened up on the road to Rockport a while back." She glances at me again. "A, uh, fertility clinic."

I nod. "Yeah. I've noticed it."

More than noticed, actually. Every time I pass it, it seems to pull my eyes magnetically, like one of those accidents you try not to look at but can't help. It has some cheesy motto emblazoned over the entryway like *Bringing You the Family You Deserve,* which is so insincere it just makes me want to scream. How do they know what kind of family I deserve? For all they know I'd be a lousy mother.

Maybe I would be.

Maybe the universe knows something I don't.

I sigh and look down at my mimosa. I thought it would feel like a pick-me-up, but I guess I'm not really in the mood.

Dinah's looking at me, waiting for my thoughts. She and I talked about IVF once before, although back then Oliver and I hadn't been trying for quite so long and I didn't feel so desperate.

I shrug. "Oliver's still pretty...you know."

"Ah," Dinah sighs.

We both know why my husband's so leery when it comes to any kind of medical "intervention." Dinah's husband Jeff is a bit like that too, although not as much as Oliver. Their mom struggled with depression for decades and it affected them a lot, growing up. Oliver's terrified of putting anything into your body that could upset its fragile, "delicate" balance. I've tried to convey to him that although I appreciate his concerns, it's my body and I'm willing to take the risk, but he seems to think the hormones will turn me into some kind of monster and will put everything in jeopardy—my mental health, general wellbeing, and maybe even our relationship. The thing is, he's not being totally paranoid: we saw it happen to a couple we knew. They went through years of unsuccessful fertility treatments that left them in a mountain of debt, and ultimately divorced.

I look down at the bubbles in my glass. "Plus, you know...it's expensive. And we've had expenses this year already that we didn't exactly budget for." Like the burst pipe in April, and

Oliver's surprise root canal in July. Yep, it's not been a great year. But here's the other thing I don't say to Dinah: that it would feel like failure. It would feel like failure and humiliation to me, to sit there in front of some shiny, white-coated professional and say *please can you help me, my body won't do what a woman's body is supposed to do.*

I know I shouldn't feel this way. I know if I said all this out loud, Dinah would remind me that this is in no way my fault; that this isn't failure, it's just life. But there's a voice in my head that says otherwise.

"I hear you." Dinah sips her drink, then gives me a tentative look. Dinah's pretty forthright; she'll say things others wouldn't. But even she's aware how sensitive this particular ground is.

"What about"—she clears her throat—"just, you know, getting tests done? Have you and Oliver ever had that stuff, um, checked out?" She flushes, and I probably do too. But I know she's being helpful. She likes to find solutions, it's her way.

I hesitate.

"Not exactly." I mean, my OB-GYN has

checked out the usual stuff, but that's not the same as the tests I know they can run in these fertility clinics. I lighten my voice, trying to joke. "Oliver would likely freak out at that too, though. You know how he thinks all genetic testing is basically the government trying to steal our DNA."

Dinah gives me a half-smile. She's aware of Oliver's somewhat paranoid tendencies from when she and Jeff did an Ancestry.com thing a few months back and tried to get us on board.

"You never did use those discount vouchers we got for you, huh?"

I shrug apologetically. "Unlike you, I won't be able to go around telling everyone I'm 5 percent Portuguese now."

She laughs at that and lets me off the hook—I guess she can tell I'm about ready to get off the subject. The thing is, if I'm being honest, it's not all about Oliver. I just don't know what I'd do if they ran those tests and then came back with the worst kind of news. What if they confirmed that the reason I'm not pregnant yet is because I never will be; that there's something fundamentally wrong?

Dinah swirls the last of her mimosa around her glass.

"Do you have time for another?" I check.

She nods.

"Jeff's taken Josie to the ice rink. I'm all yours."

I top up our glasses and get some snacks from the refrigerator, and we settle into our usual topics of conversation. I ask her about her family and how the holidays have been so far; if both her sisters were home for Christmas and what weird gifts her stepmother managed to find for everyone this year. She fills me in and asks about Oliver and the brewery.

My husband quit his job last year to co-found a brewery with his friend Dev, which is a dream the two of them have had for years now. I'm proud of him—it's not just a dream, it seems to be a sound business plan, too—but I have to say it's taking its toll. They're still just in the process of getting things off the ground, and his hours are longer than ever. And right now, while a busy day at work might be exactly what he needs to take his mind off our recent disappointment, I don't have that option. For once, I can hardly wait for school to start up again and provide a distraction.

"It's going well, I think," I say, and hand her my phone with the selfie Oliver sent me earlier: him pulling a pint of their first winter ale.

Dinah smiles, hands me back the phone.

"Cute," she says. "They're going to be a real success, those two."

I wish I could be as confident about that as she sounds.

Then as I'm about to put my phone away it starts ringing in my hand, so startlingly loud that I accidentally drop it. Dinah's mimosa topples in a gush of foam and she jumps up, pulling her now-wet top away from her.

"Oh no! I'm so sorry. Let me get you a towel..."

She fishes my phone from the puddle forming around it on the countertop.

"Answer it. It's your mother."

I take the dripping phone from her and steel myself. I'm not in the mood right now, but I know if I don't pick up she'll leave me one of those rambling, ten-minute voicemails which I still have to listen to, because sometimes she buries the one important thing right at the end like some kind of test.

I guess this is what happens when you're the reliable daughter. Sometimes I can't help but think how much easier it would be to be my sister.

I hit Accept.

"Mom?"

She doesn't answer right away. There's something about the pause, something about the way the air seems to crackle around me, that makes my stomach turn over and takes me back to fourteen months ago, when Mom rang to tell me about Dad. That same molasses, slow-motion feeling of reality slowing down. I steady myself. I'm just imagining it, I must be.

"Gillian," she says finally, her voice clear but taut as a wire. "It's your sister. She's..." Mom inhales. "She's gone."

Gone? My mind whirls.

"What do you mean, *gone*? Gone where?"

Mom's words come slowly, like she has to line them up in her head before she can speak them.

"Well, that's just it, Gillian. We don't know.

She's just...gone."

Chapter Two

I fire off questions to Mom that deep down I know won't get answers. I'm backed up against the fridge door, leaning against its cold, hulking mass as though it can cool my suddenly overheated brain. Dinah frowns at me from her bar stool, looking concerned.

"I don't know, Gillian," Mom repeats. "All I know it what Dennis told me. Apparently your sister left the house this morning and hasn't come home. Dennis says she left a note on the kitchen table."

"Saying *what?*" I demand.

"Well, I don't have it word for word, Gillian, but it sounded very odd to me. Something about 'needing to do something.' That there was somewhere she needed to go, and she couldn't explain right now, but she'd be back." She hesitates. "Dennis read it out to me. It sounded a bit, well, *hyper*, if you ask me. I'm not sure she was in the best state when she wrote it."

Is Mom implying my sister was on some kind

of medication, or drugs?

Was she?

I can't say I really know much about how Abigail's been doing lately. Now I wish I'd asked—but would she have told me if I had?

"What time this morning?" I say. "Why is Dennis only calling you now?"

I hear the crack of Mom's lips parting and I realize how dry my own lips are, how parched my throat is. My brain seems to have dried out too—all I can feel is a faint whirring up there like a badly wired connection.

"Well, Gillian, you know how your sister is. He probably thought..."

She lets the sentence hang, because of course I know what she means. Abigail's the impulsive one. Erratic. Unpredictable.

Selfish, my brain adds: *you forgot selfish.*

"I didn't think she did this kind of thing anymore," I say limply. It's true, my sister has changed over the years—she's one of the wealthy wives of Westchester now, not some wayward kid—but apparently, she hasn't changed quite as much as we thought.

"I know," Mom sighs. I shake my head.

"Have you tried calling her?"

"Well, of course we've tried calling her," Mom says. "Dennis has been calling her the whole time. I tried her just before I phoned you."

"I'll call her now," I say, even though if she hasn't picked up for Mom or Dennis, there's no way she's picking up for me.

She'd have picked up for Dad, an unhelpful inner voice says. No doubt it's true. But Dad isn't around anymore to untangle my older sister's chaos.

Across the kitchen, Dinah's still frowning at me, looking concerned.

"I'll call you back, Mom."

I hang up.

"Is this about your sister?" Dinah says, all agog.

"Who else." I shake my head and explain what little I know to Dinah as I scroll through my recent calls for Abigail's number. It gives me an uncomfortable feeling, seeing how very far down the list it is. We haven't really been close for years, to be honest, and things have only been worse since Dad died. Abigail did stop by on a kind of surprise visit a couple of months ago, though, which in itself was a bit odd. Westchester's more than a two-hour drive from Birch Bend so it's hardly the kind of visit you make on impulse, and I basically spent the forty-five minutes of her visit waiting for her to tell me why she had come, until she got back in the car and drove away again with me none the wiser. It was around the week of Dad's anniversary, so at the time I put it down to that. Now, though, I wonder if there was more going on beneath the surface.

Dinah glances at me as I wait, the dial tone whirring against my ear. I think back to what Mom said about this note my sister apparently left. "Somewhere she needed to be"? Where could she possibly need to be—a woman who hasn't had a job since her ten-year-old son was born and who so far as I know barely even goes to the grocery store anymore, now that she has everything delivered?

One more ring and the call times out.

I slump onto the stool beside Dinah.

"This isn't exactly the first time she's done something like this," I say. "But it's the first time since she had Sam."

Dinah grimaces.

"Right, she has a kid. How old is he?"

"Ten, I think. I haven't seen him in a while." *No answer,* I text Mom, and drop my phone back onto the counter with a slightly shaky hand. I'm thinking about Sam now, and what must be going on in his head.

Back when my sister and Dennis lived on the West Coast, she'd usually bring Sam back in the summers to spend a couple of weeks with our parents. But the last few years, she and Dennis started sending him to some expensive summer camp instead. I conjure up Sam as I last saw him—a bright-eyed kid with my sister's striking, almost Scandinavian looks. His hesitant laugh and wide eyes.

"That poor kid," I say aloud. I think of my sister, casually conceiving him a mere month after her wedding, and now casually walking out of their home, apparently without a backward glance.

And meanwhile, me with my bathroom drawer full of pregnancy tests and my kitchen cabinet full of overpriced prenatal vitamins.

She'll come back, I tell myself. Of course she

will. She always comes back.

Right?

"Here." Dinah pushes a re-filled glass my way. "I think you're going to need it."

*

My sister was eighteen when she disappeared the first time. It wasn't like we thought she'd been kidnapped: she'd taken a duffle bag and all her favorite sweaters and CDs. She left just a few days after graduation.

It was a pretty bad time for my parents. It seemed to age my father by years, and my mother barely spoke to either of us during that time. As for me, all I felt was guilt, like I'd wished this on us. Because I had, really.

As kids, we'd been close—I adored her and she protected me like a lioness protecting her cub, though the difference between us was just eleven months. But things changed. Or maybe they *didn't* change: instead of growing out of the willful, headstrong child she'd been, Abigail's defiant side only seemed to grow as she got older. What I guess had been charming in a small child turned into an ongoing battleground with my mother. By the time I was ten, it seemed like those days-long, door-slamming altercations between Mom and Abigail were a regular part of all our lives. Sometimes I'd lie in bed at night longing—guiltily longing, but longing all the same—for the day when my sister would leave home. I used to fantasize about what it would have been like to be an only child, to be the apple of both my parents' eyes and live in a calm and peaceful, sibling-free world. When Abigail took off that day, without preamble or follow-up, it seemed like all my basest wishes had abruptly come true.

She was fine, of course, in the end. She'd made her way across the country, right to the West Coast, and found a job there in a restaurant. She stayed there for a decade and a half, give or take. Never looked back. I guess my dad got over it, though I'm not sure Mom ever quite forgave it—although it appeased her somewhat that my sister had settled down with someone like Dennis, a person as composed as my sister was chaotic. Some people are drawn to chaos, some people love it. I don't. Mom never did. And it always kind of surprised me that someone like Dennis would. Dennis is one of those people that seems like life is an animal they've quietly tamed, and Abigail was always the opposite.

When they finally moved back to the New York area with young Sam in tow, I thought things might finally be different for us all; that with the benefit of all those years and all that water under the bridge, we'd be able to knit our way into being a different kind of family than the one we'd always been. But I guess you don't free yourself from the past that easily.

Then there was the time she was pregnant, and just got in the car and drove away—all the way to Big Sur, without telling anyone. In that case, though, she at least picked up the phone after getting there. It was my dad she called, not Dennis, which to be honest wasn't surprising. That's the way it always was, with Abigail and my dad. She said later she didn't know exactly why she'd done it, she'd just felt so restless and agitated. I guess everyone was all too willing to put it down to pregnancy hormones at the time. Abigail was about to become a mother, after all. We all wanted to buy into the narrative that my sister had changed, calmed, settled into herself at last.

And I guess for ten years we got to keep believing it.

*

I'm still in the kitchen, feeling dazed and a little day-drunk, when Oliver gets home. He takes one look at my face and sits down, eyeing the empty bottle of prosecco uncertainly.

"Did Dinah leave?"

I nod.

"Gillian...it's going to be okay, you know."

He's talking about the not-pregnancy. Which, yes, is probably still where *most* of my mind is at the moment, but now there's something new to worry about. I tell Oliver about Abigail and his eyebrows shoot up.

"But where does she 'need' to be?" he says. "What's that all about?"

I shrug: search me.

The doorbell rings then, and Oliver goes into the hall—the frosted glass panel is useful like that—and comes back to warn me.

"It's your mother," he says.

Oliver and my mom don't *not* get along. He just, shall we say, prefers her company at some times more than others, and I think the day we're having would definitely fall into the category of "others."

I stand up. "I'll get it."

Mom's standing on the doorstep with an agitated look on her face.

Mom's one of those very put-together older women. She's let her natural grey come in but she still gets highlights to create streaks of silver and ash, her hair sitting in an ultra-sleek bob just grazing her ears. She doesn't like to leave the house without lipstick—daytime lipstick of course, because "red before 6 would be gauche"—and I don't think I've ever once seen the woman in a pair of sneakers, and I probably never will.

"Mom..."

I hold the door as she strides in and follow her through to the kitchen, where I see Oliver has removed the prosecco evidence. I hadn't told Mom about the positive pregnancy test, and now I'm glad I didn't.

"Gloria." Oliver nods, gives her a smile I know

well—the polite one, not the warm one.

"Hello, Oliver." Mom sinks down into one of the kitchen chairs. "Gillian has filled you in, I suppose?"

"Just now." He glances at me.

"Well," Mom sighs. "I've been talking to Dennis. And to add to all this...*mess*," she pauses. "I'm afraid he's due to leave the country tomorrow."

Oliver and I exchange glances.

"Well...he'll have to cancel, won't he?"

I mean, he obviously can't leave Sam right now...

"Well, he really *can't*," Mom says. "You know how important his work is, Gillian."

Granted, Dennis's work *is* pretty important. He does something—I'm not quite sure what, I just know he's pretty high up the ladder—in the humanitarian field, and every now and again he'll have to fly at short notice to Haiti or Afghanistan or South Sudan or somewhere. It kind of reminds you to put things in perspective—I mean, this guy literally saves lives for a living.

Even so, on this particular occasion...

"You've seen the news, Gillian," Mom says. "What's going on in Myanmar, it hardly bears thinking about. His experience is needed on the ground."

"But...what about Abigail?" I say. "What about Sam?"

Mom shakes her head. "You know your sister, Gillian. She'll be back in a day or two, expecting us all to get over it and act like nothing happened."

I sure hope so, I think. I can't help but feel Mom's reconciled herself to this latest stunt of my sister's quicker than I have. She's still taking it seriously, right?

"And, well," Mom goes on. "We were thinking, since it's the school holidays...maybe Sam could come up here for a few days."

I feel my eyes widen, and across from me Oliver's do the same.

"Up here? Sam?"

"Well, I'd thought perhaps I could go down to Westchester," Mom says, "but that drive really takes it out of me, with my back how it's been lately." She looks between Oliver and me. "And to be honest, I think it would be better for Sam this way—getting him out of that house altogether, you know. More of a distraction."

"Right..." I say, absorbing all this. Because here's the other thing: Mom's been doing renovations on her kitchen for the last six weeks, and keeps talking about how her house is a building site. I'm pretty sure she doesn't intend for Sam to stay with her.

Mom eyes me. "Your sister will *have* to start answering our calls sooner or later."

I wonder then if that's part of her plan; that Sam being up here will coax Abigail home faster, hostage-style.

"I mean—" I glance at Oliver. "We'd love to have Sam, but..."

Mom nods rapidly.

"Oh good, good. Dennis will be so relieved. And that poor boy—it'll be much better for him up here. That big house in Westchester, it's so *cold,* you know."

Oliver's grimacing at me from over Mom's shoulder. All I can offer back is a little shrug. I don't think we're going to have much luck fighting the current on this one.

I knit my hands together beneath the tabletop.

I just really, really hope my sister starts answering her phone.

Chapter Three

Oliver removes the sheets one by one from the linen closet: fitted sheet, top sheet, pillowcases, duvet cover. With his free hand he pushes back his mop of brown, greying-at-the-temples curls.

"I don't get it, Gillian. Seriously, why can't Dennis just cancel his business trip?"

I keep my voice patient.

"You know it's not a 'business trip,' Oliver. It's not like he's off wining and dining some bankers in Dubai. He's literally trying to stop kids from dying."

Oliver's just always had a chip on his shoulder about Dennis, as far as I can tell. My sister's husband is what my mother's generation might call a catch. He's smart, dresses well, doesn't drink too much; the kind of guy people vote for to run things. The kind you meet and think, *he's got this.* And he comes from a pretty wealthy family, I gather—you don't get to own a big house in Westchester on a humanitarian aid salary. Meanwhile, Oliver was the student who had to wait tables every night to put himself through college.

"Of course: Dennis the hero." Oliver raises his hands in the air. "Okay, I get it, Dennis's work has meaning and ours is just boring old Joe Schmo stuff. But he's not the only person in the world who does this, right? He has a whole team. Can't they just send someone else?"

"Apparently not," I say through gritted teeth.

I wish he wouldn't act like this whole situation was somehow my idea. I'm nervous about Sam staying with us too. I don't really know my nephew terribly well, and this is obviously going to be hard on him. Ten is too old to fool him into thinking everything about this is normal.

I follow Oliver into the spare bedroom, dragging the duvet and pillow inserts with me.

The spare bedroom that wasn't supposed to still be a spare bedroom. I resent everything about this room now: the futon where a crib should be, a mobile hanging overhead, twirling in the breeze. The blinds at the window where there should be white, gauzy curtains. The blank walls that stare flatly back at me.

"I'm just saying"—Oliver apparently doesn't

want to let this go—"in his shoes I would want to be looking after my own child."

Suddenly I can't bear for him to keep talking. I can't bear to hear what kind of a father he thinks he would be in the universe where he actually was someone's father.

"Why is this so hard for you!" I burst out. "This is my nephew! We babysit for your niece *all the time.*"

Oliver looks momentarily startled.

"I'm not complaining," he snaps back. "I'm saying it's a bad idea. Besides, one evening of babysitting is different from a *week* of full-time parenting."

A week is how long Dennis is supposed to be away. I guess Oliver, unlike Mom, isn't expecting Abigail to walk in the door tomorrow.

"Good to know how you feel," I mutter. "I'm glad *eighteen years* of full-time parenting wouldn't intimidate you or anything."

Oliver gives me this betrayed look then, as though what I've said is cheating. Maybe it was.

"Obviously this isn't *our kid* we're talking about, Gillian."

I look around at the blank white walls. The

tired-looking futon in the corner.

No, this isn't our kid we're talking about.

As if I needed reminding.

*

The morning is windy and overcast, and sporadic gusts buffet the grass by the highway. Oliver turns the radio to his country music station.

"Can we not?" I say, even though our Car Rule Number One is that the driver picks the playlist.

He gives me a long-suffering look and turns the dial back, and the music stops abruptly.

It's over twenty-four hours now since Abigail left home. I called her number again this morning, and once more before we got in the car.

"Oliver..." I say. "We think she's fine, right? I mean—she's *safe,* right? This is just one of her little things."

He looks over at me.

"Okay, no one seems to be saying it," he says. "Gillian, it seems pretty clear to me she's having an affair."

I blink back at him.

"An affair? Abigail?"

Come to think of it I don't know why that idea feels so surprising, but it does.

Oliver shakes his head. "I mean, come on. This 'somewhere else I have to be' stuff…what does that say to you? I guarantee you."

I look at him, uncertain. I guess it *is* the most obvious assumption. Maybe it's just some kind of naivety on my part to think otherwise.

Oliver looks at me.

"What, you just can't imagine any woman being unsatisfied with Dennis?"

I roll my eyes.

"She'll be okay," Oliver says, and glances at me. "It's your sister. She'll be fine."

I guess I should try finding that thought reassuring.

Two hours later, we turn off the highway and switch on the GPS. We've been here—we've been *invited* here—exactly once since Abigail and Dennis moved back from the West Coast, so it's not like either of us remember the way that well. We drive through the quiet streets, and into their lush, leafy Westchester neighborhood that fills me with a mix of envy and discomfort. Big houses with mansard roofs, still bedecked with tasteful—oh so tasteful—Christmas decorations. Porsches and Teslas and BMWs. Even the dogs are designer.

We take a left, then a right, then we're turning onto their gravel driveway and the house is in front of us, ivy curling across it like some kind of artist's rendering of the American Dream. An oblivious, self-congratulating kind of American Dream, maybe, but I admit I still feel its pull. All it needs this time of year is for some robins to descend and start singing a chorus.

"Has it gotten bigger?" Oliver says. "Or is it just me?"

"It does kind of feel that way, doesn't it?"

He kills the engine, and we walk up to the front door and ring the bell. I feel oddly small in front of it. Then the door swings open.

"Sam!"

He's probably a head taller since I saw him last, and there's so much of Abigail in his face that in the circumstances it feels a little startling. His chaotic halo of pale hair reminds me of hers, and he looks at us now from eyes just a few shades darker than my sister's, with a flattened gaze that makes me shift my weight and smile too widely.

"Good to see you!" I say, my heartiness falling flat even to my own ears.

Sam runs his eyes over us, one hand on the door, the other buried in the pouch of his grey hoodie.

"I'll get Dad," he says.

He does it the usual way: by going to the foot of the stairs and hollering, "Dad, they're here!" But somehow even his yell sounds flat and emotionless. I glance at Oliver, who gives me a *don't look at me* shrug.

The clatter of heavy brogues sounds from upstairs, and Dennis rounds the landing. Classical, aquiline features, broad shoulders, and sandy hair that, unlike Sam's and Abigail's, sits neatly in place.

"Gillian! Oliver! Sorry to keep you. Please come in."

He leads the way into the kitchen while Sam slinks off back upstairs—probably for the best, so we can speak freely—and gestures for us to take a seat. There's a bottle of what looks like an expensive French red open on the bar behind him and he pushes a couple of glasses our way.

"Driving." Oliver shakes his head.

"Right. Right. Sure." Dennis is all energy. I get the feeling he's relieved to have us in the house just to have something to focus on. He pours wine into the glass nearest me without actually checking, then takes the other one and pours for himself.

"I'm sorry about this," he says. "If I didn't absolutely have to be there tonight..."

"Of course," I say, keeping my eyes away from Oliver's.

"Her timing, as ever, is impeccable. Can you believe it?" His voice is grim as he takes a swig from his glass. "I don't know," he scoffs. "Maybe I shouldn't even be surprised."

"You don't...you don't have *any* idea?" I say. "Any thoughts on where she might have gone?"

Dennis meets my eyes. *Don't expect me to make sense of this.*

"I'm not convinced there's any rhyme or reason to this, Gillian," he says. "She took off because she felt the urge, and she'll come back when she's done. That's the way your sister works, isn't it?"

"You don't think there's anything to it?" I say. "This 'I have somewhere to be' thing?"

Dennis grimaces. "If it's a reason she can't say out loud, Gillian, I don't think it's one I'm going to like."

Now I feel like I need some of that wine too. I take a sip—I was right, it is expensive—and replace the glass on the beautiful black-granite island. So I guess Dennis is thinking an affair as well. Oliver's bouncing his leg beside me, the way he does when he's agitated.

"And she hadn't been," I say, "you know, acting strange?"

Dennis sighs, shrugs. I hear the words he's not saying out loud: *strange isn't strange for Abigail.*

"What about a friend—is there a friend she might have gone to stay with?"

Dennis shakes his head.

"I doubt it. I wish she had, they might be able to talk sense into her. I've called the few people I could think of—which was humiliating, obviously. But they say they haven't seen her and I don't believe they would lie to me."

I don't believe they would either. Dennis is not the kind of guy you lie to.

Unless you're my sister, a little voice reminds me.

"Anyway, it's not like she really has friends here."

"She doesn't?" They've been here for two years now.

"I mean," Dennis sighs, "she knows Sam's schoolfriends' moms and stuff. But that's it, and I wouldn't say they're exactly close. She doesn't really go out."

I frown. This doesn't exactly sound healthy.

And if she doesn't go out and doesn't meet people, how would this affair Oliver's so convinced about even begin? I picture my sister hunched over the blue light of a laptop, flirting with some guy on a dating site. It's possible, I suppose. Anything's possible.

I hesitate.

"I know how this sounds, but...you're not *worried*, are you? I mean, of course you're worried, but...worried she's okay? I mean, that she's not..." I trail off, not quite knowing what to say. Depressed? In danger of doing something bad?

I can't see my sister doing anything to harm herself. I don't *think* she would. But Abigail's always been...emotional. Impulsive. I have no idea how she's been recently; how her mood has been. I berate myself now for not knowing—for not even having a shot at knowing, because we almost never talk, and it's a long time since I really asked her how she was.

What kind of a sister am I, I think.

What kind of a mother is she, a harsher voice answers.

Dennis swallows another swig of wine.

"I have a buddy in the police force. He said this kind of thing happens all the time; you wouldn't believe how often. He says families always think something bad must have happened, but the truth is, you just don't know the person as well as you thought you did. You don't know that they're capable of being that selfish." He shakes his head, and I see for the first time how much anger there is behind his eyes.

"Since she's an adult who went away of her own accord, she's not a missing person. But my buddy said if we were worried, I could get a call list of all the hospitals in the surrounding area and try them, just to be sure." He shrugs. "I tried, but I knew. There's no sign of her."

I nod, swallowing. I don't feel relieved, though I guess I should.

Oliver glances at me and takes the list.

"Thanks," he says.

Dennis nods, puts his wine glass back on the table.

"She just walked out that door and got in the car," he says, voice dark. "With her son upstairs. Who does that?"

I feel the hairs prickle on my neck. Sam was upstairs when she left? That's the part I really don't understand. Say what you like about Abigail and what might or might not be in character for her—Sam's the apple of her eye.

There's a thump from the doorway. Silhouetted in the light from the hall, duffel bag at his feet, stands Sam. His gaze passes over his father and flickers to a halt between Oliver and me.

"I'm ready," he says. "Let's go."

Chapter Four

Pulling up outside our house, I see it through Sam's eyes. The white clapboard siding is more weathered than I realized. The window panes could use a cleaning. And we could have done a better job of raking leaves this fall.

"Well, here we are," I say. I glance in the rearview. Sam says nothing, just looks out impassively at the scene before him.

"We'll have you back home before you know it," I continue, which once I've said it, doesn't really sound right.

"But we're so happy to have you in the meanwhile!" I compensate. "Really happy!"

Now I sound manic.

I glance at Oliver. Sam spent the whole ride staring out the back window, answering in monosyllables whenever I said something. I ended up asking Oliver to put that country music station back on.

"Well, come on in."

At least I tidied up a bit before we left. My

eyes scan the hallway, the doors that lead through to the kitchen and living room, and the downstairs bathroom. It's a smaller house than Sam is used to, by a long way.

"You can put your coat here," I say.

He's already taking off his shoes, aligning them neatly on the rack.

"Come on upstairs, I'll show you to your room."

Sam trails obediently behind me in his socks. I show him the upstairs bathroom, point out Oliver's and my room, and open the door to the spare room. I show him the space we've cleared in the chest of drawers for his things, and the hangers we've put in the wardrobe. I'm starting to feel like some kind of hokey tour guide, introducing these items of furniture to him like he's never met a chest of drawers before. My voice is too bright and I know I'm over-compensating, but Sam doesn't roll his eyes or smirk. I kind of wish he would. I don't know what to do with this detached, robotic attitude. Should I talk to him about Abigail, or is that the last thing he wants right now?

I pull the blinds all the way up and notch

them against the wall.

"You look out over the garden, see?"

We bought this place almost two years ago—Oliver's and Jeff's mom had finally sold the family home, and ended up gifting some of the income to each of the boys. The house is nothing fancy, but the garden is lovely, in my opinion—old and weather-beaten and graceful, with plants that have clearly been growing there for years. The realtor thought we'd want to cut down the big tree outside the window, but in the end it just didn't feel right. That tree had been around so much longer than we had. I've always liked the view from this room, perched at the top of the house, looking out on that big tree.

Sam nods, glancing out with me, and I see his fingers drum a silent little pattern on the sill. His face still gives nothing away. Then in the silence his stomach rumbles, and for the first time there's a break in that careful neutrality and I witness his look of embarrassment.

I clear my throat.

"So we should think about dinner, shouldn't we? Do you like pasta?"

"Sure," he says, with about as much commitment as if I'd asked about dog food.

"Okay, great," I say. "So you can unpack, or—or do whatever you like. I'll call you when we're ready to eat, okay?"

Downstairs, Oliver's sitting at the kitchen table with a freshly cracked beer. It wouldn't have killed *him* to think about dinner, would it?

I go to the fridge and start looking for things to put in a salad. We're a bit slack about the five-a-day thing when it's just the two of us, but I feel a sense of responsibility now with Sam in the house. I find some tomatoes that still look relatively firm, and turn on the tap.

"He's just so *silent,* Oliver. Do you think it's all because of Abigail, or is it his age?"

Oliver looks at me over his beer, and offers the same exasperating kind of shrug that Sam did a minute ago.

"Both?"

I get out a knife and chopping board, trying not to sound irritated.

"Well, either way, maybe you could help me out a little. Talk to him, you know, get him out of his shell, instead of leaving me to prattle on."

Oliver frowns.

"What if he doesn't want to be taken out of his shell, Gillian? Do you remember that age? Shells could be nice, comfortable places."

"Oh come on, Oliver. Just help me out a bit here."

He sighs, puts his beer back in the fridge, and comes over to help with the vegetables—which isn't exactly what I meant, but I'll take it. I push the onions his way, and soon we're chopping in silence.

Mom suggested coming over tonight—she's eager to see Sam, obviously—but I asked her to hold off until tomorrow. Now I'm glad I did. I think it might all be a little tense, adding her to the mix right now.

When the pasta's almost done, Oliver starts setting the table and I go up to call Sam.

"Ready to eat?" I knock. His door's ajar. Inside I can see he's just sitting on his bed, doing nothing, seemingly staring out the window. My voice seems to startle him.

He follows me downstairs.

"Can I wash up?"

I point him towards the downstairs bathroom,

then join Oliver in the kitchen. I look at our table set for three. Two adults and a child—but someone else's child.

"D'you think he's all right in there?" Oliver says.

Sam's taking a long time just to wash his hands. I hope he's not crying in there or something. I don't want to go out there and embarrass him.

"Just give him a minute," I say.

When Sam rejoins us he glances around and sets his napkin neatly on his lap.

"Smells good," he says. He just mutters it, barely looking up, but it still gives me a feeling of hope. I look at his head bowed over his food as he eats, the deep blond coloring he gets from my sister. She was always the striking one in the family. I tried not to mind that, growing up.

"So, Sam," I say, as my nephew silently forks rigatoni into his mouth. "Oliver and I...we're not really used to having a boy your age around. What do you like to do for fun at home?"

Sam swallows his mouthful of pasta and looks from Oliver to me. I want to tell him that this isn't a trick question.

"Um. I like watching basketball. And playing video games."

Oliver nods. "I used to play a lot of video games. Stuff you've probably never heard of."

"Maybe you could play something together," I suggest.

Sam frowns.

"Dad wouldn't let me bring my Xbox. And I don't have a second handset, anyway."

Oliver waves his hand. "I'd only cramp your style. We do have cable though, so you can watch all the basketball games you want."

Planting my nephew in front of the TV isn't exactly what I was trying to encourage, but Sam nods.

"So, how long do you think I'll be staying here?" he says then, putting down his fork and eyeing the two of us.

My heart skitters. I wish I knew how to answer that properly.

"I don't know, Sam. I'm sorry." I glance at Oliver. "If we knew what your mom's plans were exactly...We just don't know quite how long she plans to be away. But of course your dad will be back in a week." I look at him pushing his pasta around his plate, and brighten my voice. "I'm glad we could make this into a little family visit though. Your grandma's really looking forward to seeing you."

Sam nods, and pushes the remaining pieces of pasta to the side.

"Thank you for dinner. May I be excused?"

I glance at Oliver, but he just nods to Sam.

"Sure, buddy. Don't worry about it. Go do your thing."

I shoot him a reproachful look. He's practically *encouraging* Sam's withdrawn ways.

When my nephew's trudged out of the kitchen and upstairs, Oliver spears the last few pieces of rigatoni off Sam's plate and into his mouth, then gathers the dishes.

This is going to be a long week.

*

When I go upstairs to bed at nearly midnight I see a light still on in Sam's room; his door isn't all the way closed.

"Sam?" I tap, and hear him clearing his throat.

"Yeah?" he says.

I crane my head around the door. He's on his

phone; I don't know whether I should say something about it.

"It's bedtime, Sam," I say. "In fact it was bedtime an hour ago."

He looks at me.

"I can't sleep."

I can believe that.

"Well… can I get you something?" I say. "A… glass of milk, or something?"

I don't know if ten-year-old boys drink milk anymore, and I suspect I sound a bit *Little House on the Prairie*, much too wholesome and woefully out of date. When I was a teenager I always imagined myself being a young mom, a young cool mom. One who didn't use all the wrong slang and get constantly confused about what was in or out of fashion. I figured I'd just know these things.

I pictured myself getting married soon after college, having a big family—nothing too rushed, we'd have time because we married young. Four, I used to think. Four would be nice and comfortable and noisy. I pictured sons, their forever dirty boy-hands, the raucous overlapping voices; the ketchup stains and clumsiness and unrepentant curiosity.

If that fantasy timeline had worked out, Sam would be the age of that eldest son now. I look at him, bleary-eyed, sleepy or just faking it to get me out of here. He turns on his side, away from me.

"I'm not thirsty," he says.

"Okay." I contain a sigh. "But please turn out the light, all right?"

The night is cold and in the main bedroom I pull an extra blanket onto the bed. I hope Sam's warm enough next door; I left some spare blankets on a chair for him in case. I settle into bed and turn onto my side. Out the window, the moon is a tiny crescent.

The lights are off but I don't think Oliver's asleep yet. I say his name and he grunts.

"Did you really mean it earlier, about Abigail having an affair?"

I know they have actual apps now just for married people who are looking for affairs, people who get a thrill out of cheating on their spouses.

"Probably," Oliver mutters. "I don't know, Gill."

I roll over. "Is that what you would think if I disappeared—that I was having an affair?"

He sighs.

"You're not going to disappear, Gillian."

I blink into the darkness. It's true, of course. Is it odd that I feel somehow slighted? As if I'm not...interesting enough to disappear.

I roll back over on my side and stare at the tiny fingernail of moon.

When I fall asleep I dream that I'm on a beach, and my sister's in the water. The tide's pulling her out and I can't tell if she knows it; if she's trying to float away, or trying to fight it. I call her name and she shouts something back at me but I can't hear the words. I call and keep calling her, but she's farther away, bobbing in the distance, her graceful arms moving.

All I hear is the sound of waves, the crash of the ocean, and my own hollow, fearful voice.

Chapter Five

It's morning and I'm in the upstairs bathroom, peering at an ovulation test strip and waiting to see if the line darkens, when the doorbell rings.

The line doesn't darken.

I throw the strip in the trash and jog down the stairs. Oliver left early this morning, didn't even wake me before he went.

Downstairs I can see Mom's fuzzy outline through the glass door. I know she thinks it's a little hostile that we haven't just given her keys to let herself in. It's just, Mom is inclined to have an opinion on things and even if the doorbell just buys me an extra fifteen seconds, I like having those seconds to get the place Mom-proofed.

"It's your grandma," I say, when I spot Sam coming out onto the landing. He's wearing a hoodie that looks identical to yesterday's barring the logo, and he's got those giant earphones hanging like a padded collar around his neck.

I unlatch the door.

"Mom—come on in."

She swings into the hallway and spots Sam on the stairs.

"There he is! Sam, you're so tall!"

"Thanks, Grandma." He plods across the hall to us and tolerates my mom's embrace without flinching. She pulls back and beams at him. I'm startled to see Sam not just smile, but almost grin.

"I made some caramel apple pie. Is that still your favorite?"

Sam offers another from his vocabulary of shrugs, but my eye's been getting some practice and this one definitely looks on the more enthusiastic side. How is Mom getting this reaction out of him?

She leads us into my kitchen like a victorious general at the head of her troops, then starts divesting herself of the Tupperwares under her arm. This is a new thing for Mom ever since she got the diabetes diagnosis. She loves baking, but doesn't like to have baked goods in the house, so that's where Oliver and I—and now Sam, I guess—come in.

"Shooting up like a bean sprout," Mom says,

stepping back from Sam again to look at him afresh. She's clearly aglow, and I try to forgive myself the tiny pinch of envy. Mom has softened so much over the years. I see that joy on her face now that older people get when they're in the company of the young—the truly young, not twenties-and-thirties kind of young—like just the sight of Sam quenches some kind of thirst in her. But Abigail and I never got greeted like that, hugged like that. It felt like Mom was always checking us over, inspecting us, making sure we wouldn't let ourselves down in any way. Her little brand ambassadors.

She took her duty as a parent very seriously, I don't mean to undervalue that. She worked hard to make us into good people. But seeing the easy way she enfolds Sam in her arms now, like nothing is expected of him except that he continue to just *be*...I won't lie, it gives me a little pang.

I don't know. Maybe if I had a kid I'd be vigilant like Mom was too, always looking for something to correct, some flaw to diagnose and fix.

But will you ever find that out?

I push the savage thought away. I can't deal with it now.

"Coffee, Mom?"

"That would be lovely, dear."

I put on the kettle and she maneuvers the slices of caramel apple pie onto plates. Cake for breakfast definitely wouldn't have flown back in my and Abigail's day, but there you go.

Sam disappears to wash his hands before eating again—he may not be that into conversation, but he's sure into hygiene—and Mom glances at me.

"Did you call this morning?"

I nod. I left Abigail a voicemail and a text. No response.

"It's *Monday*, Gillian. How long do you think she plans to keep this up?"

It's odd the way Mom says it, as though Christmas weekends are a great time for disappearing but Mondays are just inappropriate. I take her point though. How long can this go on?

Sam walks back into the room, and Mom pushes the plate of pie his way.

"How are you holding up, dear? This is all

very disruptive, isn't it? I'm sure you're very upset with your mother."

"Mom—" I say.

"Always so restless," she goes on. "It was always in her."

"Sam," I say. "Would you mind fetching us some napkins? They're over there." I indicate the shelf above the silverware and my nephew un-slumps himself from his chair without making eye contact. I give Mom a look as he pads across the kitchen.

Stop it, I mouth at her.

"Well, who should he blame, himself?" Mom mutters back, mutinous, but she's quiet when Sam comes back to the table.

"Thank you, dear." She takes the napkin from him. "This *is* rather sticky."

She turns to me in what I guess is an attempt to change the subject.

"I'm going to visit your dad after this. If you want to come along."

Mom is always inviting me to go to the gravesite with her, and I rarely do. The truth is, I don't like how it feels there. I understand that it *should* feel peaceful, and like I'm closer to

Dad in some way, but the reality is it just makes me feel sad and raw. It bothers me how Mom seems to have come to terms with his death while I haven't. She already speaks about Dad with the easy fondness of someone used to his absence.

"I'd like to come," Sam says, surprising us both.

"Well, if you're sure, Sam," Mom says. "That would be lovely."

So once Mom finishes her coffee and Sam has gorged himself on more sugary breakfast items than I thought a person could, they head out to her car. Sam takes forever just lacing up his shoes but Mom waits serenely—another way in which she's apparently mellowed since Abigail and I were kids.

"You're sure you won't join us, Gillian?"

"No, I have some jobs to get done here."

Jobs like moping around the house. I guess at least my anger at my sister is giving me something of a break from the anger at my own body, which is basically all I've been feeling for days.

I watch Mom pull out of the driveway and find

myself calling Dinah. The florist shop where she works is busy during the holiday season, but sometimes she takes an early lunch break.

"Hey Gill." I hear the *cling* as she leaves the shop and goes out onto the street. "How's it going—how are things with Sam?"

"I don't know, he's pretty...withdrawn, to be honest. But it's been ages since I've spent any real time with him, Dinah. I don't know. Maybe that's just how he is these days. He's ten now. I just wish I knew him better, you know?"

"Ten is a hard age," she says. "I'm not looking forward to when Josie hits it. It'll be all cliques and sleepovers and tears, believe me."

I know she's trying to cheer me up, she's good at that. But today it's not quite working.

"Di, there's still no word from Abigail," I say. "And I admit this kind of thing isn't totally out of left field for her, but still." I wish someone would tell me exactly how worried I need to be. Oliver seems to think I'm freaking out more than I should be, but what if he's not freaking out enough? I move to the window, looking out over our garden. "Ollie says she's having an affair. I suspect that's what Dennis thinks too."

"But you don't?"

I sigh. "I don't know."

I hear the creak of my friend settling into one of those wooden benches they have along Main Street.

"She *adores* Sam," I say. "That's what makes it all so hard to understand."

Dinah stays on the line, silent.

"You're worried she won't come home, aren't you?"

I swallow. Apparently all it took was for someone to name the fear for it to arrive, fully formed, in my throat.

"I am," I say. "I am worried about that."

Dinah hesitates.

"You know...it might sound a little crazy, but you could always hire a PI."

"A what?" I frown down the line.

"A private investigator," she says. "I know it sounds a bit kooky, but real people do it, you know. Remember Philip Preston from high school? He's a PI now, I think."

"Okay..." I say slowly. "I mean, it's an idea. But it feels a little..."

Intense?

Premature?

Overly dramatic?

Who hires PIs in Birch Bend? I sigh, looking out the window.

"I mean," Dinah goes on, "the police won't be able to do anything. Unless they believe she, you know, left under duress, or is in danger somehow."

"I mean, she *might* be in danger," I say. And I'm not just being dramatic. That's the thing about my sister. Abigail carries a grain of danger with her wherever she goes, it's how she's always been. The truth is that what's inside my sister has always been the most explosive force in the room.

"I say just keep calling her," Dinah says. "Keep texting. She'll crack. She'll have to."

"Thanks, Di," I say.

"Keep me posted," she says.

I hang up, and sit there with my phone in my hand. Dinah's probably right, I think. We just need to wear Abigail down. Likely she's already regretting whatever impulsive decisions led her to drive off like that, but doesn't know how to go about undoing them.

I swipe open my message history with Abigail, and then to my shock I see three little dots flickering in the bottom corner. She's there. She's writing back to me, right now. I feel the flutter of relief, then anger, and it's an effort of will not to start typing something myself right now. But I don't want her to know I'm right here waiting; I don't want to make her skittish. So I just wait and watch the three dots pause, disappear, then start again...and pause, for longer this time, and once again flicker into motion. I clench my hands to avoid the temptation to just hit Call. I hold my breath, waiting. A car passes and I look out the window.

When I allow myself to look down at my phone again, the dots are gone...and I wait, but they stay gone. What feels like a full minute more goes by, until it becomes clear my sister doesn't mean to send that message after all.

Abigail, I text. *What is it? What's going on?*

Silence.

Just tell me, I text. But this time when I hit send, instead of showing up blue, my message turns green. *Not delivered.* I catch a breath. This better not mean what I think it means.

I hit Call, and sure enough, after just one ring it goes straight to voicemail, confirming all my worst suspicions.

She's turned it off. My runaway sister's gone and turned her damned phone off.

Chapter Six

I've channeled my nervous energy into a full deep-clean of the kitchen when I hear Mom's car in the driveway. I'm so angry at my sister right now. I'm beginning to think Oliver was right about the affair. If whatever was going on right now was halfway acceptable, she would just *tell* us.

I hear the door close, and then Sam's voice indistinctly in the corridor. Mom says something and then there's the crackle and swell of the television turning on, and some sports presenter speaking. I hear Mom's footsteps in the hall, and then she appears in the kitchen doorway.

"Gillian...Sam and I were talking in the car." She looks at me. "It sounds like Abigail was acting rather oddly for a few days before all this happened, according to what he said."

I was about to share my rage with her over what just happened with Abigail's phone, but now I hit pause on that.

"Sam says," Mom goes on, "that she was on

her laptop and phone all the time during the past couple of weeks. Very distracted, he said; hardly knew he was in the room sometimes." Mom pauses. "And apparently on a few occasions her eyes were red like she'd been crying." She looks at me, frowning. "What do you make of that?"

I don't know what to make of it. I don't suppose Sam's misremembering. So what was Abigail crying about? Was it guilty tears, if she already knew what she was planning to do?

"I wish I knew," I say. On the kitchen table my phone lies face up, its silent screen like a taunt. "Mom, she's turned off her phone. While you were out. I saw her starting to write something, and then she stopped, and then...she just turned her phone off."

I think of all the messages and voicemails we've been leaving for my sister, trying to trigger her guilty conscience. I guess we did. And now this is Abigail's way of dealing with it.

Mom blinks at me for a moment. But then she turns her gaze out the window and her face resets to a determined calm.

"She'll be back any minute now," she says,

her voice firm. "She's done this before. We just have to take it in stride."

I look at her.

"And what about when she does come back?" I say. "I can't see things just going back to normal. Not with her and Dennis, anyway."

Mom frowns. "Well, perhaps they can try therapy or something."

Mom thinks the world of Dennis. Oliver, on the other hand, I'd say she accepts rather than adores. His giving up a steady paycheck to become a self-employed brewmaster hasn't exactly won him any bonus points, either. I guess she's not willing to let Abigail's "perfect marriage" go just yet.

She sighs, dabs at her mouth as though she's been eating—she hasn't, and her light, shell-colored lipstick is still perfectly intact—and looks at me.

"Well, I suppose I'll get going. I'll call you tomorrow, Gillian." She picks up her bag from the table. "And by the way, we put flowers on your father's grave for you."

And with that parting line which I assume isn't intended as a jab but somehow still feels like one, she's on her way.

*

My sister was the last one to see Dad alive. Dad and his prodigal daughter.

It was last year. He'd been visiting her for the weekend. Abigail had told us she wouldn't be coming up for Thanksgiving—surprise, surprise—so Dad had decided he'd go down for a short visit to Westchester. Mom didn't go. She had a charity dinner for the library to go to, although I think it was mostly a question of pride. If Abigail couldn't make the effort to come up, why should *she* go down?

The embolism came out of nowhere as Dad was on the road home, back to Birch Bend on the Sunday night. He was somewhere just outside of Albany. Mom got a call from an EMT.

I picture my sister waving him off, standing on the front steps of her beautiful Westchester home. I picture Dad with a hand out the car window, his goodbye salute. Tooting the horn in his jaunty rhythm: *shave and a haircut, two bits.*

As for me, the last time I saw Dad I didn't even see him. I was over helping Mom apply for her absentee ballot and Dad was upstairs clearing out the spare room. As I was going out the door Mom called up, *Gregory, she's leaving,* and Dad hollered back, *Bye, Gillie.*

And that was it.

It was my sister who got his last *I love you.*

Of course it was.

*

I hover outside Sam's room and call his name again. When I've said his name a third time to no answer, I crack open the door. He's lying on a neatly made bed—hospital corners and all—with his headphones on. When he sees me he sits up, startled.

"Wow," I say, as he pulls off his headphones. "It's so tidy in here, Sam. I think it might be cleaner than when you moved in yesterday."

He doesn't smile back.

"I was wondering if you'd like to help me with dinner?" I say. Oliver's going to be late at the brewery tonight, so we're eating without him. "We could cook something together," I offer.

Sam looks at me, face blank, and I feel the unique discomfort of being found embarrassing by a younger generation. What was I expecting? For him to bound out of bed exclaiming about the joys of cooking? There's probably nothing he wants less right now than to spend an hour putzing around the kitchen with his aunt.

But then to my surprise he says, "Okay," takes off his headphones, and comes to the door. It's not enthusiasm exactly, but I'll take it. I lead us back downstairs to the kitchen, where I've pulled out a couple of recipe books and stacked them on the kitchen table.

"Do you like burgers?" I ask him. "I got some nice organic minced beef at the store the other day."

"Um." He looks around, hands wedged in his hoodie pocket. "I could. But I actually eat more vegetarian food these days."

"You do?" I say, surprised. Nobody mentioned that. I try to remember if last night's pasta was vegetarian.

"I mean—" He shrugs. "It's okay. I can eat meat. It's just something I'm trying out."

I shake my head.

"No, that's great. That's great, Sam. We should totally..." I look at my little recipe book collection. My mind's suddenly blank. What's vegetarian besides pasta?

"We could make veggie burgers?" Sam offers.

Make them? I've only ever seen them in the freezer aisle, along with those other mysterious meat-substitute items. Don't we need, I don't know, soy protein or something?

"We just need some beans and some breadcrumbs, and some mushrooms," Sam says, reading my mind. "And some egg."

I hadn't expected this from him. He's just a kid, but standing here in the kitchen, telling me what we need and how to go about it, he seems...competent, even confident, and it gives me a small, lifting feeling in my chest.

I inventory our fridge and cabinets: beans, breadcrumbs, mushrooms, egg.

"Okay. Can do," I say, and Sam smiles at me. I think it startles us both, that smile. It quickly falters and Sam busies himself looking through the different sizes of mixing bowls, then carefully rinsing each one three times even though they're already clean. Still, the smile happened, and something warms in my chest.

"Want to put on some music?" I say, remembering those giant headphones of his upstairs. "You could hook up your phone to our speaker."

He looks at me, dubious.

I smile at him. "Otherwise we'll end up listening to *my* music, and I doubt you'll like that."

He may or may not catch the teasing, but he gets his phone out and connects it to our Bluetooth. I ask him questions about his favorite artists, and he proceeds to give me a blow-by-blow discography that would make Wikipedia proud. I'd much rather listen to him talk about the music than listen to the actual music, it turns out, but I keep my opinions to myself and we chop and mix in what feels like a new, easier silence. When they're done we pat the veggie burgers into place on a baking sheet, and I stand back, suppressing the urge to say *careful* while Sam maneuvers the tray into the oven. He shuts the door and looks at me, a flush in his cheeks.

Then as he puts the tea towel neatly back over the oven rail his demeanor changes, and he casts a quick, awkward glance at me. At first I don't understand why, and then I follow his eyes to the plastic bottles lined up beside the stovetop. The pre-natal vitamins seem to broadcast themselves so loudly all of a sudden, that big picture of a pregnant belly looking so...*pregnant.*

Sam turns my way, visibly flustered.

"Aunt G? Are you, um..."

I shake my head.

"I'm not pregnant, Sam." I clear my throat, aiming for brisk. "I'd like to be. It just hasn't worked out so far."

He blinks.

"Oh." There's a long pause as he turns back to the sink. With our burgers in the oven, there's nothing to busy ourselves with now. "Um," he says. "I'm sorry. I mean, that it hasn't worked out."

My throat swells.

"Thank you, Sam."

He flushes again.

I clear my throat, and pull open the freezer drawer.

"So, we have some oven fries here. What do you say we cheat a little?"

*

After we eat, Sam hovers around the kitchen

while I rinse the plates and stack the dishwasher. I take it as a good sign that he hasn't immediately retreated to his room or gone into the living room to watch basketball on ESPN, but now my brain's wishing it could quickly Google *how to entertain motherless vegetarian ten-year-old*.

"How about a movie?" I say. "I could make us popcorn..."

"Yeah, okay," he says.

"There's a ton of DVDs inside. See if there's something there you like."

Oliver's a bit of a film addict, or used to be at least. When I met him we used to go to the movies at least once a week, although now it seems like a long time since we've done that. I know all couples say that kind of thing, but of course, most couples we know have an excuse these days: children.

When I join him a few minutes later, Sam's poring over a handful of DVDs he's pulled from the shelf.

"*Lord of the Rings*." He holds them up for me to see. "Grandpa used to love these. He had all the books. Remember?"

He's looking at me as if waiting for this to mean as much to me as it does to him, and I feel guilty that it doesn't.

"He loved *Lord of the Rings*," Sam says. "He used to call me Samwise. After the character in the books—Samwise, Frodo's friend. You know."

I guess I totally missed this hobby of Dad's. I remember him as being an avid reader of the news and adventure memoirs, but I don't remember him reading fantasy, or fiction at all really. Now I wonder what it was that spoke to him in these stories of Middle Earth and elves and dragons; were they books of his childhood, did they evoke old memories?

Dad's childhood wasn't a particularly happy one. He was the eldest, and his mother seems to have been a flighty sort of woman who then tragically died young. Dad spent a lot of time taking care of his younger siblings—three boys and a girl—but none of them stayed close. Mom says it was always a pretty dysfunctional family. One of the other brothers died quite young, and I guess the sister's been estranged for decades. She sent flowers to Dad's funeral—beautiful, extravagant ones—so I guess someone's in touch with her, but I've never met her. The two other brothers live in Montana and Texas now, and they did make it to the funeral, but it was almost like meeting two strangers. I could count on one hand the amount of times I've seen them, growing up. One of them has kids, not that I've ever met them. My Texan cousins that I couldn't pick out of a line-up.

Mom says that was why family meant everything to Dad: he'd never had enough of it when he was young. And Dad really was a family man. He was never that interested in going "out with the boys" like the other men he worked with. He preferred to come straight home to Mom and his girls.

"Well." I force myself out of my reverie and look at Sam. "Shall we watch one?"

Sam nods. "*The Hobbit.* So we can start at the beginning."

I make the popcorn, though Sam barely touches it. It's too greasy, he says, and the oil gets on his hands. He likes the movie, though, and I'm enjoying it too, until I accidentally fall asleep about two-thirds of the way in. I wake up to my nephew tapping me politely on the shoulder.

"Aunt G? You fell asleep."

I glance groggily at the rolling credits, and then at the time.

"Wow. Eleven o'clock. I guess it's time for you to be in bed, Sam. And me too, apparently."

Sam complies and starts heading upstairs while I put the DVD away, then I go and check if the dishwasher's finished its cycle. I decide to leave the unloading for the morning. I have a message from Dennis, I notice—just checking in and letting me know he's arrived safely. I want to ask him if he's tried Abigail's phone recently, if he knows she's turned it off, but now's not the time for that conversation.

I plod up the stairs and lie on my bed, waiting for Sam to finish up in the bathroom. He's not quick about it, and I reflect wryly that our water bill is going to increase considerably while he's here. I sigh and shift my gaze out the window, watching the moon above the tree line. I think about how Oliver left this morning without waking me and how now I'll be asleep before he comes home. It's not great, this new cycle we seem to be getting into.

The longer I lie here, the more my thoughts spiral outward, moving back in time and space. For some reason I picture Abigail and me coming up the drive of our old house after school, pausing at the mailbox. Back in those days I'd fish out the school letters that used to get sent home, complaining about Abigail's "disruptive" behavior or some fight she'd gotten into—snagging it before Mom could open the mailbox. I was always the shrimpy one, and I'd dig down with my skinny wrists into the locked box, bold with the thought of rescuing my sister.

I don't know when it changed, exactly—when exactly I stopped trying to defend Abigail or be her ally. Maybe over time I just got tired of it. And then there was Dad—he was always right there, ready to come to Abigail's aid.

Neither Dad nor I were fighters. Abigail seemed animated by some other spirit, something neither he nor I knew how to be, and I think he marveled at her a bit. "A spitfire," he used to chuckle when she was little. He stopped chuckling as she got older, but he still took her side. *Gloria,* he'd say to Mom, *she's just being a teenager.* I didn't point out that I was a teenager too, that I had been for years—Abigail and I were a mere eleven months apart, after all—and that I'd never once been outside the principal's office, never really caused trouble at all. Even though maybe I'd have liked to, sometimes.

I didn't set out to be "the good child". It wasn't something I wanted. But apparently Abigail had chosen "bad" and there was a role that needed filling.

Abigail had Dad. So Mom needed me. Those were how the lines got drawn, though when they were drawn and who first drew them, it's hard for me to say. But then sometimes the memories come so clearly, of Abigail and me back in grade school, how I'd look for her bright hair in the playground at recess and how I was comforted when I found it, and I wonder if there was a different way it could have all played out.

I hear Sam's door close and the house go quiet and then, much later, just as I'm drifting off to sleep, the sound of Oliver's key in the door.

Wide awake again, I decide to get up. I throw

on my robe and pad downstairs. But when Oliver glances up at me from the hallway, there's a sweaty sheen to his face and a slightly frozen look in his eye that makes me stop.

"Ol?"

He frowns at me, but it's almost like he's looking through me.

"Oliver..." I pause, feeling a shiver of disquiet in my stomach. "Is everything okay?"

Chapter Seven

Oliver frowns.

"I'm fine," he says. "Why are you looking at me like that?"

"You look like you've seen a ghost...Are you *sure* you're okay?"

He heaves a sigh, shifts his eyes from mine. "Of course, Gill. It was a long day, that's all. Some of the distributors aren't playing ball, and Dev was on the phone non-stop...it's just a bit crazy right now."

It feels a little like a reproach, as though I couldn't possibly understand what a crazy day at work looks like. Which, having heard the stories I bring home from Birch Bend Elementary, he knows is not the case. Oliver's always valued my work though, always respected it, I remind myself.

"Okay, well...I hope it gets better," I say. "I know this is a tough time."

He nods, but seems distracted.

"So in other news," I say, "Abigail turned off

her phone earlier." I checked my messages again after Sam was in bed. "My messages aren't delivering."

Oliver grimaces.

"Well, I guess if she wanted you to know where she was going and why, she'd probably have told you. The way you and your mom and Dennis must have been blowing up her phone, it kind of makes sense that she doesn't want to deal with it."

True, I guess. But not that comforting.

"Dinah was saying maybe we should get a PI," I say. "You know, to track her down. Is that crazy?"

Oliver looks at me in a way that makes me think that yes, it probably is crazy.

"I don't know, Gill. Maybe it's best to just wait it out. Wait for her to, you know, wind down."

The thing is, my sister isn't a wind-up toy, or a toddler with too much sugar in her system. I understand what Oliver's saying, and I understand why. He's the *let it run its course* guy; he believes in letting things shake out, and that somehow it'll be for the best. But what if that's not the approach we need right now?

Oliver hooks a finger around the back of his shirt, freeing it from his neck. He really does look exhausted.

"How's Sam?" he says finally.

I glance up towards the landing.

"I think maybe he's adjusting a bit," I say, hoping I don't jinx the small shift between my nephew and me that I thought I felt earlier. "We watched a movie after dinner."

Oliver looks up at me as he steps out of his other shoe and moves them to the rack.

"He probably needs to get out of the house a bit more."

A suggestion that would probably sit a little better with me if Oliver had made any alterations to his own schedule since Sam arrived.

"Mom came by earlier, actually," I say. "Sam went to the cemetery with her."

"Uplifting," Oliver says, and thumbs his phone to check the time. "Yikes, Gill, it's late." He drops his phone on the console table and moves in socked feet towards the kitchen. "Want some water?" he says over his shoulder.

"Sure."

I linger in the hallway, feeling the wave of night air Oliver brought in with him. Beside me on the console table, his phone is still glowing. When I glance down I see the Recent Calls list— two missed calls from Jeff, followed by one that Oliver evidently managed to answer.

"Everything okay with Jeff?" I say when Oliver comes back, a glass in each hand.

He just stares at me.

I point towards his phone, the screen now dimming again beside me.

"There were a bunch of missed calls?" I say.

"You were going through my *phone?*" Oliver's voice is sharp, and confusion mixes with defensiveness in my tired, late-night brain.

"Of course not," I say. "It was on; I glanced down."

He looks at me, not exactly with disbelief, but somehow angry all the same. But beneath it I glimpse that exhaustion again, and something else—fear?

"It was nothing," he says finally. "He was just calling for a chat. Wanted to know how the new IPA launch was coming along."

He dredges up a smile, and because I can see

it was an effort for him, I manage to smile back. But something feels off—it's not like him to be this way, accusatory, questioning my motives. If this is what the brewery and being a small business owner is doing to him, I'm worried. All this time away from home already hasn't been great for us. This was supposed to be an exciting new adventure for him, not something that would run him—or *us*—into the ground.

Upstairs we get into bed, burrowing under the covers quickly in the cold night. I hesitate, then shift closer to him under the sheets, and slide my arm over and down his chest. He takes my hand and pats it, places his own hand firmly over it.

"I'm too tired, Gillian," he says. "Not tonight."

*

It's 3 AM when I wake up—my phone on the nightstand informs me of the late hour—and I look over at Oliver's sleeping face. The tension from earlier is gone now, and only the tiniest frown between his eyes remains, so small I could smooth it with my pinkie. How does he look this peaceful? It's as though in sleep he's passed his burdens onto me.

A little before 4 AM I give in and go down to the kitchen to root around for the cookies I know are there: the unopened packet bought especially for insomni-mergencies. My collection of overpriced vitamins winks back at me from the counter, white plastic bottles glowing in the filtered streetlight from outside. I shake cookies onto a plate and pour a glass of milk from the fridge, hoping for a post-snack stupor to send me back to sleep.

As I eat, I stare out the window at our garden. There's a snowstorm forecast for tomorrow but the garden is oblivious, its bare branches delicate in the faint streetlight. I snap a cookie in two, and suddenly I'm picturing Abigail and me as kids, each of us down to our last Famous Amos, competing to see whose stash would last longer. My sister's fine hair in messy pigtails, pink fingers snapping her bounty in half.

Now I have two *cookies!*

I sigh, and pop a last cookie into my mouth. When I'm done I wash up my plate and glass and climb the stairs as quietly as I can, then pause outside Sam's door. It's slightly ajar, and I push the gap a little wider and look in.

Faint streetlight filters through the blinds, illuminating a room so neat and tidy that my heart breaks a little to see it. Even his few belongings on the shelf seem to be arrayed at perfect intervals. I feel a squeeze in my chest for this child who's trying so hard. It's an impulse I understand. I look down at his face, its angles illuminated in this watery yellow light: his slight frown, still soft and childish, not yet a teenager's; my sister's golden hair and lashes, colorless now in this night.

We'll bring her home, Sam, I find myself saying, the voice in my head suddenly clear and determined. *We'll make this all okay.* It's a risky promise, albeit a silent, unwitnessed one, and I'm struck then by an unexpected feeling.

It comes over me in a wave, this bone-deep desire to protect, a feeling both sweet and heavy, and it feels new and yet not new, like a long-ago debt suddenly being called in: a blood-vow I didn't know I was making, ten years ago when my only sister brought life into the world.

We'll bring her home, the voice in my head says again, daring me to contradict it.

The problem is, it's a promise I don't know

how to keep.

Chapter Eight

It's still dark when I wake the next morning and Oliver's at the end of the bed, putting on his socks.

"Morning," he says, still tugging one sock over his ankle. "Hey, I have game night tonight, so I'll be home later."

"You're going to game night?" I say.

He looks at me. "I always go."

It's true, he always does—it's a once-monthly thing he does with his three best friends, and I know it means a lot to him.

"I know..." I say, "but we have Sam." *And I've hardly seen you these past weeks.*

Oliver swings his leg back down onto the floor, turns more fully towards me.

"Gill, this is our one night a month. You know how hard it is to get the guys together since Pat and Jamal became dads."

Way to hit me in the solar plexus. I close my eyes.

"Yeah. Okay. But can you not stay super-late?"

"Yeah, I mean, I figure Dev will kick us all out pretty early anyway." He stands up, brushes down his pants. "So what are you gonna do for the day?"

"I don't know," I say. "Maybe Sam and I will go check out the farmer's market." Sam's got some foodie interests, maybe he'll like it.

Oliver kisses me on the cheek and heads downstairs, and soon after I hear the front door close. I sigh, and glance over at the nightstand, where my phone is. I check my messages—no surprise there, Abigail's phone is still off. I navigate to my emails and type in her email address. Maybe it's something about the memories that I kept having last night, maybe it's something about how tender and bruised the sky looks outside as we wait for snow—but what I feel for my sister right now isn't anger.

Whatever it is, I type, *you can tell me.*

I hit Send.

Then, phone still in hand, I hesitate, and pull up the browser app. Apparently I forgot to plug in my phone last night after my midnight cookie raid so it's low on battery, but I type *finding someone who doesn't want to be found* and hit Search.

There are so many entries. So, so many stories. Forums upon forums of people wanting to find someone they've lost: missing spouses, absent parents, vanished children; old flames, high school friends, legal beneficiaries. The list is endless. It's overwhelming, to see how many people are out there searching for someone they may never find. And then all the professional services advertising to those people: psychics and support groups and, yes, private investigators.

I find myself on a series of websites, private investigators with headshots that make them look like corporate lawyers, boasting about their success rates and all the various methods they use to find our missing loved ones. It's startling, actually, to realize how much information about private citizens is available to buy and sell. Even just on our two-hour drive down to Westchester, it sounds like our license plate was probably recorded by a variety of private companies, automatically storing data about us and where we were driving. I start to have a bit more sympathy with Oliver's general paranoia about everything from DNA testing to Amazon's Alexa.

Soon my phone battery is on the verge of giving out and I know I should take it as a sign to abandon my weird internet rabbit hole and get out of bed, but I'm in too deep now. Feeling sheepish, I slide Oliver's laptop off his nightstand—mine's all the way downstairs—and flick it open.

It opens to his Gmail inbox, and to an email he's started composing. When I say "started," it's virtually blank: it's addressed to hannah.g.feldman@gmail.com, the subject line is *Meeting up,* and all he's written so far is, *Dear Hannah.*

I frown.

Who is Hannah G Feldman? And why is Oliver planning to meet up with her? The subject line is highlighted, the cursor blinking beside it, as though Oliver can't make up his mind what it should say and has been changing his mind.

I take a breath, telling myself not to get agitated. For all I know, Hannah Feldman is just one of the distributors he's been trying to connect with, or some consultant Dev wants them to talk to. Oliver's never given me any reason not to trust him, and there's no call for me to start now, just because some stranger he's emailing happens to have a pretty name. He was wrong to get so hot and bothered about me seeing his Missed Calls list last night—but he was right about me having to trust him.

I swallow, and with some effort of will, close the laptop and slide it back onto the nightstand. I'm startled to see it's already noon.

I throw on some jeans and go knock on Sam's door. He opens it fully dressed, those padded earphones around his neck like they're surgically attached.

"Morning," I say. "So, I was thinking it'd be nice to go to the farmer's market today—what do you think? We can pick out some stuff for dinner."

He nods with what I decide to interpret as understated enthusiasm.

"We'll have to hustle," I say. "They start packing up at one. See you downstairs in ten?"

I leave him to it and head down to see if there's any coffee left in the pot from this morning. Ten minutes later, though, there's no sign of Sam. Fifteen minutes later, I tap on his door.

"Sam, if you want to go to this thing, we need to get a move on…"

"Two minutes!" he calls back, and I retreat downstairs, reflecting that my nephew's dawdling ways definitely don't come from hyper-efficient Dennis. Sam finally makes his way down the stairs but the dallying still isn't over; I swear I see him actually *untying* his perfectly tied laces and starting again.

"We're not visiting the Queen of England, Sam," I say, and he looks at me, confused.

"Never mind," I sigh. "Maybe you can tie your shoes in the car?"

He shakes his head.

"No, I've got them. It's fine."

We get in the car finally, and drive out towards the main square where the market's on. They're still forecasting snow later and although the day is bright, you can almost feel the ice in the air.

"Radio?" I say to Sam, and he nods.

"It's set to WGNA," I say. "But you can change it to something you prefer."

He does, after grimacing a little at the country music. I glance over as he fiddles with the dial and notice how his fingers are all chapped at the tips.

"Sam, your hands—does that always happen in winter?"

He moves his hand away, looking self-conscious.

"It's fine," he says. "It just happens."

"I have some cream at home," I say. "Remind me to get it for you when we go back."

"I don't *want* your cream," he snaps, and I stare at him, wondering where this outburst is coming from.

"Nobody's forcing it on you, Sam," I say calmly. "I'm not trying to be your mom here or anything. I just want you to be comfortable."

He shrinks into his hoodie, turning away from me to stare out the window.

"Sorry," he mumbles after a while, so quiet I can barely hear it.

We make it to the market in time for the organic, outdoor version of Supermarket Sweep. All the usual stalls are out—only a couple have started to pack up—and I wave to Dinah's sister, who's at her usual stall in the far corner. Lottie went off to some culinary course a while back, and nowadays has her own stand with homemade breads and baked goods. She does this raisin twist bread that Oliver likes a lot.

"Hey, Lottie." I go over with Sam in tow. "This is my nephew, Sam. He's staying with us for a few days."

She smiles at him.

"Hey, Sam. Tell your aunt to buy you some treats for later, okay? I think you might like the apple turnovers."

I shake my head.

"You're a hard sell." It's all in jest; she knows I never pass her stall without buying something. "So," I say, "how were your holidays?"

Lottie gives me the rundown, which is more or less what I'd already heard from Dinah, and then tells me that business is going well: she's even looking at getting her own pop-up store on Main Street, since apparently the woman who owns Dinah's florist store also leases the small building next door.

"Speaking of which, have you been talking to Dinah recently?"

"Just yesterday," I say, wondering if she's driving at something. Dinah and I talk all the time, so it's hardly unusual.

Lottie nods, looking slightly flustered.

"Right. Right, of course. Hey, did you want one of the raisin breads? I saved the last one for you."

"You did? Oliver will thank his stars." I turn around. "Sam, what do you want? I recommend the apple turnovers, Lottie's right."

"Sounds good."

We collect our bags and head to the produce section and I put the odd comment from Lottie out of my head. I have enough sister drama of my own going on without getting involved in whatever's happening between her and Dinah.

"How about one of these for tonight?" I say, as we get to a stand filled with fat butternut squashes.

Sam nods, and I pick up a couple, weighing them in my hands.

"Hey, Aunt G—how come you're not wearing your ring?"

My gloves are stuffed in my pocket and Sam's right about my bare ring finger. After putting myself on this gluten-free, sugar-free, fun-free regimen—not to mention giving up alcohol for a couple of months—I've lost weight from all the places I didn't want to lose weight from. My wedding ring's been slipping off my finger recently, so I finally decided to leave it on the little jewelry tray by my bed for now.

"It's not fitting anymore," I say.

Sam looks at me from beneath his messy hair.

"The ring?" he says, his voice very quiet.

I glance at him. Did he think I meant my *marriage?*

"Sam," I say. "Everything's fine. I promise. I just need to put a bit of weight back on these fingers." I wiggle them, trying to make a joke. "Come on, let's get what we need and get out of here. It's cold." But despite myself, as we walk back to the car, I flash back to the Hannah Feldman email and wonder how long it will take Oliver to notice that I'm not wearing my wedding ring.

*

Sam agrees to stop in at Mom's quickly on the way home, so we take a different route back from the market.

To my chagrin we hit a red light at the intersection beside the fertility clinic. I try not to glance over, ignoring the building that dances just outside my field of vision, daring me to look.

"Um." Sam's voice cuts through. "The light's green."

"Right, thanks." Embarrassed, I hurry up before anyone starts beeping.

As we drive on I point out the "landmarks" on the rest of our route, among them the school where I teach. Sam pulls on the strings of his hoodie and stares out at the low-slung, redbrick building. It looks so quiet, so dormant during the holidays—as though it's been empty for months, not days.

"Do you like teaching?" he asks.

I nod. "I do. It's hard though. Harder than it seemed when I was your age. I thought teaching looked easy back then. And there's a *lot* of homework."

"There is?" He looks nonplussed.

"Way more than you get."

Sam grimaces.

"Your grandpa encouraged me to become a teacher, you know," I say.

Dad always thought teaching was a wonderful profession. He fully understood that the real job was teaching students *how* to think, not just ramming their heads full of facts. *God bless curiosity,* he'd say—most of the time sincerely, but some of the time jokingly, like when we'd see nosy Mrs. Harding's curtains twitching as we drove by.

"Curiosity is being skeptical of the right things," he told me once. "It means being skeptical of ideas, but not of people. Someone tells you to swallow an idea whole, you just have a think about where that idea comes from. But spend your life being skeptical of people?" He shook his head. "That's a quick way to corrode the soul."

Dad loved people: even the people he didn't like, he kind of loved. Even Mrs. Harding and her twitching curtains.

"What about you, Sam?" I say. I feel like I'm treading cautiously. We haven't talked much about Sam's "real" life, back home in Westchester. I'm afraid that asking him too much about it will just rub salt in the wound.

"What do you mean, what about me?" He glances back out the window.

"Well, what would you like to do for a job one day?" I avoid using the term *when you grow up,* because the older I get the less that term makes sense to me.

"Um." Sam looks at me. "Promise you won't laugh?"

"I would never."

He fiddles with his hoodie strings again. "I think I'd like to be an astronaut. I mean," he goes on, "I know it's really hard and there's lots of training. But it would be so awesome, seeing the earth from super far away. Seeing everything." He pauses. "Plus you get all those special meals. And astronaut ice cream."

"It would be pretty spectacular," I concede. "Wouldn't it be a little lonely, though?"

Sam considers it. "I don't think so. I don't feel lonely in Nature, and Space is like Nature, just bigger."

I smile, turning that one over as I pull up into Mom's driveway. "I guess it is, Samwise."

He looks at me, surprised.

"Your grandpa was right." I shrug. "It's a good name for you."

Mom gives Sam a hero's welcome, and leads us into the kitchen. She's left her novel planted wide open on the table to keep the page—it's a sign of her enthusiasm to see her grandson that she didn't even take the extra second to use a bookmark, because Mom always says she can't abide a cracked spine.

"I was thinking," she says, "we should all do something for New Year's, since Sam's here this year. What do you think?"

New Year's Eve is in two days' time, and Dennis is due to fly back on the first. I look at Mom, wondering if she's expecting to have heard from Abigail by then; if she's imagining Abigail sitting down for a New Year's celebration with us.

"Sure," I say tentatively. "What do you think, Sam?"

"Yeah, I guess."

"Excellent," Mom says, and I remind myself to tell Oliver we have plans. I'm not sure he'll be exactly thrilled to spend New Year's Eve with Mom, but he'll get over it.

Mom's just putting on some tea when my phone rings: Dennis.

I look up at Mom and Sam.

"I'll just take this quickly."

I go out into the hallway in case there's anything Dennis has to say that shouldn't be overhead. Outside, the sky is low and heavy now, the promised snow storm on its way.

"Gillian?" He must be on a Wi-Fi connection: his voice sounds unnervingly close, yet hollow, and I picture it bouncing down those hundreds and thousands of miles of fiber-optic cable.

"Dennis! Hi."

"So I have an update," he says. I can't read his voice right now, but I can tell it's not an update he's happy about, and my heart jitters with anticipation.

"We know where she is," he says

"You *do*?" I so want this to be good news. But the way he's saying it, I don't feel like it will be.

Dennis clears his throat.

"Apparently—" He pauses. "Well, apparently, Gillian, your sister has found her way to Miami."

Chapter Nine

"*Miami?*" I picture Ocean Drive, fishbowl-size cocktails. "But we don't know anyone in Miami," I say stupidly.

The line hisses with a sharp exhale.

"I didn't think you did," Dennis says.

My brain is starting to tick. "Wait, how do you know?" I say. "Have you spoken to her? Did she call you?"

"No." His voice is taut as a wire. "I know because a credit card transaction came through online."

"Okay," I say, my brain whirring. "Let's...let's not jump to conclusions." Even though I can't figure out what conclusions, exactly, those would be. "The main thing is she's safe, right?" *She's not in the hospital. She didn't step in front of a car or jump off a building.*

"Well, get this," Dennis says. "The credit card charge? It was at a florist's store."

Now I'm truly at sea.

Food, gas, a RiteAid pit stop, any of those

would have made some sense. But a florist store in Miami?

Buying rose petals for the love-motel, I hear Oliver's wry voice saying.

The momentary relief has passed, and like an ocean filling a hole in the sand, my brain rushes in with other feelings. Angrier ones.

"I...what do we do?" I say finally.

"Well, I'm cutting off her credit cards," Dennis says. "I should have done that before."

It feels surreal, this conversation—like my sister is a rat in a maze, some creature we're trying to force down an exit route.

"Do you...do you think we should hire someone?" I say. I can't believe I'm saying it. "Someone like a PI, I mean—a professional."

There's a silence at the other end of the line.

"I don't know, Gillian," he says after a while. "Maybe."

We're silent for a moment.

"What about Sam—do we tell him? About Miami, I mean?"

Dennis hesitates.

"Better not. Not until we know more."

I nod, even though I know he can't see it.

"Can I talk to him?" Dennis says.

I walk back into the kitchen and motion to Sam, who looks up from his phone.

"Your dad."

He takes the phone, tentative.

"Hey Dad."

I go over to where Mom's standing by the kettle, her hands cupped around a mug. She raises her eyebrows at the look on my face.

"I'll tell you outside," I murmur, as Sam's monosyllabic answers punctuate the conversation with his dad.

Miami, I think.

What is she doing?

*

Guess I picked the right sister, Oliver texts back when I message him about Dennis's news. He can joke about it, but I can't. Why hasn't she even attempted to offer us any reassurances besides that note on the kitchen table claiming she'd be "back soon"?

A butternut squash risotto is cooking on the stove, and I sit at the kitchen table and stare out the window. Outside the storm is coming in as forecast, the sky a tender grey-purple. The first flakes are so delicate that it's impossible to tell the exact moment it begins.

Life's like that, isn't it? You never see the beginning of things. Even looking back, sometimes it's impossible to pinpoint. To say, *there: that was the moment when everything changed.*

I look out at the tree branches slowly frosting with snow, the harmony of light and dark. I think about how I could wind back the past like a film reel and still not know the starting points of any of the things that have changed my life. Like this chasm between my sister and me—when exactly did that begin? When did our family become the way it became?

As impossible as pinpointing the moment you fall in love, or the moment that love ends. Most of the time there's no clear before and after when your world changes—only a slow landslide, quiet as a lullaby.

Inside in the living room, Sam's TV show has given way to a commercial break, and I sink onto the sofa to the sound of perky voices touting car insurance, followed by the Grinch advertising the Christmas gift of 23AndMe. Sam chuckles along as the cranky Grinch uncovers his genetic history.

"Hilarious," Sam says of the ad and turns to me.

"Aunt G, can you do Spock hands?" He demonstrates one of those it's-in-your-genes party tricks I've never been able to manage.

I shake my head.

"This guy in my grade can wiggle his ears," Sam adds. "All his brothers can too."

I sigh and wonder why this stuff even matters to us.

I remember the first time I heard that Kahlil Gibran poem: *Your children are not your children,* it begins. *They come through you but not from you, and though they are with you yet they belong not to you.*

So why does it matter to everyone—and why does it matter to *me*—that a child I raise should have my smile, or Oliver's nose, or our love of pistachio nuts? Is it just some kind of narcissism? And if it is, why do I want it so much?

*

It's only as I'm getting ready for bed that I remember I never did my ovulation test this morning. I'm usually really careful around this time of the month, but admittedly I've been pretty distracted the last few days.

I get the test strips out from under the sink where they live next to the army of pregnancy tests I bought in bulk online, back in more optimistic days. I thought I was overdoing it; I never thought I'd need this many.

And there it is: a dark blue line. I verify it on the digital reader, picturing Oliver over at Dev's house with his buddies. I guess Dev didn't "kick them out early" after all.

Are you coming back soon? I text.

Oliver doesn't text back.

Fifteen minutes later I decide to call—I don't care if it's embarrassing for him, he can make something up—but the call goes to voicemail and I grit my teeth. Of course it would be tonight.

I go to bed intending to stay awake until he gets home, but once it's midnight I decide there's no point and I might as well get some sleep. But now, of course, I'm seething so much that I can do nothing but toss and turn until I hear the car, the footsteps, the swing of the front door.

He takes long enough coming up the stairs that I know he's drunk. He shuffles into the bedroom as I sit up and turn on the light.

"Son of a-!" Startled, he grabs the door frame for stability. "Gillian! You scared me. I was tryna be quiet."

He smells like beer and his words sound loose.

"Did you get my voicemail?" I say, even though it seems pretty clear that he hasn't.

He looks puzzled.

"What voicemail?"

His obliviousness makes me want to scream. Instead I just hold up the digital reader lying on my nightstand and his mouth widens into an O shape.

"You're ovulating?" he stage whispers.

Seconds later his pants are on the floor, he's pulling his T-shirt over his head.

"Oliver..."

"Let's do this," he pants. "You're ovulating."

I wince.

"Can you just, I don't know, brush your teeth first?"

He stares at me like *I'm* the one who just ruined the moment, and sulks off to the bathroom. When he comes back I will myself to forget the evening it's been, and the fact that my husband has turned into a bleary-eyed frat boy. *Business not romance,* I tell myself. Maybe tomorrow we can have romance.

But after about ten minutes, Oliver rolls away from me, panting.

"I'm sorry," he wheezes. "It must be the beer. I...yeah, I don't think this is going to happen tonight. I'm sorry, Gill."

I close my eyes and lock my voice down in my lungs so this feeling inside me doesn't emerge in a neighborhood-waking scream.

"Gillian?" His breath is hot on my chin. "Gillian, it's not that big a deal, we'll try again tomorrow, okay?"

I turn away from him. I'm afraid of what would come out of my mouth if I spoke. The feelings inside me—humiliation, anger, disappointment, and who knows what else— have fused together in some lava-hot ball. But Oliver, on the other side of the bed, doesn't seem to notice. Soon his heavy breathing lengthens, and I lie there, alone, seething in the darkness like a fire.

Chapter Ten

I wake up to an empty room and silence in the house. I roll over and check my phone to see I've slept much later than usual. I guess my rage-filled tossing and turning caught up with me at some point.

It's not like I'm expecting an email from Abigail, but still my stomach sinks when my inbox reloads and there's nothing there from her. I hesitate, then hit Compose.

New Year's Eve is tomorrow, I type. *Don't you think Sam deserves to have you home?*

I don't know if they're doing any good, these attempts to guilt my sister into a homecoming, and I suppose it's possible they're doing harm. But what can we do? I wonder if the stop on her credit cards is active yet. I know it won't magically fix things, but I'm so relieved that Dennis will be home in two days.

I pad downstairs and into the kitchen. To my surprise, there are signs of brunch preparations all over: a bowl of pancake batter resting on the counter; a bowl of washed berries beside it; a carton of eggs waiting by the stove.

I raise my voice. "Oliver?"

"In here."

I go into the living room, and he and Sam are seated at the coffee table, a travel chess set on the coffee table between them. It must be left over from some camping holiday years ago—I remember us packing it, though not actually playing it. We were still a pretty new couple then: sex was usually more interesting than chess.

"Where'd you even find that?"

"Garage," Oliver says, eyes on the board. "Sam's kicking my ass."

Oliver looks up, meets my eyes. If I'm expecting to see some recognition of last night, whether it's apology or defensiveness or even camaraderie, I don't find it. Instead I see something I don't understand. He looks...nervous? It reminds me of that rabbit-in-headlights look he had two nights ago, when he came in late from work and so very tetchy.

"Are your brother and Dinah coming over?" I don't remember making that plan, but they're our usual brunch guests.

Oliver nods.

"For early New Year's. Don't you remember?"

I don't, but my brain feels full of holes these days. I look out the window to where yesterday's snow still lingers, thick across the lawn.

"I used to play chess with Grandpa," Sam says. I look down at the chessboard and Oliver's right: my nephew's winning.

"You remember Jeff and Dinah, right, Sam?" I say. I figure they've met once or twice over the years. "And Josie, your..." I try to work out it out. "Cousin-in-law?"

Sam glances up.

"Cousin-in-law's not a thing."

"Sure it is," I say. I don't know why I feel compelled to insist. I guess given how depleted his family seems right now, some extra can't hurt.

"There they are." Oliver rises from the sofa as Sam says, "Checkmate," but Oliver doesn't even hear him. He's got that weird look on his face again, marching towards the door even though Dinah hasn't even parked the car yet.

What's going on with him?

Hannah Feldman, a voice whispers, and I brush it away irritably. Oliver's not like that and I know it.

Sam looks up at me.

"I win, right?"

"You win. Come on. Let's say hi."

Our guests trudge up through the carpet of new snow, and as they draw closer I see something in my brother-in-law's eyes, something that flickers as he looks at Oliver and then at me.

Is *this* it; is this what Oliver's on edge about? Have they argued? Jeff and he almost never argue.

Josie reaches the door first, stomps her boots to get rid of the snow. She's getting tall these days, and even starting to look a bit like Jeff. She's always been like a carbon copy of Dinah, so it's odd to see that change.

"Hi, Josie. How's the snow out there?"

"Good! How are the birds?"

We have a bird-feeder out back which we always let Josie fill when she comes over. She knows it's a task Oliver saves for her; I've sometimes even known him to go empty it before she arrives.

"Hungry," says Oliver, and she grins at him.

"Josie, you remember Sam, right?" I say. "My nephew?"

Josie looks at him.

"No...Hi, Sam. Are you coming to feed the birds?"

"Uh." He readjusts the headphones around his neck and I swear I hear his voice get deeper. "Yeah. Sure."

Oliver leads them off to get the bird food and Dinah and Jeff follow me into the kitchen.

"So...?" Dinah says.

I tell her the latest: how Abigail's in Miami, and we still haven't heard a word from her.

Jeff whistles. "Your sister knows how to keep things interesting, Gillian."

"I won't argue with that. All I can say is, I'm glad Dennis is flying back in a couple of days."

Out in the garden, Josie and Sam are getting to work with the birdfeeder. They look so lovely against the snow—so fresh, so young, Josie in her red parka and Sam in his blue one. I feel a small pang in my chest.

As if on cue Sam looks up, gives a tentative wave. I raise my hand in response.

"Earth to Gillian?"

I turn around. Jeff's smiling at me.

"Sorry, what was that?"

He smiles at me. Jeff, the younger brother, is basically a leaner, taller version of Oliver. He's the rambunctious one, and has always been the golden boy in that family, but somehow Oliver's never held it against him. I've never liked comparing their relationship to Abigail's and mine.

"I was just asking," Jeff says, "how it feels to be free of those rugrats at Birch Bend Elementary for a couple of weeks."

"*I'm* not a rugrat," Josie says, coming in through the garden door.

Jeff reaches for her ponytail, pulls on it affectionately.

"You're the rugrattiest."

I can't help a moment of imagining: of picturing Oliver with his own daughter, teasing her like that. I swallow the thought.

"Oops," I say, looking around. "Bad hosts. What's everyone drinking? Juice, beer, seltzer? I could make mimosas?"

Dinah waves away the mimosa offer.

"Seltzer's great," she says. "You have those fancy flavored ones, right? I love those."

"I'll take a beer," Jeff says. "None of that goji berry-pomegranate stuff for me, thank you very much."

We laugh, and the kids place their orders as they slide off their snow boots and come over. Then after Oliver's handed out the drinks, Dinah clears her throat.

"We, um, have some news," she says.

She glances over at Jeff before turning back to us, and in that moment, I *know*. I see it in the tense, apologetic look in her eye, and in the suppressed excitement that's there too. I see it in the faint flush of pride on Jeff's face, and in how Josie's buzzing with the awareness of someone who knows big news. I remember Lottie at the farmer's market: *have you spoken to Dinah recently?*

Dinah hesitates, that look of apology flickering again.

"We're having a baby," she says. "We just confirmed it."

I inhale, and push out the words.

"You are?! That's wonderful! Wonderful. Congratulations!"

I sound manic. I *am* manic. I'm pretty sure that if I stop firing out good wishes or let my face stop smiling, I'll have some other, mortifying reaction that Dinah and Jeff really, really don't deserve.

"We...we weren't really planning on it," she says. "I mean, we were *open* to it, but..."

I know what she's trying to tell me. She thinks it'll feel better for me to know that this took them by surprise; that they didn't do it "on purpose." But it doesn't make me feel better. How can it just *happen* for them, when they're not even trying? When they're not even *thinking* about it?

Oliver's offering his congratulations now, and there are smiles all around. I see the shadow behind Dinah's smile as she looks my way. *I'm sorry,* it says. *I didn't mean for it to be this way.* I draw air through my nose, marshal the feelings until I'm confident the tremor won't show. But on top of everything else, here's what I'm thinking: Oliver knew.

He *knew.* That's what this whole thing with Jeff was about. The missed calls the other night. His agitation this morning. But instead of telling me, he just let me walk into this bombshell unawares. And now he has the gall to act surprised.

I could kill him, I really could.

Dinah gets me on my own a few minutes later.

"Gillian...please don't think I don't appreciate how...well, unfair this is. The timing is terrible, I know that. It just happened. I...I wasn't sure when to tell you. Jeff said we had to tell you both together—brothers, you know how it is."

I swallow. I don't bother telling her that Jeff obviously let the cat out of the bag to Oliver already, whatever he said.

"You shouldn't apologize. I *am* happy for you. I just..." I shrug, because I can't manage the words, and because she already knows.

This is not about you, Gillian. I remind myself that this was never going to be *my* baby. It's not as though this little embryo made it into the wrong body by mistake.

But at the least, at the very least, couldn't my husband have told me?

I hold it together until they've left and Sam's parked in front of the TV inside. There's a tremor in my fingers as I close the kitchen door and look around. Oliver glances up from the dishwasher.

"You didn't *tell* me?" I say.

He blinks back at me.

"Tell you...?"

"About *that,* Oliver." I jab my thumb towards the hallway. "About the pregnancy!"

His eyebrows knit in what looks like real consternation.

"G, I didn't know. I had no idea." He shakes his head. "I'm sorry...I know how hard that must have been on you. We were kind of put on the spot."

I search his eyes.

"You didn't know?" I say skeptically. "You're telling me you didn't know that Dinah was pregnant?"

He spreads his arms by his sides in a helpless *of course not.*

"So those calls from Jeff the other day—they really weren't about this?"

He looks even more pained; opens his mouth,

shuts it.

"No, babe," he says. "They really weren't." He steps into me, pulls me against him. "Gill, I know. I know how much you want this. I do too."

I repeat his words in my head. He wants this too. Sometimes it *does* feel like I'm in this alone, and I have to remind myself that I'm not the only one who's feeling it.

I pull back and Oliver squeezes my hand.

"Go join Sam for a bit. I'll finish this up."

Sam looks up from the television as I come in.

"Hey, Aunt G."

I see something tentative and awkward in his glance, and I'm pretty sure he's aware of it too, and remembering what I said about those pre-natal vitamins by the stovetop.

I give him my best *everything's fine!* smile, which probably reeks of denial, and sink onto the sofa. I try my best to turn my brain off, and just follow the convoluted plot of this action movie Sam's watching. Later Oliver comes in and joins us in front of the television, and in a while we order pizza for dinner, as nobody wants to do any more cooking. Apparently

Oliver's taking the day off today in lieu of tomorrow, but is planning to spend the afternoon of New Year's Eve back in the brewery.

I bring the pizza inside when it arrives, and we eat in front of the television, strings of cheese stretching as we tug our slices onto plates.

That stupid 23AndMe ad is playing again, and I close my eyes and do my best to tune it out.

"Last slice?" Oliver says. I shake my head and he and Sam decide to split it. Then Oliver takes our plates into the kitchen and I look out the window to where the light has all but faded. The trees in the front yard stand quiet and strong, supporting their snowy branches as if they've never known tiredness. And I decide something.

I decide that it doesn't matter why I feel what I do. I'm not selfish for wanting a baby that shares my DNA. It doesn't make me a bad person if I'm yearning for a child with Oliver's dimples, or my love of music, or Dad's laugh. And this waiting, and hoping, and not knowing— it can't go on. I take a breath, and get off the couch.

In the kitchen Oliver's just finishing cleaning up. I shut the door, and he looks at me, sensing a change in the air.

"Oliver..." I meet his eyes. "I know how you feel about IVF. But this can't go on. I need us to go to that clinic. I need us to try."

Chapter Eleven

I see the look on his face, he takes no pains to hide it.

"I thought we had talked about this, Gillian."

"Well in that case," I keep my voice calm. "I want to talk about it again."

He keeps his gaze on the window, brows drawn.

"We wouldn't have to be like Rakesh and Lisa," I go on. *Just because it tore our friends' marriage apart, it doesn't have to be the same for ours.*

He glances back to me.

"Gillian, it's not as if this is some, you know, *herbal remedies*," he says, his voice sharp. "It's not like just popping a sleeping pill or something. They pump all these synthetic hormones and chemicals into you. You'd be shooting yourself up with these fake laboratory hormones all day long. That stuff changes you, you know? It changes your body. It changes your mind." He looks at me. "People just don't understand how fragile the mind is, Gillian. You don't even realize how *lucky* we are, you and me both, that we don't have to medicate ourselves just to get through the day. And now you want to throw a bunch of chemicals in there and mess with all that? You don't know what'll happen. You don't know how it's going to change you."

I close my eyes.

"Ollie, I know what you're saying, but this isn't some experimental drug we're talking about..."

"And what about long-term effects?" he continues. "I read that some studies have shown links to cancer, Gillian!"

"Ollie," I say, my voice tight. It exasperates me that he's willing to fall back on "internet science" all of a sudden—he's smarter than that and he knows it. "Please don't throw around this 'studies have shown' stuff as if you'd done the research. You *know* those headlines are clickbait. Suggesting that things 'are linked to cancer' is the internet's favorite pastime."

I go through a list of just a few of the things which have been linked to cancer in the last five years. Vitamins. Birth control. Childbirth. It's true: *childbirth* has literally been linked to increased rates of uterine cancer, but do you see anyone not having kids because of that?

Of course not. Because the "increased rates" are minuscule; because the science methodology is questionable; and because people need to get on with their lives.

Oliver just shakes his head, like he can't believe how stubborn I'm being.

"Ol," I say. "I get why you're so...non-interventionist about this stuff. I do." *But you're blowing this way out of proportion.* "But tons of women," I continue, "tons of couples, do IVF."

"Name someone," he says. And I can't, because Rakesh and Lisa are the only couple that actually told us they were going through it. I bet there are plenty of couples we know casually who've done it and just haven't mentioned it to us. There's a lot the world doesn't talk about when it comes to women's bodies in particular.

"Don't put me in this position, Oliver," I say.

He exhales sharply through his nose.

"Put you in this position? Gillian, don't act like this is just about you," he says, and I feel my blood rising.

"I thought we weren't supposed to make this a me versus you thing," I say. "You're the one who's always saying we shouldn't get adversarial about this."

"Exactly," he shoots back.

"Well, you're the one being accusatory!" I say. "And, and anyway—it *is* about me more than you, because you don't care as much as I do. If you did, I'd be pregnant by now."

He stares at me, then looks away.

"You know what I sometimes feel like?" he says. "I feel like some stud bull on a farm. Like I'm just kept around for the purposes of insemination. Like that's what I'm *for* these days."

My blood simmers.

"How do you think *I* feel? How do you think last night felt for me; do you think it was particularly *affirming*, that it did wonders for *my* ego? Do you think I don't feel like a barnyard animal myself? Like a walking uterus instead of a human?"

Oliver stares at me. Then he grabs his coat from where it's slung over one of the kitchen chairs.

"Where are you going?"

"Out."

"Out *where?*" I say.

"Out anywhere, Gillian. I can't do this right now."

Seconds later I hear the front door close. I sit down at the table, trembling a little.

Oliver's always said he doesn't want us to get adversarial over this like Rakesh and Lisa did. I remember how they got about it all in the end: everything was about who was the "problem"; were the eggs defective or was it the sperm? *We have to be playing on the same team*, Oliver says. But that's all very well for him to say when that team's not even on the field, just sitting benched on the sidelines where he wants it. *Not* doing anything is a choice too, and it's not my choice, it's his.

And it isn't fair.

I take a breath, and pull up the browser on my phone. I look up the fertility clinic, and the address and phone number comes up, and their hours. I close my eyes and hit Call.

"Good afternoon, Freedom Fertility," a

woman's voice picks up.

"Hi," I say. "I was wondering if I could come in for a consultation. What's the first appointment you have available?"

*

I pretend to be asleep when Oliver comes back in. I lie facing the wall, eyes closed. I have no intention of telling him about the appointment I just made tonight. New Year's Eve—I thought they'd be closed tomorrow, but they're not. They have an opening first thing, nine thirty in the morning. Just thinking about it, I feel goosebumps. I'll tell him about it when it's over. I don't know how, but I'll cross that bridge when I come to it.

Oliver slips into bed beside me, and I'm pretty sure he knows I'm not really asleep but if he does he says nothing. My stomach roils with guilt and the thrill of deception: I have a secret and I hold it to myself like armor—and soon, despite my certainty that racing thoughts will keep me awake till the small hours, I'm sinking under like I haven't a care in the world.

It's a shock, then, to wake up in the morning

and find I've overslept. I pick up my phone from the nightstand and check it in a panic. The stupid screen is declaring *Alarm* in bright orange, but I didn't hear anything. I jump out of bed—Oliver's gone, of course—and knock on Sam's door.

"Sam? Are you up? I have a doctor's appointment I forgot about. We have to rush, sorry. I'm going to drop you off at Dinah's, okay?"

He cracks the door open, looking slightly alarmed.

"I have a doctor's appointment that I'm late for," I explain. "Just an hour or so, I think. Depends on traffic. Can you be ready to leave ASAP? Just throw on some clothes, you can brush your teeth later."

He gapes at me as though I've suggested the unspeakable.

"I have to brush my teeth."

Just my luck to have the most hygiene-obsessed ten-year-old in the world under my roof this morning.

"Fine, brush your teeth. Just be downstairs in ten minutes."

Ten minutes later, I'm outside his door.

"Sam? I'm not kidding. We need to move. Do you want me to leave you home alone?"

When I was a kid, leaving a ten-year-old home alone for a couple of hours wouldn't have been a problem. But things are different these days and from what I understand about Dennis's parenting philosophy, I don't think Sam would be used to that at all.

Finally he opens the door, looking agitated. He's not the only one. I wish I knew what was so hard about throwing on a hoodie.

"Great!" I say, trying to conceal my impatience. "Let's go." I snag the keys from the hall table and marshal him into the car.

"Cereal bars are beside you," I say. I glance over as I pull out of our driveway, and the hair on my neck prickles. Sam looks...I don't know how to describe it. He looks *stricken.* Like he's just seen a puppy get run over.

"Sam?"

He looks at me.

"What's the matter?"

He shakes his head.

"I didn't get to..." He stops. "I just needed

more time."

Sam would never have made it in our house growing up. How did everything always seem to be so frantic back then? Mom's voice always yelling up the stairs: *You'll be late for school! Late for church! Late for swimming!* But now my nephew looks on the point of tears, folding his arms into the kangaroo pocket of his hoodie, shoulders hunching.

"More time for what?" I say, because it feels like I must have missed something.

"It doesn't matter. I just don't like being rushed," he mutters.

I shake my head. This definitely seems like an overreaction but we don't really have time to talk about it. Soon we're pulling up at Dinah's. I called her last night and gave her the line about a medical appointment I'd totally forgotten. Luckily she's working the afternoon shift today and didn't miss a beat to say she'd watch Sam. I figure she feels she owes me right now. I could have dropped him at Mom's, of course, but I figured Mom would be apt to ask me more questions.

I honk once from the driveway, and Dinah

opens the front door, waving out at us.

"I'll see you in an hour or two, Sam, okay?" I say. "Thanks for bearing with me."

He extracts himself reluctantly from the car, and I try not to feel like a horrible person as I watch him move slowly up the path towards Dinah's door.

"Thank you!" I signal to her. When the front door closes I turn the car around, and fifteen minutes later I'm in the parking lot outside the clinic. I turn off the engine and take some long, deep breaths. And then some more long, deep breaths.

Behind me, the traffic lights change and an engine guns.

Get in there, Gillian. Before you lose your nerve.

I get out of my car and slam the door.

*

The reception desk is long and white and sleek—this whole place feels a little like being inside an iPhone. I give my name quietly to the young woman behind the desk, who smiles and invites me to have a seat.

"Dr. Tremain won't be long."

I eyeball the other people here as discreetly as I can. I get the sense we might *all* be eyeballing each other, actually. Most of the folks here are women waiting alone, although some have partners with them—male partners, female partners. A few are reading books or magazines, and the rest have their heads buried in their phones, swiping and scrolling with absorbed frowns on their faces. Or maybe they're not absorbed at all; maybe they're just trying to pretend to themselves and to everybody else that this is all no big deal.

I wonder how long these people have been trying for a baby? Are some here for the first time, like me? Have others been coming here for years, trying and failing, watching their money get swallowed by this sinkhole of hope?

My palms grow damp and I clamp them over my knees.

I start scrolling through my phone like the two women next to me, mostly to numb my anxious thoughts, and see an email from Dennis. I open it. He's letting me know he's hired a PI.

"Gillian Gerritsen?"

I blink. A woman is calling me over to the

doorway, and smiles quickly as I approach.

"Dr. Tremain," she introduces herself as she leads me down a warren of corridors and glass-paneled offices. She's wearing smart, tailored clothing, not a white coat or scrubs. She's probably a few years older than me, and sleeker. She looks like the kind of woman who probably "does it all" and still somehow has free time in her day, but it makes me want to trust her instead of dislike her.

She opens a door into one of the offices and wheels a seat out from the desk for me.

"Water?"

I decline, since nerves are already playing havoc with my bladder, and take the seat she's offering me. She sits down behind her desk and folds her hands and smiles at me. It's a professional smile, but warm. My eyes drift to the photograph frame on her desk, a large silver one, turned away from me with its velvet back showing. I imagine the family portrait inside. A husband, or perhaps a wife. Children, one or two or even three. Chestnut-haired, maybe, like the doctor. I imagine one smiling, another one sulking, fat cheeks pouched in an adorable frown.

"So." The doctor rests her hands on the desk and seeks my eyes. "Tell me about what brings you here today."

I know she doesn't need the obvious answer.

She doesn't need me to tell her why I, and all the other anxious women out there in that room, showed up today. She wants to hear about *me,* and suddenly it feels like a long time since anyone has wanted to hear that, or since I've been looked at with such quiet, patient focus.

I feel it all well up in me. All the words, all the feelings. I have an urge to pour everything out in this little office with its generic wall art and bland beige furniture.

My sister's gone AWOL.

My husband's unreachable.

My nephew's lonely.

I miss my father.

But none of that is the reason I'm here today. None of that has anything to do with the fact that the mere glimpse of a toddler-sized anything—tiny gloves abandoned in the park; miniature gumboots stacked on a porch—fills me with a loss I can't explain. Or the fact that

I've switched pharmacies because the one nearest to me now has moved its greeting card rack to right in front of the sliding doors, and the ambush of pastel blues and pinks is sometimes too much to deal with.

I take a breath. A beat passes. The doctor pushes a box of tissues my way.

Her eyes meet mine.

"Take your time," she says.

Chapter Twelve

Dr. Tremain has statistics for everything, and she doesn't get defensive when I ask hard questions. *If Oliver were here right now, she could convince him,* I tell myself.

I look through the brochures she's placed in front of me. Bar graphs, numbers, statistical probabilities for different age ranges. Indicators, but no guarantees. Like everything in life, it seems the answers boil down to *it depends*.

The doctor asks me about my family history, and I tell her about Mom struggling to conceive and then having two pregnancies almost back to back when she was in her mid-thirties. The doctor raises her eyebrows.

"Unusual. But I take it you don't feel comfortable relying on something similar."

I shake my head. I used to reckon I was a lucky person; now I'm not so sure.

Dr. Tremain talks about preliminary tests they can run: an ultrasound, blood tests. It'll take about forty-five minutes to do both, and the blood tests will definitely be covered by my insurance. Apparently that's all it takes to get a "baseline assessment of my fertility." She says if I want, she can fit me in for the bloodwork and ultrasound today, or I can make an appointment to come back in the future.

"Of course," she says pointedly, "this is only one-half of the equation. According to our statistics, of the 80 percent of couple infertility cases where we're looking at individual fertility issues, it's split straight down the middle between what we call 'male factor' and 'female factor.'" She looks at me, and I think the look in her eyes is meant to remind me that I have a somewhat irresponsible husband who decided that a work meeting was more important than showing up today. That's what I told her when she asked me about my partner—that he had an unavoidable work thing come up last minute.

"Society does a lot of messaging about the female biological clock," she continues, "but the reality is that fertility issues occur at approximately the same rates for both sexes. Men don't have the hard cut-off point of menopause, but male and female fertility dwindles at about the same rate up until the mid-forties. Increased risks of genetic disorders follow a similar pattern."

Huh. Everyone talks about "advanced maternal age" when a woman's having kids in her forties, but I've never seen anyone point fingers at the mid-forties husband.

"So," Dr. Tremain smiles briskly. "I do hope you'll urge your husband to join you on your next appointment so we can get a better snapshot of the whole situation."

I clear my throat. "I'm sure he'll want to come in at the earliest opportunity," I say. "Meanwhile, I'd like to go ahead with those tests today."

Tests. Why do they have to call them tests?

"Absolutely." Dr. Tremain folds her hands on the desk. "There may be a small wait but we'll fit you in." She reminds me that although the follicle count will be immediate, the blood tests results will take a few days, then leads me back to the waiting room where I fill out some more forms, and after a while a nurse calls me through a different door. She leads me into a small examination room with one of those crinkly paper-covered beds.

"Dr. Tremain will be right with you."

My heart skitters as I disrobe. It feels like a long wait until the doctor comes in, and when she does she looks a whole lot taller now that I'm all the way down here.

"Okay," she says. "Let's see what we can see."

The ultrasound isn't pleasant but at least it's quick—and no one goes *uh-oh* while looking at the screen.

"This looks very healthy," Dr. Tremain announces when we're done. She says I have an "average-to-good" follicle count for a woman in my age bracket and that, pending bloodwork results, she would say I'm an excellent candidate for IVF.

Excellent candidate, I can hear Oliver's wry voice in my head saying. *It's hardly the Ivy League.*

"Share those brochures with your partner," Dr. Tremain says. "And have him come by when he's able. Then we can go from there. I'm sure he'll have questions of his own."

After she's gone I take my time in the examination room, slowly sliding my feet back into my shoes. I shoulder my coat on, and head back out into the waiting area to settle up for today's visit. In the car outside, my body feels light and strange, like it's not yet fully my own again. But there's also a kindling sense of hope: I'm healthy, I'm "normal," I'm an *excellent candidate*. I brush my hair back from my damp forehead and start the engine. Then a new worry burrows into my momentary relief.

What if Oliver's not a "good candidate"?

What if it's him? What then?

I start the car and turn onto the road.

Don't meet trouble halfway, Gillian, I tell myself.

Needless to say, the pep talk doesn't work.

*

"Hey, Gillian!" Jeff calls from the kitchen as Dinah ushers me indoors.

"The kids are downstairs," Dinah says. "I let them bring sandwiches down to the basement for lunch. Apparently Sam's an Xbox fan."

Jeff and Dinah had some big anniversary this year, and Jeff's present was an Xbox; Dinah's was that DNA kit. Oliver kept joking it was grounds for divorce, but it turned out Dinah thought it was a great gift.

"Sam will be thrilled," I say. "He has an Xbox back home that he's been missing."

Dinah gives me a slight smile, since we both know that's not really what Sam's been missing.

She walks me into the living room.

"Did your appointment go okay?"

I nod. Behind the words, her eyes are asking something different: Are *you* okay? I wonder if she suspects the doctor's appointment wasn't just the usual kind. If it had been a week ago, I'd have told her everything. Now, though, it all feels too raw.

"Fine," I say. "Seems like I'm in pretty good shape."

Knock on wood.

I hesitate. This is hard. "How are you doing?" I say. "I mean, the pregnancy. How are you feeling?"

She flushes, not quite meeting my eyes.

"Okay. I'm...a little nervous, honestly. It's been a while."

I nod, despite the kick of jealousy in my chest. What a luxury those nerves would be. How much I'd love to be downloading one of those pregnancy apps right now, the ones that tell you every week how big the baby is in fruit-size equivalents. To be able to say to Oliver, *it's a kumquat this week* and then, later: *almost a grapefruit!*

So Dinah's jitters are hard for me to empathize with right now.

"Anyway." She glances towards the basement stairs. "Dennis is back soon, right?"

"Tomorrow," I say. New Year's Day. It feels sort of symbolic, but not in a good way. Abigail should be here. What will it be like for Sam, starting the new year without her? Meanwhile for New Year's Eve Mom's made us a dinner reservation at Brannagh's, a local restaurant that's a bit of a Birch Bend institution. We were lucky they still had tables this close to the day.

It's probably good that Mom made the effort. If Sam weren't here, Oliver and I would likely just have ordered takeout and watched the ball drop on TV.

I glance toward the basement staircase. While I *am* relieved that Dennis is coming home, I feel like I'll miss having Sam around. I feel like I'm just starting to make up for lost time with my nephew, and though it's only been a few days, I'll miss the space he takes up in our home. The way the house's silence feels rounder and fuller when he's in it; the way he makes our household into a little triangle.

And I really, really thought Abigail would be home by now.

"Dennis hired a private investigator," I tell Dinah.

She gapes at me a little, even though she was the one who first came up with the idea.

"Wow. This is serious, huh?"

Is it? I wish I knew. Is Abigail just making a statement as she's wont to do, or is it something different this time? I wonder afresh at my sister, at her talent for delaying the inevitable. Doesn't she know the price of coming back is that she'll have to account for where she's been? That she'll *have* to face up to all this one way or another?

I guess she does know that. And maybe that's the reason she's gone so silent—because she realizes she's thrown a bomb into our midst and now she's scared she can't just put it back in the box. She can't afford to stay away and can't afford to come home.

"Well, anyway," I say, "I should probably get Sam."

Dinah nods. There's an awkwardness between us today, and I wonder if this is just the beginning of me losing another friend to the whirlwind of pregnancy and new maternity.

She drops her eyes from mine and goes to the top of the stairs. "Kids? Gillian's here!"

Ten seconds later Josie's bounding up the steps, then flops onto a beanbag, arms wide.

"I'm exhausted! Dance Challenge is *so hard*!"

Sam doesn't seem to be following her, so I head down and find him shelving the handsets for the Xbox console. He doesn't turn around as I enter.

"Hi, Sam."

"Hi."

He still doesn't turn.

"Everything okay?" I say.

He nods his head the tiniest bit.

"Sam? Did something happen?"

He turns sharply.

"Can you just leave me alone? Why does everyone always have to make a big deal of everything! It's just a game!"

I start backwards.

"Well, excuse *me.*"

Sarcasm probably isn't the best tone to take but Sam's already stomping up the stairs. *He's a kid*, I remind myself; he's hurting, this is normal. But I'm surprised at how wounded I feel.

Come on, Gillian. Be the grown-up here.

"Well," Dinah says uncertainly as I reach the top of the stairs. I guess neither Sam nor I are at our sunniest right now. "Get home safe."

"Thanks," I say, a little more crisply than I mean to. I turn to her daughter. "Bye, Josie. Happy New Year."

Outside we get into the car, and Sam doesn't speak so I don't either. I don't have it in me right now to be snapped at again. When we park in the driveway he slams the car door, and once I let him in, goes up to his room without a word. I figure the wise thing might be to let him cool off for a bit before I go talk to him. Hopefully I can rally him a little for our New Year's Eve dinner with Mom.

I pull out my phone and text Oliver.

Don't forget, 7:30 for tonight.

We still haven't actually spoken to each other since he walked out on me last night. I'm still smarting from that if I think about it too hard—but it's layered now with all the guilt from where I've been today. I just don't know how I'm going to bring this up with him again, including the fact that I went rogue with my solo visit to the clinic and that I lied to the doctor about Oliver being on board.

It feels kind of like a game of chicken, neither of us acknowledging where we left the conversation last night. Ignoring all that probably suits Oliver, though—I bet I'm going to have to be the one to bring it up again.

Can I just meet you at the restaurant? he texts back. *Sorry, today is crazy.*

I clench my teeth.

I know this game. He just wants to avoid me right now, and then when we get to the restaurant we'll be in front of Mom and Sam and we'll have to make nice. Maybe he thinks if enough time passes without us talking about last night, it'll get too awkward for me to raise again.

I'm flexing my fingers, deliberating between

writing back a terse *Fine*, or something more combative, when my phone lights up with a call in front of me.

Dennis.

"Gillian?" he says when I pick up; I can tell he's somewhere loud.

"Hi! What's going on?"

"I'm afraid we're running into some issues here," he says, with the air of someone who's trying to keep the show on the road while the show has other ideas. "They're demonstrating again," he goes on. "At the airport."

"What? Who's demonstrating?" I try to keep up.

"The rebel groups," he says, and I realize I might have known more about all this if I'd been paying attention to the news the last couple of weeks. "We're all being issued with a travel advisory to avoid the airport for the next twenty-four hours."

He clears his throat.

"Gillian, my flight's canceled."

Chapter Thirteen

"*Canceled?*" I say.

"I'm not in any danger," he clarifies, which hadn't really occurred to me until then. "It's just unclear when they're going to be able to clear the demonstrators and reschedule our flights. Last time they demonstrated right through the night."

"So...you're not going to make your flight." I'm stating the obvious, but my brain's still a little behind.

"No, Gillian. I'm sorry. I'll keep you posted, but I'm expecting this to be resolved within the next twenty-four hours tops." He clears his throat. "Is it okay for Sam to stay with you an extra day?"

"I mean...of course." I feel a bit dazed. I hope he's right about those estimates. "You really think this will be cleared up soon?" I say.

He assures me that it will.

"It's all par for the course out here, I'm afraid. They might even be rescheduling the flights by tonight."

"Okay," I say, wondering what Oliver's take will be. "Well...just keep us posted, I guess..."

"I will. Is Sam there?"

"I'll get him."

I walk the phone upstairs to Sam's room, wincing a little in anticipation. Sam's mood has been such a tempest today and this I'm sure is not going to help.

"Sam? It's your dad on the phone."

Silence.

"Sam?"

"I'll talk to him later."

"He needs to talk to you now, Sam. It's important."

The door cracks open and Sam's flushed face glances up at me, a hint of anxiety behind the belligerent look.

"It's okay," I say. "He just needs a word."

I'm back downstairs in the kitchen when Sam reappears with my phone. He slides a look my way as he puts the phone back on the table.

"Too bad about your dad," I say, and he glances up at me.

"I don't care," he says.

"No?" I say.

Sam's jaw sets. "Why should I? I hate them anyway," he says. "Both of them."

I look at him.

"I don't think you do, Sam."

He looks back at me, eyes narrow.

"They don't even like each other, you know. They act like we're a family but we're not."

"Sam..." I don't know what to say to that. A few weeks ago it would have shocked me to hear it. I'd always assumed Abigail and Dennis had a basically successful marriage, even though they seemed so opposite to each other.

Sam hovers, casting a quick glance towards the window and then back at me.

"She told me she was leaving," he blurts.

I don't absorb the words at first, and it takes a couple of seconds before they make sense to me.

"Sam...what exactly are you saying?" I ask, in case despite the obvious interpretation I've somehow got it wrong.

He looks at me.

"Mom," he says, his words careful and hard. "The day she left. She came upstairs and told me she was leaving."

I stare at my nephew, wrong-footed.

"What did she say to you?"

He looks away.

"She said she was sorry. That there was something"—his brow scrunches—"that she needed to find out about herself. And it meant she had to go away for a few days." He looks at me. "I asked what it was about and she said she couldn't tell me just yet, that she needed to learn a little more about it first." He swallows. "She said she had to leave while Dad was gone or she wouldn't be able to leave at all. But she said that it would just be for a few days," he repeats.

My head's spinning.

I look at my nephew.

"And she told you not to tell us this?"

According to Dennis, Sam was upstairs with his headphones on and heard nothing, not even the car pulling out.

Sam drops his eyes again.

"No...I just thought everyone would be mad at me. For letting her leave."

I exhale.

"You didn't try to stop her?" I say. "You didn't...try to make her stay?"

The corners of his mouth turn down.

"Oh, Sam, I'm not blaming you—"

"She said it was important," he says, his voice fierce for a moment, but the fierceness quickly dies, and his eyes move towards the window.

"She said she'd be back before I knew it. But...maybe she won't."

I sigh. At least she spoke to him, I suppose. At least she gave him *some* reassurance before vanishing into the ether. But I'm just not sure how much that reassurance counts for right now, and I guess Sam's starting to feel the same.

Something she needed to find out about herself. Does that actually mean something? Or were they just empty words to make her feel better about all this?

"So she didn't tell you *anything* about where she was going?" I say.

Sam sighs like it's painfully clear we've been over this ground.

"No."

We sit in silence a moment.

"Okay," I say. "Well, we should tell your

father, Sam. I think everyone's been pretty angry with your mom for disappearing without a word. Especially without a word to *you*."

Sam's shoulders slump.

"He won't be angry," I say. "It wasn't your responsibility to make her stay."

"Can you tell him?" he asks.

I study his face. "I can, if you want me to."

He doesn't look up at me. I clear my throat. "Sam...I know this is all a bit mysterious about your mom, and it's not fair of her to expect us all to be so patient. But what's *not* a mystery is how much she loves you. You know that, right?"

He steals a quick look at me, then shrugs.

I sigh internally.

"Want to help me break into my late-night cookie stash?" I ask. "We have a few hours before dinner to spoil our appetites."

*

As we snack in front of the television, I find myself going over Sam's account again; over those words of Abigail's. Oliver would probably scoff at it all, reminding me that "there's something I need to find out about myself" is probably just a loftier way of saying "I'm leaving my marriage."

But still it goes around in my head like a refrain, the "finding out" and the needing to "learn more", and soon I'm back to doubting this whole affair theory. A nasty thought worms its way into my mind. She couldn't be *ill*, could she? Some world-upending diagnosis; one of those slow, debilitating diseases—Parkinson's, Huntington's, something like that...

And then something else flickers into my mind. Not a memory exactly, but a half-memory. Those Ancestry.com vouchers we had lying around for weeks...I'd left them on the console table in the hall; I pretty much flogged them to anyone who came to the house, knowing that otherwise they'd go in the recycling. Didn't Abigail comment on them when she came over a couple of months ago, that strange visit of hers that I found so odd at the time? Did I try and foist those vouchers on her, too? And if I did, did she take them?

I don't know all that much about those tests, but I do know that they can tell you if you carry genes for certain conditions—like the one that makes it 85 percent likely you'll get breast cancer. And other things too: those scary, degenerative diseases...

I shake my head, reminding myself that there are plenty of other less dramatic conclusions to come to. It's like Oliver's favorite saying: *when you hear hoofbeats, think horses, not zebras.* Abigail might keep a lot of things from us, but she wouldn't keep *that.*

But still, the unease doesn't quite leave me as Sam and I chomp our way through the packet of chocolate chip cookies.

I'm just about to suggest that we start getting ready to leave for our dinner reservation when my phone lights up again, this time with Dinah's number. That's odd. I dust cookie crumbs off my fingers and swipe to accept.

"Dinah! Hi."

"Hey, Gillian."

Her voice sounds a little off.

"Is something up?"

She hesitates, and I pick up my phone and leave the room. The sound of Sam's program follows me out the door; I shut it behind me.

"Di?"

She sighs.

"I'm thinking maybe I shouldn't have called now. I feel kind of stupid. But Gillian, I just thought maybe I should pick up the phone after listening to some stuff Josie said to me earlier."

I swallow.

"Stuff? What stuff?" I'm assuming she means some kind of argument between Josie and Sam. That seems likely enough, just based on how tetchy he was earlier when I went down to the basement to get him.

"He didn't do anything bad, Gillian. This isn't a complaint." She pauses. "And maybe I'm overstepping here...but I guess from what Josie described, it seemed like Sam was behaving in a somewhat unusual way...And I guess I was just wondering, well, if that was something you had picked up on too?"

"Unusual?" I say. "Like how?"

"Nothing big," she hurries to say. "And nothing that would matter on its own. But just all together, it sounded a little...well, I guess you might say, compulsive."

"Compulsive?" I echo.

I can hear the awkwardness in her voice.

"Stuff with the video games, for example.

Josie said he had these funny little rituals when he was playing. Buttons he had to hit in some particular order even though it was nothing to do with the game. And she said he was starting to find the game quite upsetting at one point because he didn't get a chance to complete all the moves correctly. I mean, *exactly* correctly; in some particular way that he seemed to have decided was necessary."

I wrinkle my nose. Okay, this does sound a little...eccentric. But that's hardly a crime. And Sam, well, he's fussy. He's just a sensitive, fussy kind of kid. Maybe a bit of a perfectionist.

"I gather Josie started asking him about it and he got a bit upset."

Ah. No wonder he was so defensive when I went downstairs.

"And..." Dinah hesitates. "She also said that when they went to wash their hands before lunch, Sam washed his for an unusually long time. I asked her what she meant and she just said he washed his hands 'a bunch of times.'"

I feel annoyed now. Sam *does* wash his hands kind of a lot. And a minute is clearly unnecessary. But...

"I'm 100 percent not an expert, Gillian. It's just that one of Josie's school friends got this OCD diagnosis recently and his mom was chatting to me about all of that last week, and I guess it was on my mind. I just thought I would pass it along, in case it was worth flagging."

I pause.

"I mean, thanks Dinah, I hear you; I think Sam's hygiene concerns might be a tad excessive, and yeah, maybe he's a little on the neurotic side...but, well, nobody's perfect." I force a smile. "I mean I'm just not seeing how it's 'that' kind of problem. The kind with a diagnosis, you know?"

"Right," Dinah says, her voice growing more distant now. "You're right, and if it's not a problem for him, then it's not a problem. I just...well. If I was overstepping, I'm sorry. I just thought it might be information I should pass on."

"Okay," I exhale. "Well, I appreciate you calling."

"Gillian—"

"I appreciate it, Dinah." I cut her off. "But I've got to go."

I hang up, shake my head, and look at the time.

"Okay, Sam?" I stick my head inside the living room. "Ready to head to dinner?"

Chapter Fourteen

Brannagh's is all decorated for the holidays, bright yellow light spilling out the windows as Sam and I walk up. I see our table from outside: to my surprise Oliver's already there, sitting next to Mom and chatting with her; actually smiling. We go inside and I indicate to the greeter that we're joining the window-side table.

"Hello, you two!" Mom exclaims as we approach. "Happy New Year, Sam!"

"Happy New Year, Grandma," he says, a little louder than the standard mumble.

I look at Oliver, who to my surprise has shown up in a blazer and tie, and his hair freshly gelled. When he said he was coming from work I assumed he'd be dressed in jeans and some ratty old sweater. Now I'm wishing *I'd* made more of an effort. Just a quick bit of lipstick or eyeliner or a spritz of perfume wouldn't have gone amiss.

Mom has already ordered a round of drinks for the table, and after the day I've had it feels earned.

Oliver readjusts his seat and I smell just the faint waft of nicotine, or I think I do.

"Have you...have you been *smoking*?" I say. Oliver hasn't smoked in years.

He looks at me.

"Just the one," he says. "I...I've been really stressed lately, Gill. It's not going to become a habit, don't worry."

Stressed about what, I don't ask. And then: *Maybe Hannah Feldman smokes,* a nasty voice says before I can push it away.

"Gill..." Oliver says. "I'm sorry about how things ended up last night. I know you meant what you said."

I glance across the table at Mom and Sam, who, for right now, are occupied in conversation. But Oliver and I can't talk in undertones like this all night.

"But," Oliver goes on, "I just don't really feel able to resolve all this right now. There's just so much going on. I don't think I can really deal with this too."

I swallow. What's to deal with? I've told him that I can't not do this. We can afford it, if we make the effort. But he's making it sound like there's this big decision weighing on his shoulders and it's all down to him. I take a long gulp of prosecco.

"Well," I murmur to Oliver, "I don't feel able to *not* resolve it, so it sounds like we have a problem."

He sighs.

"Gill...it's New Year's Eve. Can we just take it easy for tonight? Can we just try?"

I look at him, his shirt and blazer and tired eyes.

"We can try," I nod, and he leans in to kiss me.

When he does, I smell smoke.

*

The food is good, Mom's buoyant, and even Sam appears happier than this afternoon. I get the sense that after all, maybe he's happier not to have to go home just yet. It's probably easier to pretend that things with his mom are under control if he doesn't have to be in the Westchester house without her.

Mom is wide-eyed as she hears about Dennis's flight cancellation.

"My, how dramatic," she says, and I see Oliver glance at me. He's not impressed by the delay, and I can see it grates on him that for Mom, it apparently adds to Dennis's exotic charm.

"Can I stay up to watch the ball drop when we get home?" Sam says, and I figure why not. Given how all over the place everything feels right now, sticking to bedtime doesn't seem like a huge priority for tonight.

Back home, Oliver pours himself a drink and joins Sam in front of the television for the "New Year's Eve Spectacular" that consists of a camera panning across screaming twenty-somethings crowded into iron pens in Times Square, inter-cut with vacuous banter from the two celebrity co-presenters.

"New Year's Eve is weird," Sam says.

"How so?" I say.

"Well, everyone acts like it's such a big deal," he says. "But it's not like anything really changes."

I'd meant to stay and watch the TV special with them, but somehow I feel restless, uneasy. I'm thinking about the stuff Abigail said to Sam again, and then when I put that out of my mind I flash back to the call with Dinah. It's like my brain has just decided to be in worry mode for the night.

I retreat from the living room for a bit and open my laptop at the kitchen table. The snow outside is still all but pristine, not yet slushy.

No email from my sister—not that I expected it, really. I sigh and sit back from the computer, watching the garden for a moment. Then I get up and pour myself a cup of hot water—limiting my daily caffeine intake is a part of the pregnancy-aspiration diet I haven't given up just yet—and sit back down in front of my screen. I hesitate, then open the browser and type in *OCD in kids.* I blow on the hot water, and sip as I click on the first article. I read it all the way through, then go back to the search page and read the next one. Then a third. Then a fourth.

One of the take-home messages, of course, is that everybody's different: OCD looks different on different people. But there are common threads.

"Rituals," as Dinah called it, are the biggest one. These are the compulsive behaviors, and excessive hand-washing is a common one. But they can be just about anything, these rituals. Sometimes it's doing a perfectly normal thing more times than is necessary, until you reach a certain pattern or number—like flicking a switch seven times instead of just one. Often the rituals are just exaggerated, overly completist versions of normal daily tasks, like brushing your teeth one by one, or saying evening prayers that take forty-five minutes. It says that children with OCD may have rituals of getting ready in the morning or going to bed at night which get debilitating because they become so lengthy and complex. I feel the hairs prickle on my neck, thinking of how difficult it's been to get Sam out the door in the mornings, and how agitated, almost tearful, it seemed to make him when I rushed him. How I swear I saw him re-tie a shoelace three times the other day.

I think about his exceptionally neat room, the precision of how he's arranged it all. I think about the things Dinah mentioned earlier.

Maybe we do need to talk.

"Gill? You okay?" Oliver comes into the room, turns on the light. I hadn't even noticed how dark it was in here, and now I blink like a mole at Oliver standing in the doorway.

"Oliver—" I swivel the laptop screen towards him. "Does this—does any of this remind you of Sam?"

He looks at the article headline, then back at me, surprised. But then he takes a seat and reads through it. He frowns at me.

"I don't know. Maybe. Where did this come from?"

I tell him about Dinah's call earlier.

"At first I thought...well, I thought she was just being alarmist." I keep my voice down, conscious of Sam in the next room. "Sam's been going through so much, and everyone can be a little, you know, a little odd in their own ways. But now that I've started reading about it...I don't know. A lot of it reminds me of him."

"I figured he was just a perfectionist," Oliver says. "I mean, have you seen his room? Hospital corners, Gill." He glances at the screen again. "Half a million kids in the United States have this?"

"Apparently." I close the lid. But is Sam one of them?

Oliver looks at me.

"So...what are you going to do? You think you should talk to him about it?"

Despite the "truce" Oliver extracted from me earlier, this just rankles me.

"Why do you say that like it's just up to me to do something?" I say. "What about you?"

Oliver looks incredulous.

"You want *me* to talk to him about this?"

I shrug. "Well, you're the guy. He likes you. It's less embarrassing than talking to me." I look over at the way my husband's frowning, almost recoiling. "Why does it always have to be me?" I burst out.

Oliver blinks at me.

"Why does *what* always have to be you?"

"You always leave me to fix things!" I say. I'm thinking of last night, of his response to the whole IVF conversation. And of course it's not *just* that. If there's ever anything to be smoothed over with our relatives—with my mom, or Oliver's mom even—or with our friends, the occasional tensions and awkwardnesses that crop up, Oliver always somehow sidesteps his way out of it. Literally or figuratively, he finds a way to leave the room.

"When things get awkward," I say, "you check out. You just leave me to handle them."

Oliver's staring at me. I see the defensive, angry cloud that moves across his face. Then he stands up, and I think he's about to leave the room but he doesn't. Instead he walks over to the window, his back to me.

"I didn't realize you felt that way," he says.

"Well," I say more quietly. "I do."

There's silence for a while.

"Gillian...maybe this sounds like a cop-out, but...I've always known you were better at those kinds of things: people, dealing with people, saying the right thing. I never really know what to say, and you always seem to know."

I feel some of the tension leave my shoulders. But though his admission softens me a bit, it's not enough. I think about the hours of my life— probably days of my life at this point—that I've spent worrying about how to say the right thing the right way; how to keep the peace, or soothe a conflict, or avoid giving offense. Oliver makes it sound like it's a gift I just happen to have;

something that just comes naturally. But if it comes naturally then why would it be so damned tiring?

Why would I be so damn tired?

"It's not magic, Oliver," I say. "It's not just some 'female intuition' fairy-dust thing. It's that I make the effort. And yes, maybe by now I'm better at those things than you are but if I am, it's because I've spent a lifetime *making the effort*."

The kitchen door opens and Sam stands in the doorway, eyes narrowed.

"Did something happen?" he asks.

I guess our voices—or my voice, at least—got pretty loud there for a minute.

"Everything's fine, Sam," I say.

His eyes flick between Oliver and me.

"Are you gonna come watch the ball drop?"

Oliver looks at me, and I look back at him.

"Sam, honey," I say. "Could you sit down for a minute?" I take a breath. "There's something I want to ask you about."

Chapter Fifteen

"Sam?"

He looks at me warily, then at Oliver.

"You're not in any kind of trouble," I say. "You've done absolutely nothing wrong."

He doesn't quite believe me, but slowly he lowers himself into one of the seats.

"Sam," I say carefully, "this might sound odd, but I"—I glance at Oliver—"*we*, just noticed some things you've been doing recently, and we wanted to ask you about them."

He stares at me.

"Things?"

"They're not bad things," I say. "We were just hoping you could tell us more."

Sam stares at me. Over by the window, Oliver isn't meeting my eyes. A few minutes ago, reading that article on OCD, all my intuition was whispering that Dinah was right. But now, I wonder if I've been barking up the wrong tree.

"Okay..." Sam draws out the word, making it clear how weird he thinks I'm being.

"Well, just to take an example," I push on: "your hands."

"My *hands*?"

He's trying to keep up the you're-so-weird tone, but is it just my imagination or is there a new, prickly energy in the room?

"Okay, just humor me," I say. "About how many times a day do you wash your hands, Sam? Ballpark."

I'm remembering, now, our day at the farmer's market, and the pink, chapped fingertips. How I put it all down to the winter weather.

He doesn't answer.

"Dunno," he says after a while.

"Just very approximately, Sam."

He's still silent.

"Is it more than ten?" I say, and he shrugs. I take a breath.

"More than fifteen?"

I don't get to ask about twenty, because Sam interrupts me angrily.

"Why do you even care? It's just being clean. Being clean is a good thing."

It's the sharpest, the angriest I've heard Sam

be, and I try not to wince. I knew he might get angry; I was even expecting it. But I'm not sure how to get around it. I hesitate, and then to my surprise Oliver clears his throat. He moves over to the table, puts his hands on the back of a chair.

"Sam...what happens if you *don't* wash your hands when you feel you're supposed to?"

Sam blinks like a rabbit in headlights, and suddenly I feel so much anguish for him. I almost want us to stop, because it's easy to see this interrogation is becoming painful for him. But now that I know we're onto something, I know that stopping isn't the right thing.

For a long time Sam says nothing.

"Sam?"

Another silence. He closes his eyes.

"I can't help it," he says finally. It comes out not much above a whisper. "I know it's crazy but I can't."

"Sam," I say. "It's okay. Whatever you're feeling is okay."

"No, it's not," he says, his eyes flashing wide open now, as angry as if I'd lied. "It's not okay. I'm a freak."

"*Nobody* is a freak," I say. "You hear me?"

He doesn't look at us.

"Then what am I—crazy? If you hear voices you're crazy, right?"

I glance back at Oliver, who's frowning.

"What do you mean, exactly?" I say, forcing my voice to stay steady. "What kind of voices?"

Sam shrugs. I can see the effort it takes him to force out the words.

"Well...it's one voice, really. And sometimes it's more of a feeling than a voice. But sometimes I feel like I can actually hear it, you know, speaking. Telling me that I have to do things again even though I've already done them. Or that I have to do things a certain number of times or in a certain way."

"And if you don't?" Oliver prompts, his voice quiet. I can see the look on his face. He's shocked at what this conversation is uncovering, probably more so than I am. I'm pretty sure just staying here at this table, he's having to override all his instincts to just get up and leave. He doesn't like going to dark places.

In other words, he's trying.

Sam looks at us.

"Well...the voice says bad things will happen if I don't do things just right. I don't even know *what* bad things. I just know they'll be bad...really bad."

He looks at me, his face full of doubt. Is he waiting for us to backtrack; to agree that after all, there's something really wrong with him, something unfixable that we don't want to be part of?

"Sam..." I say. "We're not doctors so we really don't know. But it sounds like you might have a similar condition to one that a lot of other people have. A lot of people say they hear a kind of 'voice' that makes them jump through hoops like that, so that bad things won't happen."

It's actually pretty much an exact reflection of what most of those websites were saying. These little rituals, they're not just personality quirks, and they're much more than regular perfectionism. What makes them so bad is that they come alongside this anxiety or dread that Sam's describing. Performing the rituals is what gives the person relief from the dread—but it's only temporary, of course. The dread comes back, and the cycle keeps going.

Sam looks at me, skeptical.

"What other people? You mean crazy people."

I sigh.

"Sam, honey..." I try to tread carefully. "'Crazy' doesn't actually mean anything, you know. It's just a word. A mean word, that people tend to use for things that scare them. I'm going to let you in on a secret," I say. "We all hear voices. Everybody on this planet. Okay? It's just, the voice you're hearing is louder and more unhelpful than most."

Sam looks at me, narrows his eyes.

"So *you* hear voices?" His voice is skeptical. "You're telling me..." I see him casting around for someone even more unlikely. "That—that the *President* hears voices?"

"Sam," I say. "I guarantee you the President hears voices."

He raises his eyebrows at me.

"Well, what about a conscience?" I say. "Isn't that a voice?"

Sam looks irritable.

"Okay," he says. "So what does your voice say?"

I hesitate. Given where I've been leading this conversation, it's not really a question I can avoid. But my hands are suddenly sweating. And because of how much I don't want to answer this question honestly, I realize just how brave Sam is being with us right now.

"Well," I say slowly. "Sometimes I'll make a mistake, and then my voice will tell me how stupid I am." I clear my throat. "It'll tell me that everybody *knows* how stupid I am and that they think I'm a fool. And ridiculous. Or..." I hesitate. This really is humiliating, and I'm starting to wish Oliver wasn't in the room. "Or I'll look in the mirror and the voice will say things like *look at all those wrinkles*, or *look how fat your arms are. Nobody wants to look at you.*"

I feel Oliver's startled eyes on me, but I avoid meeting them. Sam, meanwhile, is agog. I've come this far now.

"It also likes to tell me," I say, forcing out the words, "that I'm letting everyone down. That I'm not a very good daughter, or sister, or aunt." I take a deep breath, and say the last part. "And it tells me the reason I'm not a mom is...is because I wouldn't be a good enough one."

I feel Oliver shift in his seat. I focus on Sam's face instead, his high-alert eyes scanning mine. Children aren't used to getting admissions like this from adults. Maybe it's too much. I wonder whether I've unnerved him, or made him lose respect for me.

He sits silent for a while, then frowns.

"That's a different kind of voice, though," he says finally. "It's not the same as mine."

"Well...no," I agree. "It's not the same. My voice doesn't give me orders. Or threaten me. And it's not always there." *Just on bad days. Just a little too often, recently.* "But," I say, "it's still a person that lives in my head, that I didn't invite in, and that doesn't want the best for me even though it pretends it does. Doesn't that sound a little crazy to you?"

Sam looks to me, then Oliver, then the floor.

"I don't know. No. Maybe."

"They're just bullies, you know," I say. "Those voices—they try to tell us they're our friends. That they're protecting us; that we need them. But they're actually just bullies."

Sam's silent for a while. Slowly, he nods. We

sit for a while, saying nothing.

"I guess you haven't said anything about this to your parents?" I ask quietly.

He looks away.

"There's nothing they can do. I'm just like this."

I swallow a lump in my throat.

"Sam...for one thing I don't think that's true, that you're 'just like this.' I think it's something that's happening to you, and that you can get some help with. There are experts out there who know way, way more about this than we do." I look at him. "And as for your parents...even though they're not experts, they'll want to help too in whatever way they can."

Sam juts out his jaw.

"I can't make it go away. I've tried."

Oliver clears his throat.

"Sam," he says, "I think...I think the hard part is, the voices never really do go away, not all the way away. But over time, we can try to show them who's boss, you know?"

"I mean, I've tried being the boss." Sam shrugs. "But the voice is...it's really strong."

Oliver considers him.

"So...I'm not an expert, Sam, but I think we can do exercises for the mind, like we can for our bodies. You can train to make it stronger. You start with really small weights. Then when the small weights aren't so hard, you level up." He looks at Sam. "Nobody gets strong overnight."

Sam narrows his eyes.

"What kind of exercises?"

I glance at Oliver. "We're not the experts on that, Sam," I say. "But I bet your parents would like to find a really great expert to answer that question for you."

Sam scowls, and kicks his toe against the table leg.

"I don't want to talk to them about it," he says. "I don't want them to know."

"Sam...they have to know. Keeping a secret like this is too hard, it's too much work. You've already been keeping it for too long a time."

Sam keeps his gaze on the floor, not looking at either of us. Somewhere outside, distantly, I hear a bell ring, and cheering. The New Year is here.

"You really don't think I'm crazy?" Sam says,

not looking up.

I move to the seat next to him and put an arm around his shoulders. He pulls away a little, then doesn't.

"I think you're something very different," I say. "What I think you are, Sam, is a brave person going through a hard time."

Chapter Sixteen

It's late, long past the time for me to be asleep, but I don't feel tired, or even frustrated to still be awake. I roll over and stare out the window, the glinting snow that still clings to the branches outside.

I've been thinking all night about our conversation with Sam. And what keeps coming back to me about this condition—OCD, I guess, if that's what we're calling it—is how *normal* it is, even as it's also not normal at all. Haven't humans been doing this kind of thing since the dawn of time: crossing our fingers and knocking on wood, trying to ward off bad luck any way we can? Evil eyes to stop boats from sinking, and horseshoes over the door...we tell ourselves we can keep life's chaos at bay by offering the darkness this odd little dance. Because accepting that terrible things can—and do, and *will*—happen, and that in the end we cannot protect ourselves against them or trick them into leaving us alone, is sometimes more than our minds can accept. It occurs to me that it doesn't really matter all that much whether a therapist ends up putting the label "OCD" on whatever Sam's going through. What matters is that he's dealing with something that's hard and hard to control, and that we have to make sure he knows he's not alone.

When I asked him if he could remember when all this had started, he said it was probably not that long after Dad died. He told me how he said goodbye to his grandpa and then went to basketball practice—and a few hours later, Dad was dead. *It happened out of nowhere*, Sam insisted, looking at me. *For no reason*. Of course I could have reminded him that there was a reason: that there was something that wasn't working right anymore inside Dad's body; that Dad wasn't young anymore and that these things happen. But I didn't, because I knew Sam was right: what he meant was that Dad wasn't *supposed* to die, and he was right. No one we love is ever supposed to die.

I don't think Dad's death "caused" it, exactly. From what I read on the internet, it seems like OCD is mostly one of those things that you either get or you don't, rarely something you cause through bad parenting or even a traumatic experience. But still, there can be triggers.

I think about how I never put together the little clues in Sam's behavior, and it's not that I didn't notice them; I just didn't see this meaning in them. And for that matter, neither did his parents. But I think there are probably good reasons Josie noticed it and we didn't, and not just because Sam was perhaps less on his guard around her: it's because it's been a long time since we were children, and adults probably *expect* children to be baffling, with their own rituals and preoccupations that we don't understand. And then, so much of what's been going on with Sam looked like things we recognize and tend to reward—like being tidy, or careful, or hygienic.

But maybe most of all, we didn't notice because of love. Because for the children we love, we want a life with no bad fairies: with only the good fairies, who hand out futures of all charms and no curses, all light and no dark.

Which is impossible, of course. Darkness can't

be banished, only walked through.

And it's darkness that gives depth to light.

I roll over and prop myself up on my elbow. Oliver's fast asleep, his back to me, pale in the darkness. I watch his slow breaths rise and fall; the curl of hair around the nape of his neck.

A new year, I think. What darknesses will it bring us; what light?

*

Sam sleeps late the next morning, which after the intense talks of last night, doesn't surprise me. Meanwhile, I've sent an email to my sister. I figure we can talk this all through with Dennis when we see him and there's no point making him worry from a distance while he's still in air traffic limbo. But Abigail...she needs to wake up. If this shocks her, so much the better. And if it *doesn't* shock her into coming back home, I don't really know what will.

I text Dinah too: just a short message saying thank you and that she was right about talking to Sam. I don't think I was very gracious when she called me yesterday. I feel grateful this morning, that I have a friend who I can trust to say the unwelcome things.

Oliver's making breakfast, slouching around in his tracksuit bottoms, and it feels almost like it used to be—back before the brewery, and the late nights and working weekends, back before the stress of waiting every month to see if the pregnancy test came back positive. I wonder how long we can make it last. For a few hours more, at least, I'm going to savor this: the smell of pancakes, the snow on the trees outside, the coffee cup warm beside me on the table.

Then my phone pings with a message. I figure it's Dinah but then I see the name and almost spit out my mouthful of coffee.

Oliver turns around, spatula in hand, but he's just a figure in my peripheral vision as I open the message from my sister and stare at the screen.

Are you serious, Gillian? OCD?

I swallow.

Oliver's behind me, reading over my shoulder.

"Damn!" he says. "Gillian, just call her. You need to have an actual conversation with her, stat."

I hesitate, then hit Call.

It rings, then stops. Another message comes

in.

I'm sorry, Gillian.

Three dots flicker.

Mom will be there soon.

I stare at the screen, and behind me I can tell Oliver is too.

"What the hell?"

"'Mom will be there soon?'"

Oliver shakes his head and looks out the window.

"Well, she wasn't lying, at any rate."

I follow his eyes, and when I look out the window, I see Mom in the driveway. She's hesitating, standing very still, as though she's tempted to just do a one-eighty and march away again.

I go down the hallway, swing the door open.

"Mom," I say. "Abigail texted me. What is this? What's going on?"

*

Mom sits at the kitchen table, a mug of coffee in front of her. She looks, well, she looks positively *rumpled,* and Mom never looks rumpled.

"Sam's upstairs?" she says. I nod.

"Asleep. Mom...what is it? Is somebody sick?"

She shakes her head. Glances around at Oliver, who's still standing by the stove.

"Should I...go?" he says, but Mom shakes her head again.

"Stay with Gillian."

My stomach turns. Bad news. Not that I doubted, by now, that it would be. And not just bad news: I see it in the way she holds herself, in the way her eyes move. This is a confession.

Mom puts her hands around the cup of coffee, looks up at me. Her eyes are calm, now, almost defiant. "Your father and I...we made a decision in a very different world, Gillian. We did what we thought was best. We never dreamed she would find out."

Those alarming, extraordinary words hang in the air.

"Find out what?" I say, my own voice sounding like a stranger's.

Mom swallows.

"Your sister's gone to Florida, Gillian—" Mom takes a breath, looks at Oliver, and then back at me. "To meet her birth mother."

Chapter Seventeen

My head's spinning. The words don't make
sense. Of course they don't.

Your sister's birth mother.

"Abigail..." I have to push my voice out of my
chest; it's stopped working. "Abigail's *adopted*?"
And then a new thought, like a wave crashing
on top of the last one.

"Wait: am *I* adopted?"

Mom shakes her head.

"Not you, Gillian. Your sister, yes."

Those six words ring in the air. Splitting our
world into shards like a cracked mirror.

"I don't understand," I say.

Mom looks at me.

"You know how it was for your father and
me," she says, her voice low. "We'd been trying
for a baby for—for so long, Gillian."

Yes, I think. *And Abigail was your miracle.*
That's how it was supposed to be; that's the
story I grew up with. Abigail was the miracle

baby, and then there was me. Miracle Number Two.

"Your father's sister," Mom goes on. "Lorna. The baby of the family—you've heard us mention her." She looks at me. "When Lorna was eighteen, she got pregnant." Mom hesitates. "I remember when your father told me. He felt guilty, like it was somehow his fault, and meanwhile all I felt was rage. How could this...this *child,* have everything I wanted? And have it by accident; as a *mistake*, without ever wanting it? And then..." she goes on, "when your dad said Lorna was going to have the baby adopted, I just...I felt this *certainty*, Gillian. This rightness. That saying, 'God works in mysterious ways,' I'd never really felt it before, but I felt it then, in my bones." She takes a breath. "I was the one to suggest it to your father—that we'd take her, that she'd be our daughter. He was doubtful at first. Not on his own account: he was worried about me, if it would be fair to me? Would it be better to try and adopt from a stranger, where everything was anonymous? But I was sure. I was just sure." She looks at me. "You have to understand that. She was *wanted,* she was so wanted."

I can hear myself breathing. I'm hearing all the words but I can't yet believe them. I'm barely conscious of Oliver in the room, but I sense his presence nearby, his disbelief a fainter echo of mine.

"Your dad and I went to the hospital with Lorna. When Abigail"—my stomach jolts to hear my sister's name, though I've been waiting for it—"when Abigail was born and I held her, I'd never loved anyone so much in my life.

"We'd told ourselves," she goes on, "that we'd tell her when she was older. You have to remember, things were different then. A lot of adoptions were closed adoptions. A lot were kept secret. There were no children's books or online communities or information about what to tell your child. But we decided when she was old enough to understand, seven or eight maybe, we'd explain things to her." Mom closes her eyes. "But then we had you."

The words hit me like a wall. I stare at Mom, and she gazes back at me.

"Can you begin to understand? They say it happens more than you'd think, you know—

people trying for years, *years,* and then the moment they adopt: boom. But we had never even in our wildest dreams, imagined such a thing. We never imagined Abigail being anything other than an only child. And then...how were we to tell her the truth *then*? After we'd had a second child, the kind of child we'd tried to have for so long? Can you understand what that would have felt like to her to know that; what it would have done to her?" She looks at me. "How could a child in her position not have grown up thinking they were second-best? That they were 'unnecessary,' once we had you?" She shakes her head. "Of course it wasn't how we felt. We thought we'd won the world's greatest lottery, to have you both. But how could we have explained all that to a child like Abigail and expected her not to feel...superfluous?"

I sit, dazed. My brain pounds with conflicting thoughts. I know—of course I know—what Mom means. And yet I hate her right now for not telling us the truth.

Mom sweeps a hand under her reddening eyes.

"You see, don't you? How it would have felt to

her? And of course, by the time she *got* to an age where we could have begun to talk about such things..." She shakes her head. "From the beginning, Gillian, I couldn't seem to get it right with her. Even as a baby, she cried so much. So restless. It seemed like I was always getting it wrong. We were always this close to upsetting the apple cart. How could we have thrown something like that into the mix?"

I want to get up from my chair—I need water, or to move, I need *something*—but dizziness pushes me back down.

"Gill," Oliver says. "Are you okay?"

I shake my head, then stop when it feels like everything in there's going tumbling. I look back at my mother.

"Mom...this is huge. You get that, right? This changes everything? It's like our whole childhood was—was a lie."

She puts her hand to her mouth, her fingers curling in on themselves like she's protecting something, and shakes her head.

"It wasn't a lie, Gillian. It was real."

"But you and Dad kept this from us. And..." I choke up. "And now he's gone."

Mom looks down at the table. She draws a breath.

"I regret that," she says. "I regret very much, that Abigail—and you—that you never got to talk to him about this. But we made our decision long ago. We never thought of revising it. We never thought you'd know."

And yet Abigail was his favorite, I think. She was, we all knew she was, even if we've never said it out loud; even if this might be the first time I'm voicing those words even to myself.

"If you'd told us from day one," I say, "that would have been the right way. That would have been the only painless way."

"Not painless." Mom shakes her head. "Never painless. Look at how it was already, without any of that added weight. The way you two grew apart; the way she acted out. Can you imagine how much worse it would have been if you both had known the truth? I dread to imagine what her teens would have been like. I don't think we'd have been able to hang onto her till she finished high school. We'd have lost her long before."

I sit with that. Speculation, alternative

universes. None of us know what might have been, had things been different.

"You have to understand," Mom says. "When Abigail was born, there was no such thing as DNA testing. It never in a million years occurred to us that one day you'd just be able to spit on a stick and everything would come crumbling down..." She looks at me. "Your father and I, it was a sacrifice for us, too, you know—having to hide something like that from you both. But we did what we thought was best. What we thought was the kindest thing."

I drop my gaze from hers. Everything in the room seems too bright, lurching in and out of focus. Abigail. My sister. My sister and yet not my sister.

I remind myself that family isn't blood, it isn't mere genes. Of course she's my sister, of course nothing about that has changed.

But if nothing has changed, why do I feel the ground shifting underneath me like this; upending itself forever?

"She did a DNA test, didn't she?" I say. I was right. I must have been. The voucher on our hall table. I imagine a world in which Oliver and I had just used those stupid vouchers. We would have gotten our perfectly normal, predictable results, and my sister would never have discovered a secret that would turn our worlds upside down.

Imagine if Jeff had gotten Dinah a different anniversary present.

If Dinah had given those vouchers to someone else.

If I'd just thrown the damn things in the recycling.

Mom shifts in her seat.

"Yes," she says. "She said you gave her some coupon." She looks down at the coffee in her mug, which must be long cold by now. "I hadn't realized it was so easy, you know. I thought those tests were just things people did to tell you how Italian or Irish you were; that sort of thing. I didn't know you could simply tick a box and find all sorts of people on it. Only people that want to be found, of course." She clears her throat. "Evidently Lorna wanted to be found. I suppose she must have done it on purpose. She must have thought about it—about Abigail looking for her one day."

I sit there, trying to imagine what it would have been like in my sister's shoes. Getting information like that from an automated message on some internet site. Seeing a stranger flash up as a genetic match for your parent. I look over at Oliver.

"But she kept it to herself?" I say. "She didn't tell us when she found this all out?"

Mom looks away.

"I think she tried to tell me, Gillian." She clears her throat. "I...I was in the middle of the Thanksgiving fundraiser. I was barely even looking at my phone. I had some missed calls from your sister..."

Dad was driving back from Westchester ten days before Thanksgiving last year. I think it's a pretty rough time of year for all of us.

"And then," Mom stumbles on, "when I called her back...I assumed it was because of your father, Gillian, how strange her mood was, but she was just...seething. I don't know how to describe it. I felt like she was waiting to catch me out somehow but I didn't understand why. I suppose by then she'd had a couple of days to figure things out; to absorb the worst of the shock. She'd spoken to Lorna..." Mom hesitates. "Apparently Lorna said to talk to me first, but Abigail had had enough by then." She looks at me. "By the time I talked to her I suppose she already knew all the important parts, and she'd changed her mind about wanting to confront me. By then she was just angry. I think it was her way of punishing me, Gillian—and of staying in control. Feeling like she was fooling *me,* watching *me* make a fool of myself in all my ignorance..." Mom swallows.

I sit there, with this new reality swirling around me. Small truths drop like coins, plinking somewhere in my memory. Things about our world that suddenly make sense in a new way.

Like *why* Lorna has stayed away all these years; more even than Dad's other siblings.

Like how, growing up, Mom was always warning us to "be careful with boys" to a point that seemed old-fashioned and excessive. Now I know where the paranoia came from—Mom thinking Abigail's fate might be the same as Lorna's.

Or like Abigail's looks—how as a kid when plundering old photo albums, we landed on a childhood picture of Dad with his siblings , and Abigail brought it in to Dad to demand who the girl in the photograph was. The girl who looked so like her.

Oliver gets up, fills a glass of water from the tap, and comes back, pushing it across the table to me. Concern flashes in his eyes.

The water tastes cold and strange. I wonder at what point this truth will start to settle; when my brain will stop firing these strange semaphores into my nervous system, making everything feel unreal.

"When did she call you?" I say. "When did she tell you all this?"

Mom hesitates.

"This morning. Early. I think after you texted her about Sam..." Mom swallows; obviously the prospect of her grandson having OCD is painful for her too. "She's ready to come home," she adds.

I close my eyes, giving a split-second rest to my brain.

"What about Dennis?" I say. "Has she told him?"

Mom nods. "She was going to call him next.

He knows by now."

I stare out the window at the white, blameless snow.

"She told no one," I say. "Not even him. She just left."

Mom nods slowly. "I think she was angry at all of us, Gillian. All of us but Sam."

I breathe it in. So now I know.

Lorna—my dad's sister, my estranged aunt...my sister's birth mother. She lives in Miami. And that's where Abigail is now.

Mom glances back down at her coffee. There's something about the gesture, something about her eyes, about her face.

"What is it?" I say, my voice sharp. "Mom, what is it?"

Mom hesitates, and looks up.

"Lorna's....she's..."

I wait.

"She's sick," Mom says.

Sick. I hear the way she says it.

"Is she dying?" I ask, in a voice that even to my ears sounds small and faint.

Mom blinks at me, then sort of shrugs.

"She had—has—a tumor in her liver. She,

well..." Mom looks at me. "She used to be an alcoholic. Her liver was compromised. The surgery was a few days ago. It sounds like they didn't quite get it all."

Oliver shoots a shocked glance my way.

"There's still a lot they can do," Mom says. "But the prognosis is unclear. It's a question of how much time she has left. Whether it's years, or..." She swallows. "Or a lot less."

Chapter Eighteen

Unthinkable.

For my sister to discover this person and then, discovering them, to know they're not long for this world....

I stare at my mother's taut face, and then at Oliver's, which mirrors my shock. And then at my phone on the kitchen table.

"Will she speak to me now?" I say. "Now that I know?" My voice sounds bold and steady, which is not how I feel at all.

Mom sighs.

"Try her." She looks at me. "She doesn't want to hear any more from me right now, Gillian. But she gave me permission to tell you. She said I was the one who should tell you the truth."

I feel a sudden wave of anger.

"This honestly didn't cross your mind, Mom?" I say. "That this whole thing could have had anything to do with how she just took off?"

Mom flinches, and looks away from me.

"Gillian, we'd just buried it so deep."

I close my eyes.

This is what I'm starting to know: that we can bury the truth as deep as we like, but that, like heat or rot, truth rises.

It always rises.

*

Mom told me, I text. *Can we speak?*

I wait for what feels like a long time, waiting for the three little dots. But instead, the phone rings, and I almost drop it right where I'm sitting. My heart beating fast, I pick up as Mom's eyes and Oliver's follow me. I leave the kitchen and move to the living room. Thank God Sam's still upstairs....

"Abigail?"

"Gillian..."

I bite my lip to keep in the sudden wave of feeling. My sister. I'd forgotten the particular pitch of her voice. How low it is, how musical; the cold-water shock of it. And now for the first time I'm wondering where she inherited it from. If the woman who gave birth to her has a voice just like it.

"So, Mom told me," I say.

Silence.

"Well. Now you know. Now we both do."

"Abigail...I'm sorry. Are you okay?"

Another silence.

"Not really," she says. "Are you?"

"Not really."

We stay on the line: her breathing, me breathing.

"Mom feels terrible," I say. Do I really think it'll make her feel better? I don't know.

"Gillian," my sister says. "I don't give a rat's ass."

I swallow.

"Is Lorna...is she really that sick?"

"She's sick," Abigail pauses. "She doesn't have family, Gillian. She has friends, and people she loves. But she doesn't have family." Her voice slows again. "The doctors don't know. Nobody knows, Gillian. It depends how she responds to the rest of the treatment...chemo, radiotherapy." She swallows. "At first she wasn't going to do any of that at all. She said she'd prefer to just let nature take its course. But now she says she's changed her mind." Abigail takes another breath. "I heard there's about a 30 percent chance of her being alive in five years, for a cancer like this."

I swallow. Thirty percent is not a lot.

"But if the treatments don't go well..." I hear the shrug in her voice. "It could be less than a year; maybe much less."

I glance out the window. How surreal it is, all this snowy beauty. The peacefulness.

"What about Sam?" I say quietly. "What are you going to tell him?"

The words have barely left my lips when a rustling sound from the doorway makes me stiffen.

"When are you going to tell me what?" a young voice says, and I turn to see my nephew standing in the doorway.

*

"Do you understand, darling?" Abigail's saying. She's on FaceTime now, with my phone planted in the middle of the kitchen table for Sam's benefit.

I wasn't supposed to give the game away. Abigail was supposed to explain it to him all in person when she came home. But that wasn't going to work anymore; not after Sam had overheard what he did. Perhaps if I'd had my head together I could have covered it up better and found some excuse, but such an idea was beyond me today.

"Do you, Sam?" Abigail repeats. "I'm sorry I waited to tell you. I just...had so much to figure out. And I didn't want to bring her into your life unless she seemed like a good person. A safe person." My sister hesitates. "And I wasn't at my best, Sam. It was all a bit of a shock to me. I probably wasn't quite thinking straight."

Sam listens, still as a statue. He's stopped casting glances at me, at Oliver; at Mom. The past few minutes he's just been staring at a spot on the table.

I know Abigail didn't want to share this conversation with Mom; she doesn't even want to hear the sound of Mom's voice right now. But to her credit, she manages not to show that anger around Sam.

And she doesn't tell Sam that Lorna's sick. I don't know if she just intuitively feels that it would be too much or if she's thinking of the OCD thing, and how badly Dad's death threw Sam. Either way, she doesn't mention it, which I think is probably wise right now.

At a certain point, Sam raises his eyes to Mom.

"Why didn't you tell Mom?" he says, his voice small but hard as a pebble. "Why didn't you tell us?"

I see Mom swallow.

"I'm sorry, Sam," she says. "It was...it was a misjudgment. Your grandfather and I, we made a choice and once it was made, we had to stand by it."

Sam scowls.

"He wasn't my real grandpa," he says. "And you're not even my real grandma."

In a second, Mom's eyes well up.

"Oh, Sam," she says. "The way I love you is real. There's nothing realer than that."

Sam gets up, and without looking at any of us, moves past me and stalks out the door.

"Sam—"

Oliver gets out of his seat, ready to go after him.

"Leave him," Abigail says from the phone. "Give him a minute."

Sam's bedroom door slams upstairs.

I don't know if Abigail hears it but her gaze

locks on mine, and for a moment there's a bolt of some shared emotion between us.

"Maybe I should just check on Sam—" Mom starts, but Abigail snaps.

"He doesn't need you right now. Gillie"—she looks at me—"go and see if he'll talk to me, will you?"

I glance at Mom and Oliver before I take the phone and leave. Upstairs, I knock on Sam's door.

"Sam—honey? It's your mom. She's still on the phone. She'd really like to talk to you." When he doesn't answer I crack the door. He's lying on his bed, arms around a pillow. As I open the door he turns away from me.

"This makes me sad too, Sam," I say. "I liked sharing more DNA with you."

He makes a small, scoffing noise.

I take a breath. "But it *is* just DNA, Sam. It doesn't get to decide the stuff that matters most."

He doesn't say anything. I move softly to the bed, and place the phone down by his pillow.

"Just talk to your mom. Okay?"

Downstairs I walk back into a kitchen that still

vibrates with shellshock. Oliver's making fresh coffee, and pauses to glance at me with a *what the hell* look. Mom's usually straight back is slumped, and she looks folded in on herself in a way that I can't ever remember seeing before.

"He's going to hate me now," she says.

I shake my head.

"He's angry."

"He's my grandson," she says—not to me, but as a plea to the universe.

It's not just Sam or Abigail: I'm angry at her too. I'm angry that she hoarded the truth instead of being free with it. I'm angry that she gave no one in her family, including herself, the breathing room we all needed. I'm angry that we all grew into the shapes we did and that maybe it never had to be this way. But right now, in this moment, something else crowds out the anger.

I go over and stand beside her, and I put my arms around her. And I hold her the way I remember her holding me once upon a time. Back when Abigail and I were very, very young; back before she decided we'd outgrown it. The grip that says *I've got you, I've got you, and it's all going to be okay.*

And I hope so hard that that's true.

*

Sam, red-eyed and sullen, comes through the kitchen door.

"She wants to speak to you."

He hands me my phone back without making eye contact, then leaves.

I draw a steadying breath and raise the phone to my ear.

"Abigail?"

She exhales.

"Gillian." She pauses. "I...I have to say thank you. For taking care of him and, well, for the email."

"That's okay."

A silence.

"Gillian?..."

And there's something in her tone that takes me back to childhood. Back to when I used to reach my skinny wrists down into our mailbox to get those detention notices before Mom could see them. I try to keep the trepidation out of my voice.

"What is it?" I say.

"He wants to meet her." Abigail pauses. "Sam wants to meet her."

That seems natural.

"Gillian...I haven't told him that she's sick. I can't now, after everything. But if we wait...she might not even be around this summer, Gillian. Or if she is..." Abigail swallows. "We just don't know. Right now she's doing well. She looks good, healthy. But she might not even want visitors, if things...you know. Deteriorate."

I start to understand. If things go downhill fast, even if Sam *can* visit her, it might not be the same. He might be visiting someone very sick. And if he does get the chance to make memories, they might be sad memories, or scary ones.

"He really wants to meet her, Gillie."

That crackling, nervous feeling comes back into the air.

"Abigail..." I hesitate. "What are you asking?"

She takes a deep breath.

"There's a flight leaving Albany for Miami at five-thirty today."

"Abigail..." I say, my mouth going dry. Involuntarily, I glance at the time. It's noon.

Albany airport is thirty minutes away.

"Please, Gillie. I'll book the tickets right now if you say yes."

"Abigail, I can't..."

I hear her breath quiver on the line.

"Gillian...if he doesn't meet her now, he might never. And he'll blame us all for it." I hear her breath on the line. "I just don't want him to have regrets, Gillie, like I do about Dad. About what we never got to say."

That cuts me to the quick, and I think she knows it.

"Just ask him, Gillie. And if he says no then it's no. But just ask him."

I pause. I can feel myself being dragged closer to this wild plan, as if my sister's will is a whirlpool drawing me in. I've felt this feeling before many times. Sometimes it's led good places; other times, bad.

"What about Dennis?" I say finally.

"You said his flight's delayed," Abigail says. "It's still not scheduled, right?—and it'll take him at least twenty-four hours to get home. I can get in the car with Sam the moment his flight takes off. We'll still beat him home."

I pause.

"But Abigail...I don't know if he'll like this. This whole idea."

She hesitates.

"You don't *need* permission, Gillian."

I feel my eyes widen.

"You mean not tell him?"

"I'll tell him," Abigail says eventually. "I'll tell him once you're on the plane."

"*If,*" I say, trying to hold my ground, though it already feels like I've conceded too much.

"*If* you're on the plane," she says quickly.

"Abigail..."

"Please, Gillian," she says.

I close my eyes, trying to weigh it all in my befuddled brain. What's to be gained and what's to be lost. And I think of Mom earlier, folded in on herself at the kitchen table. Afraid of losing Abigail, afraid of losing Sam. I glance towards the living room door.

"If we come, Mom's coming too," I say. The words supply themselves before I can ask myself whether they're wise.

"No." Abigail's voice is curt. "I have nothing to say to her, Gillian."

CLAIRE AMARTI

"I understand," I say. "And you have every right to feel those feelings. But if you want me to bring Sam, that's how it's happening. We're doing this as a family."

She doesn't say a word; she doesn't have to. I feel her fury bouncing along the telephone wires. The silence simmers.

"Gillian," she repeats. "I don't have anything to say to her."

"That's okay," I say. "You don't have to."

Abigail's silence lasts a moment longer.

"The flight's at five-thirty," she says at last. "Text me if you're coming."

Chapter Nineteen

Oliver keeps glancing sidelong at me as he drives us to the airport: Mom and Sam in the back, me in the passenger seat beside him. He took me aside before we left the house.

"Gillian..." He put his hand on my arm. "Are you sure this is a good idea?"

It was a laughable question. Of course I wasn't sure. But I'd spoken to Sam and my nephew's reaction had been instant.

"I want to go." He'd sat up on his bed, looking at me with a defiance that reminded me of his mother.

"Sam..." I'd hesitated. "You know that...it might not be like you expect. You might be disappointed."

He'd looked at me.

"I want to go. Mom met her. I want to meet her."

And I understand, I do. When a truth springs out of nowhere—especially an earthquake of a truth like this one—you want to respond to it.

You want to *do* something. You want to throw out all the old stuff like a set of clothes that no longer fits, and remake the world according to your new reality.

So we packed our overnight cases, and downstairs Oliver purchased three one-way fares to Miami.

Now, out on the highway, snow is piled high against the side of the road, icy and blackening from traffic, a depressing charcoal color on the side that faces the highway. I'd suggested to Mom that she sit in the front seat—I figured it would be better if she and Sam didn't have to sit side by side right now—but the two of them ended up in the back anyway. Right now they're emitting the kind of silence you could cut with a knife.

"Everyone okay back there?" I raise my voice in a jolly-holiday timbre which lands jarringly with the mood in the car. Sam takes off his earphones, which I think he's been wearing as a kind of defense mechanism against Mom.

"What?" he says.

"Your aunt's just checking in," Oliver glances in the rearview. "Wanting to know if everyone's okay."

Sam tucks his hands deeper into his armpits.

"*I'm* fine," he says, in a tone designed to remind us that we may have a pathological liar in the back seat.

There's an awkward beat, and then Sam puts his headphones back on. Oliver glances in the rearview mirror, overtakes the driver ahead.

"So this is just for one night?" He addresses the question partly to me and partly to Mom, his voice low. I glance over at him.

"Probably. Or we might stay a second night, I guess. What do you think, Mom?"

"I think your sister's going to want to pack me on a return flight as soon as she can, Gillian."

"Mom..." I glance quickly towards Sam, whose gaze is turned fixedly toward the window. I don't hear the tinny music coming out of his headphones like usual. I can tell he's using them to ignore us, but I'm not convinced he can't hear us.

"Oliver," Mom turns to him suddenly, like he's the one voice of reason in the car. "What do you think? Is this crazy, me getting on this flight? Should *any* of us be getting on this flight?"

Oliver glances sideways at me and clears his throat.

"Mom, come on," I say. "Don't do this now. We're almost at the airport."

"Oliver?" Mom insists.

He shifts his eyes momentarily towards me, and I sense betrayal coming.

"I think it's rushed," he says. "And that you're letting your Abigail pull your strings." *As usual,* he doesn't say, but might as well.

"Well, there isn't much time," I bristle, "before..."

Oliver shoots me a knowing glance. "Before Dennis gets home?" he says.

He really does know how to activate my self-doubt. But he's right, isn't he? There *is* something a bit off about how I'm rushing to set things in motion before Dennis can stop them. Dennis, who after all is Sam's parent, and who's presumably asleep right now in the middle of his night-time over there.

Will he react as badly to this as Abigail thinks he will?

Surely what we're doing is for the best. Sam will be with his mom, and Mom and I will be there to make sure nothing goes wrong.

A hawk cuts through the sky overhead, and Oliver signals for the airport exit. Then we crest a hill and the airport comes into view. A plane cuts in low, the noise thunderous over our heads, and I take a breath and hope this isn't the worst idea ever.

*

We sit three in a row on the plane: mom in the aisle seat, me in the middle, and Sam next to the window. He's edgy, shifting the window blind up and down until the flight attendant asks him to stop.

"So we'll be back in Westchester by the time Dad gets home?" he says.

I clear my throat, tamping down the little nervous feeling at the mention of Dennis.

"That's the plan," I say to Sam. "It depends a little bit on his flight schedule. But it should work out that way." Even at its best, the flight from Myanmar takes almost thirty hours to JFK, with two or three different stopovers.

"Drinks?" Another flight attendant is passing with the beverage cart, rolling it to a halt beside us.

"Coffee, please," Mom says, which going by how jittery she already is seems like a terrible idea. Sam orders a Coke and I take a seltzer, though I'm tempted to ask for a large glass of hard liquor—anything to tamp down my brain from all the hectic rapid-firing it's still doing. The flight attendant hands out some cheese twists and Mom and I pass ours down to Sam.

"Thanks," he mumbles, not quite looking up. The way he's trying not to look at Mom right now reminds me of me driving past the fertility clinic, desperately trying to avoid eye contact and the feelings I didn't want to feel.

I watch Sam carefully sanitizing his hands, and feel again that flicker of concern about this whole expedition. It's all going to be pretty intense, and I hope it won't throw him off balance. But he fiercely wanted to come, and I have to take him at his word that he's ready for this.

I watch him tapping at the in-flight entertainment screen, which is pay-per-view. I see his glance flick towards me when he realizes, but he doesn't want to ask.

"Here." I swipe my card through the slot on

screen. "Knock yourself out."

He does knock himself out: within twenty minutes, he's out cold with his cheek against the headrest, mouth ajar.

"Poor lamb," Mom says. "This is all so much to take in."

I look at her.

"No kidding."

I've been operating on some kind of autopilot: on the surface moving forward in this new reality...but below the surface, most of me is floating in an ocean of dreamy disbelief. My brain flickers between two worlds—the world that I woke up to this morning, and the one I'm in now—without yet realizing that one of those worlds is dead. Adrenalin's been keeping me going for the past few hours. Now at cruising altitude it's finally starting to leak away, and like Sam, if I closed my eyes for a moment I'd no doubt be out cold. But I don't want to fall asleep, because then when I wake up I'll have to do all the work of reacquainting my brain with reality all over again.

"Mom..." I don't even know where to start my questions. There are so many things I've been thinking about since this morning. Some things that make more sense than before; others that make less. Pieces fitting together into a new, different jigsaw.

"Why was it always so bad between you?" I blurt out. "Between you and Abigail?"

Mom looks at me.

"You were always fighting," I say. I've always blamed Abigail more so than Mom for that—but now I'm wondering if I was right to.

Mom sighs.

"I tried, Gillian. And it wasn't just me, you know. Abigail could be...disruptive, at school. She didn't understand compromise, she wasn't accommodating; she couldn't just accept what was and wasn't appropriate." Mom looks at me. "She always thought I was nagging her; trying to change her. But I was trying to help her, Gillian. I was trying to keep her safe. She was always so headstrong—*so* headstrong—and the world isn't kind to people like that, especially young women. Once in ten times you break the system, but nine times out of ten the system breaks you."

I look at my mother, wondering where this is

coming from.

"I don't mean to speak ill of Lorna," Mom goes on. "But no one ever taught that girl to think ahead, to consider consequences; to just slow herself *down*. I saw a lot of that in your sister. She was always so restless, always impatient. So stubborn, and hang the consequences." She sighs. "I felt she needed someone to balance her out, and your father certainly wasn't going to do it; he never checked her, never. And I didn't want her to make trouble for herself, Gillian.

"But she never listened to me. It was like she *knew*." Mom glances over. "Maybe it sounds silly saying it, but sometimes when she was an infant I felt she knew in her bones that I wasn't the mother her body remembered; that I wasn't the one who'd carried her. And yet with your father she was different. She'd scream and scream at me, but then when your father picked her up she was quiet as a lamb."

I study Mom as she speaks, wondering how much of these memories is colored by her own fears and doubts. If Abigail really cried for her and not for Dad, or if that's just the way Mom saw it.

Mom shakes her head.

"It was like she was always trying to be gone: always walking or crawling in the opposite direction. Even before she could crawl, always with her eyes on something just outside of the room. She never wanted to just *be*; to just be in my arms."

But some babies are like that: curious, impatient. Mom didn't need to take it personally.

"Do you—" I hesitate. "Did you bond with her? When she was a baby?"

I would never have dreamed of asking my mother such a question before today. We're a private sort of family, I suppose, with a nervous sixth sense for anything taboo to say aloud. But now it's like the rules of the game have changed.

Mom sighs.

"I've asked myself that, over the years; if I failed her somehow, back then at the start." She looks at me. "I don't know, Gillian. Was it different with Abigail to how it was with you? Yes, absolutely. But it wasn't that I didn't love her as much. I just felt so much *better* about myself as your mother. You were such a relief."

She looks at me. "You were quiet, you would just sit in my lap and that would be enough for you. You never went off looking for trouble, I never had to worry about you like that. Abigail just...she *lunged* at danger. You were my little fraidy-cat."

I've heard this before—plenty of times—and I still dislike hearing it. Apparently everything frightened me as a small child: swings; the ocean; dogs, cats, bicycles, vacuum cleaners; you name it. *Mouse,* Dad called me: a nickname that no doubt he meant affectionately but which I grew to secretly hate. Abigail was the one who would throw herself at danger "like there was a self-destruct trigger inside her," as Mom used to put it.

So I've heard these comparisons plenty, and I'm not sure that they're flattering to either me or my sister, but until today I've always taken them pretty much at face value: me and my timidity, Abigail and her recklessness. But suddenly I wonder how Abigail's recklessness might have looked to another parent. If instead of self-destruction and a wanton urge for danger, they would have seen a fearless, adventurous child. If they would have been impressed by Abigail's resilience and her indifference to pain. If they would have been proud.

"What if those weren't bad things, Mom?" I say now. "I mean, what if Abigail was just...really independent? And...brave?"

I wonder if Mom even realizes the bias that was in her from the start: when she held Abigail for the first time, along with the wave of love, how much fear she felt. Not just the regular new-parent fear, but fear of what was *inside* her daughter; of whatever genes lay coded inside her, because for some strange reason we tend to think the genes we have produced are safer than the rest. Does Mom understand the difference it made that from the minute I was born she trusted my genes—and Abigail never got the same benefit?

"To tell you the truth, Gillian," Mom sighs, "I think I just thought that it would all be much easier." She looks at me, then over at Sam, mouth open, head drooping. "Wasn't that a silly thing to think? I'd just had so much time to watch other people become mothers, I suppose I thought I could do it better. And then, well...it was so hard."

I remind myself that leaving everything else aside, Mom was also just a mother dealing with two infants less than a year apart. Of course she was frazzled. Of course all she wanted was for her babies to sit still and suck quietly on their pacifiers.

"I wouldn't have changed my mind, you know," Mom says quietly. "Even if I had known we were going to have you." She looks at me. "It's the sort of thing people wonder: *If you had known, would you still have...?* But I would have, Gillian. I'd always have wanted your sister. I always *have* wanted her." Mom swallows.

"She's my daughter."

Chapter Twenty

I see her as the glass doors slide open, her hands clasped behind her back, her face taut. I'm struck again by how beautiful she is, my sister. Beautiful the way a sheer cliff is beautiful. Or a stormy sea. She steps towards us, fast and hesitant at the same time. Her eyes travel quickly over mine, over Mom's. And then they lock on the person beside me.

"Sam." His name is a question.

"Hi, Mom," he says, steady and careful. If her voice was a question, now his is the answer: *no, I haven't forgiven you yet, not completely.* I see how much she wants to hug him and instead, rests a hand over his shoulders, half-ready for him to shake her off.

"Gillian." She looks at me and I see the *thank you* in her eyes, for bringing Sam to her. But there's something else too—almost a defiance, a *so now you know* in the set of her chin, the narrowing of her eyes.

Does she still see me as her sister? I feel like

someone's taken scissors to the threads that link us together. Threads that for years we haven't truly been nurturing...but I'd always just assumed were *there,* would always be there, because you can't undo blood. But now everything feels unstable, like my sister could shake us off if she wanted, and maybe it wouldn't take so very much at all.

"Abigail..." Mom says.

My sister reluctantly meets her eyes.

"Hi," she says. Not *hi, Mom.* She says nothing to her, just looks back at the rest of us.

"Ready?" she says. "The car's outside."

*

As we drive I see Abigail's eyes in the rearview flicking towards me, skittish and questioning. *All these years*, I think, and we still haven't found a way to trust each other, she and I.

"Sam, you and I have a lot to talk about." Abigail glances over at him in the passenger seat. "A *lot.* So the two of us are going to go out for some tacos—they have a taqueria by the hotel that you're going to love—and do some catching up." She glances back at Mom and me. "And I'm sure Gillian and—and your grandma—"

she says, but the words seem to stick in her throat, "will be fine making their own dinner plans for tonight. Okay?"

The airport's not far from the downtown, and soon we're off the expressway and on city streets. It feels like another country here—people outside in summer-weather clothes, strolling, relaxed. Holidaymakers. Mom has rolled down the window and the Florida night air drifts through the car, warm even in the evening.

The hotel is low-budget and nondescript, the lobby a large rectangle with a bar at one end. We wait at reception under yellowish lights and I look around at our little group: my sister, beautiful, tired, angry; my mother, looking out of place in this slightly shabby environment and trying not to show just how out of place she feels in her whole life right now. And Sam, staying close to his mother but keeping a distance still, like a tiny force-field: the distance of not yet forgiven.

Mom and I get our key cards—we're in a double queen down the hall from Abigail's room. Meanwhile they've put a folding cot in my sister's room for Sam. We part ways outside the elevator.

"I'll text you later, okay?" Abigail says, directing her gaze at me rather than Mom. There's so much to say, so much to unpack. I just nod.

"Talk soon."

Once inside our room, Mom opens the windows and we hang up the few items of clothing we've brought with us. I take out my phone and turn it off airplane mode. A text from Oliver pops up, checking in, and then another alert: Missed call from Dennis. *Two* missed calls from Dennis. My stomach churns, and I quickly check for voicemails.

None.

I think about calling him back, but then I reason he's probably spoken to Abigail by now. This is up to the two of them.

"She hates me," Mom says abruptly, and I look over to where she's standing by the window.

"It's been bad between us before," Mom goes on, gazing out. "But not like this. She's always had plenty to say to me before. Now she has nothing to say at all."

I look at her.

"Maybe she's waiting for what you have to say."

Mom swallows, moves her gaze from the window and onto me.

"I'm not hungry, Gillian. Are you?"

I shake my head. I should be, but the day we've had seems to have destroyed whatever appetite I might have had.

"I'll tell you what though," Mom says. "I think I could use a stiff drink."

*

Mom gets reckless over her second martini.

"It probably was a mistake, coming here...but Gillian, she's my daughter. Even if she doesn't feel that way right now."

I nod, sip my own drink.

"Maybe we can all talk when Sam's gone to bed," I say, although I'm starting to doubt the wisdom of that, since Mom isn't usually a two-martini lady and alcohol doesn't necessarily help these kinds of situations.

Mom looks at me.

"It's hard to imagine," she says. "Lorna,

being...sick. Being *old*. She was just a girl when I saw her. Eighteen! A child." Mom shakes her head. "At your father's funeral, when those flowers came, my heart just about stopped, you know. I didn't think she'd have heard of his death; it was like getting a message from a ghost. And then I thought about how old she'd be by then—a woman in her mid-fifties! It seemed unthinkable." She looks down into the bowl of her glass. "But still so young—much too young for something like this to be happening."

The bartender—a young guy who looks like a student, probably barely ten years older than Sam—passes by and asks if we need anything. Mom looks doubtfully at her near-empty glass but shakes her head. I wait until he's gone and ask Mom something else that's been on my mind.

"Mom...why didn't you and Dad stay in touch with Lorna? I get that you wanted the adoption to be secret. But couldn't you have just kept in touch?"

Mom eyes me.

"Well, I don't think she wanted to, Gillian. I suppose it was more comfortable for her, leaving everything behind. *She* was the one who ran off to I-don't-know-where; Mexico I think it was, to begin with. And things were different then. People without a fixed address or a landline, well, you had to wait for them to contact you, you didn't really have a way of reaching them."

"But you liked it," I say. "Her not being around. Right? Not having to think about her. Not having to worry about her ever being around Abigail."

Mom flushes.

"I don't think that's very kind of you, Gillian."

I finish the last of my drink.

I'm not sure that it was *un*kind. But I also feel that maybe the time for kindness in our family has passed—or a certain type of kindness at least. The type of kindness that keeps you from saying things you should have said long ago.

"That family," Mom says. "Your father tried to take care of them all, but as far as I could see he was the only one to make it out of there as, well, as a fully functioning adult, Gillian. The younger ones all ran wild. Lorna was the baby, you know. The only girl. Your father adored her.

There was eighteen years between them—she was almost more a daughter to him than a sister."

The bartender passes by again—the other people lingering at the bar have left, and I guess it's not exactly a happening spot, this shabby little hotel bar, because we're now the only ones here—and feeling reckless, I push my empty glass back towards him.

"I'll have another, please."

Mom hesitates, but not for long.

"Make it two."

They're playing holiday tunes on the stereo. The playlist must not be very long, as this feels like the third time we've heard "I Saw Mommy Kissing Santa Claus" in that faux-sassy, little-girl voice that I'm coming to really dislike.

"Oh, Gillian. I miss your father," Mom says suddenly. It's not that the statement is surprising, it's just the first time she's actually said those words out loud. In her mouth—Gloria Gerritsen, the woman who shows no weakness—it sounds like a confession.

"I miss him too," I say, and apparently the

words themselves are a trigger, instantly forming a lump in my throat that only a large swallow of gin and vermouth can help me get down.

"We'd had end-of-life conversations, you know." She pauses. "I remember he said he wanted me not to grieve too long. He said, *less than six months and I'll be offended, Gloria. And a year is okay, too. But some people turn into monsters if they live alone too long, and you're one of them.*" She shakes her head, gives me a half-smile. "He didn't show it all that often but he had a good sense of humor, your dad."

She doesn't need to tell me that.

It was a sense of humor that came fully alive when he was with my sister; not quite so much with me. Instead Dad was full of praise for me, but always for the things I already knew I was good at, like being well-behaved and "such a help to your mother". For being good at school, tidy and diligent and smart. I was his serious girl. And yet I don't think I ever *wanted* to be so serious. Maybe when Abigail became the wild child I was the one who had to be the over-achiever, like a racehorse trained for the highest jumps.

Just then my phone starts ringing. My first thought is that it's Oliver, and I'm halfway to answering when I see the name on the screen: Dennis. I hesitate a moment, but pick up.

"Dennis?"

"Gillian." His voice explodes down the line. "What the hell is going on? Is this true? Where is my son?"

Nerves pool in the pit of my stomach.

"Dennis—"

"Are you *actually* in Miami?"

"Dennis, listen to me. Yes, we're in Miami. Mom's here, and me, and we brought Sam. He's fine. Everything's—"

"What the hell were you thinking, Gillian? This is *unacceptable*. I left him with you because I trusted you! I did not give you permission for this!"

I swallow, and glance up at Mom, who's staring at me open-mouthed. I'm guessing at the volume Dennis is speaking, she can hear every word too.

"I know, Dennis...it was a decision we had to make quickly. It's only for a day. They'll likely be back to Westchester before you are—"

"That is *not* the point, Gillian. You're just, just enabling your sister's insane schemes...This is the last thing my son needs right now." He barely catches his breath between words. "I expected more from you, Gillian; I thought there was at least *one* sane person in that family. Can you imagine? I wake up here, check my flight updates, and what do I see? This message from your sister, telling me my son's halfway to Florida. You're lucky I don't have you arrested for kidnapping!"

My jaw drops. Is that even possible? No one asked if we had Sam's parents' consent when we got on the plane. It was just a domestic flight...

"Dennis..." I don't know where to begin trying to talk him down, and I'm not even sure I should try. "I can understand it's been a shock, but I don't think I betrayed your trust. We—we wanted to get him home in time for your return and the school term so we made a bit of a snap decision. Sam's the one who was so set on coming here."

"And since when do ten-year-olds get to make

executive decisions about their lives?" Dennis snaps.

"I—I think it's important, don't you? This news has been a shock"—I look over at Mom—"for all of us, and this could really help..."

"Introducing him to some deadbeat alcoholic," Dennis says.

"I..." I don't know what to say to that. It's not that I have any particular loyalty to Lorna, but she was Dad's sister. And she's Abigail's birth mother, and Sam's biological grandmother.

"She *had* an alcohol problem, Dennis. That doesn't make her a bad person."

"That woman," he says, voice trembling with rage, "is not family. She has no right to be in my son's life."

"Well, this isn't about her," I say, surprising myself with an answering fierceness. "This is about Sam—"

"I don't know why I was even surprised by this adoption thing," Dennis bursts out then. "It actually makes perfect sense, you know, that my wife's real mother is some unstable—"

"No one said anything about unstable," I manage to cut in, my voice trembling now too.

"And Abigail's 'real mother,' Dennis, is the same person she's always been."

I hear the angry puff of air on the end of the line.

"What hotel are you in?"

I blink, thrown by the sudden change of direction.

"You heard me," he says. "What's the name of your hotel?"

I hesitate, then give it to him.

"I'm changing my flights," he says. "I'm leaving for Doha and I'll figure out Miami from there. None of you better move, you hear me? Nobody leaves until I get there."

I open my mouth, trying to find the right words, but he's already hung up. The tinny Christmas music plinks away in the background as the dial tone echoes. Slowly I take the phone from my ear and set it down on the bar. Mom stares at me.

"Gillian," she says, "what was *that?*"

Chapter Twenty-One

When I text Abigail that I'm in the bar, I don't mention that Mom's here with me. It's a deliberate omission, but I still feel a little guilty when I see her come in and do a double-take.

"Oh…" She looks from me to Mom, then back to me, eyes narrowing.

"Sam's in bed?" I say.

"Sleeping. We had…we had a long talk." She swallows. "So…what did he say to you?"

I texted her about Dennis's call but haven't given her the details.

"Didn't he call *you*?" I say.

Abigail flushes. "He left me some voicemails earlier, and…well, when I listened to them I figured he might need some time to cool off. I texted him, but…"

"Well, he's pretty angry," I say sharply. "As no doubt you've gathered. He basically accused me of kidnapping. He called Lorna a deadbeat alcoholic and said Sam shouldn't be seeing her. He's changing his flights to come to Miami, and wants you to stay put till he gets here. It sounds like he'll finally be leaving soon."

Abigail swallows.

"Okay," she says. "Okay. I'm—I'm sorry you had to hear all that, Gillian."

"Abigail..."

My sister's shoulders tighten at Mom's voice.

"What's going on with you and Dennis?"

I think both Mom and I are a little shell-shocked after that call. Dennis has always been so calm, so elegantly in control. The man I just talked to sounded anything but.

Abigail doesn't answer, just fixes her gaze on the bar, her jaw tight.

"Why didn't you tell him anything?" I say. "When you found out about Lorna...when you contacted her...I can understand why you couldn't tell Sam, Abigail. I can maybe understand why you didn't tell Mom or me. But couldn't you have told Dennis? Instead of just disappearing and letting him think the worst."

"You don't know Dennis," my sister says then, her voice tight. "He thinks the worst no matter what. He thinks whatever I do is the worst." She doesn't look up.

"Things had gotten so bad between us, Gillian. I just had this feeling that if I told him about...about Lorna, about what I'd found, that he'd use it against me somehow. Not at first, maybe, but later. This 'apple doesn't fall far from the tree' stuff." She glances up. "Dennis's family has always been big on pedigree. And he's...I didn't want to give him that kind of ammunition, Gillian. The truth is I haven't been doing that well, this past year." She hesitates.

"I was getting this anxiety—bad anxiety. Some days I didn't even feel good enough to pick Sam up from school. I'd ask one of the other neighborhood parents if they could do it, but one time we had a miscommunication and no one was there to get him. Dennis was furious. *You have one job to do*, that's what he says. My one job is to make sure our kid has the perfect mother—the kind of domestic, constantly accommodating mother Dennis grew up with." Abigail shakes her head. "I felt like he was already building this case against me in his head, you know? 'Fragile mental health,' 'unfit mother,' you know the kind of thing. I didn't want to give him more fuel for all that." She looks away again, folds her arms across her stomach.

"Abigail..." I say. "I'm sorry."

I can see on Mom's face that she's as taken aback as I am if not more. The idea that Abigail was dealing with anxiety like this; the fact that their marriage had eroded so far.

"I thought he was wonderful, you know," Abigail says, "when I met him. I mean, I know I've always been...messy. Hard to manage. *I* find me hard to manage. And at first I thought he did such a good job of that: managing everything, including me. I loved how neat he was. How organized, how efficient. So disciplined, you know? Never made excuses. I loved all that." She glances at me. "I don't know when it started exactly, when he began to—to undermine me. Telling me I was letting him down, letting Sam down. That I was a mess. Unreliable. Embarrassing." She swallows. "I thought, well, you can't afford to be too sensitive in a marriage. And it wasn't all the time. Then by the time I realized it was more than just a 'bad patch,' I'd already started to...to shrink, or something.

"It was all very gradual. It was like everything about me that once had seemed to charm him, he began to find irritating...intolerable, even." Abigail goes on. She looks up, meeting my eyes. "I suppose the truth is he fell out of love with me long before I fell out of love with him—and yet there's some masochistic part of him that insists on staying married."

"Abigail..."

"It chips away at you, Gillian," she says. "Living with someone who doesn't...doesn't even *like* you anymore. You get to thinking things about yourself."

I glance at Mom. I don't bother pointing out to Abigail that what she has just described, many people might term emotional abuse. Because right now doesn't seem like a useful time for labels. I want to focus on my sister, not on the man she's married to.

"You should have told us," Mom says.

Abigail shrugs.

"I know you all think it's because of me that we don't visit more, but it's mostly Dennis. He liked the way we had it in California, where I didn't know anyone except the people he introduced me to." She swallows. "I think what he wants is a wife with no family, no parents, nothing. He should have married an orphan, that's what he really wants. Someone who has no one." She looks at Mom. "He tolerates you, and he tolerates you, Gillian—because you've always thought he can do no wrong—"

"That's not true," I protest, and Abigail looks at me.

"Gillian, you treat him like he's some kind of knight—"

That's Mom, I think...but if I'm fully honest, I know I've secretly compared Oliver to Dennis many times and found my husband wanting. It embarrasses me now to think of it.

"But I guarantee you he tried a bunch of other places before he sent Sam up to you last week." Abigail shrugs. She looks at me again.

"So can you understand why I didn't tell him where I was going? I knew I'd be making trouble for myself later, of course I knew that. But I also knew that if I'd told him...I don't mean he'd have stopped me, as in, stood in the doorway and held my wrists. But he'd have chipped away and chipped away like he does, until I felt smaller than dirt; until I gave up the whole harebrained idea and saw how poorly thought through it was, how disruptive for Sam and our family; how I wasn't strong enough to handle it." She takes a breath. "I didn't trust the person I'd be after he'd finished talking me down. It's why I had to just go. Honestly, Gillian, I didn't even know if it was the right thing or the wrong thing in the end, but I knew it took every bit of self-determination I had to just get in that car and drive."

"I'm—I'm sorry you felt that way," I say. It's hard to get my head around all this. Not just that their marriage was so different from what it seemed, but this whole vision of my sister. Abigail, the fighter. The feisty one.

"I don't think he can even help it, you know," Abigail says, after a while. "He's married to someone he doesn't love, and he's so…angry. Not just at me; everything irritates him. It's like he's set to the wrong frequency."

"It's not an excuse," I say quietly.

"I know," she says. "I'm not excusing him. I can't, anymore."

I look at Mom. She looks like this is hitting her

hard. She's always thought so highly of Dennis.

"What about Sam?" she says quietly. "How is he towards Sam?"

Abigail sighs.

"He's...better. I can say that much for him. He's not a bad father. Demanding, maybe, but Sam's his little prince."

We all sit with that for a moment.

"What are you going to do?" I say finally. "Are you going to divorce?"

Slowly, Abigail nods.

"I think I needed to get away to see that, Gillian. At first I was waiting for things to get better, and then I guess I've been waiting for Dennis to see the light. I said the word *divorce* to him in the summer, and he acted like I was talking about going to the moon. I thought it would sink in: how unhappy he is, how divorce would be best for both of us. But now I see that's not going to happen, and I just have to do this alone. Even if he fights me on it."

"Abigail..." Mom sounds choked up. "I'm so sorry this has been going on. And that you felt alone. And I'm sorry for—for everything. For the secrets. They were never supposed to hurt you.

We just wanted to protect you. I never wanted you to doubt yourself."

Abigail turns her full gaze on Mom for the first time.

"Are you kidding? I grew up on self-doubt. You always acted like I was dysfunctional."

"That's not true," Mom says.

"Maybe I *was* dysfunctional," Abigail says. "You know? This whole thing with Sam, it's been making me think...Nowadays I bet I'd have gotten tested for ADHD or something—I never really could control my impulses, my emotions. I was so restless all the time. But I wasn't trying to be the bad kid, you know? Not at first, anyway."

"I never said you were—"

"You didn't have to say it," Abigail says quietly. "After a while, it began to seem like being bad was the one thing I was good at."

"Abigail..." Mom says, but trails off, looking lost.

"You thought I was so problematic," Abigail says. "Everything I did was wrong. I think I was afraid of myself, Mom, you know that? I didn't trust whatever was inside me."

"I..." Mom looks down and I wonder if she's thinking what I'm thinking: that maybe *she* didn't trust what was inside Abigail either. That she loved her, but she didn't trust her. And that children need both.

"I'm sorry," she says.

Abigail says nothing.

"We never wanted you to leave, you know," Mom says. "Never. You left us, Abigail. You took off without a word, and never came home. I was afraid it would break your father's heart."

Abigail's face changes.

"Don't *do* that!" she erupts. "Don't 'your-father' me! You were always doing that—trying to guilt me by invoking Dad. Trying to make me feel like I wasn't a good enough daughter to him."

Mom looks stricken.

"Oh no. You were good enough for him, Abigail, you were always good enough. He wouldn't have changed one hair on your head."

Abigail's face crumples, and I see how furiously determined she is not to cry.

"Abigail..." Mom hesitates. "I can apologize to you for the rest of my life, but I can't apologize for being your mother. You can be anyone else's daughter that you want to be," she says, "but you will never not be mine. You're written into my skin. You have been since the day I first held you."

Abigail stares at her for a few moments.

"I need to go to bed," she says finally, and turns on her heel. In the background, the tinny Christmas music plays on.

*

Upstairs I wait with the light on while Mom brushes her teeth, then pulls back the thin quilt and gets into bed. She's barely said a word since we came upstairs.

"I was trying to do it right," she says. "I was trying to be a good mother. I was trying to *teach* her." She looks at me. "But I don't think she wants to hear that."

"Not yet," I say.

Mom moves a hand across her eyes. "No," she says. "And I never was able to make her listen." She lets out a breath. "I don't know what's going to happen to us, Gillian—to this family."

I think of Dennis, perhaps in the air by now.

Of Lorna, probably asleep in her bed only a mile away. Of Oliver, back in Birch Bend in an empty house, the spare room dark and vacant once again. Of how we're all just wind-tossed little specks, the future a dark universe swirling all around us.

One way or another, I guess we'll find out, I think, and turn off the light.

Chapter Twenty-Two

I wake in the morning to a polite knocking on the door.

"Just a minute," I say, blinking back to reality. I roll over to see that the other bed is neatly made, and as I get up I see the note left on top of the quilt: *Gone for a walk.*

I know that's how Mom relieves stress, but the streets of Miami are not quite the same as the small neighborhood roads of Birch Bend.

"Mom, is that you?" I pad towards the door, figuring she likely left her key behind.

"It's Sam," my nephew's voice says. I swing open the door.

"Sam! Everything okay?"

He nods.

"Do you want to come for breakfast with me? Mom's still sleeping." He glances cautiously into the room behind me. "Is Grandma gone?"

"She's out for a walk. Give me a minute to get changed, okay? And leave your mom a note."

I upgrade my pajamas to some jeans and a

T-shirt and unplug my phone from the nightstand so Mom can text me when she gets back. It lights up and I see three message alerts stacked on my home screen. Oliver.

I thumb open the last one.

Tell me if you don't want me to come, it says.

I do a double take and go to the first message, wondering if this means what I think it means. It does. He says it felt wrong driving away from the airport yesterday; that he knows what an intense time this must be for me and my family, and he should be here to support me, if that's something I want.

I call him.

"Oliver?"

"Gillian—" I can hear the energy in his voice. He's on speakerphone, I think. "There's an early flight. I thought I'd just drive to the airport. I'm in the car now. Tell me if you want me to turn around."

I'm amazed. This isn't like him—so impulsive; romantic even.

"Don't turn around," I say, and I hear the faint smile in his voice as he says, "Okay, I won't."

Sam's waiting in the corridor, kicking one shoe against the heel of the other.

"Oliver's coming," I tell him, still a little dazed from the news.

"Here? Today?"

I nod.

"Does he want to meet Lorna too?"

"I...maybe," I say. *Do I? Will I?*

Downstairs the air smells of budget inn breakfasts: coffee and the hot, sweet smell of processed baked goods. We take a seat, and Sam pulls strips of flaky dough off his pre-packaged croissant and looks around, wide-eyed.

"How are *you* doing, Sam?"

He looks at me.

"You mean...you mean like with the stuff in my head?"

"Yes," I say. "And in general."

He looks down.

"Okay. Honestly I think maybe it's worse at home. It's like...it's like my mind doesn't have a map of things here yet so it doesn't know yet exactly what orders to give."

I nod.

"Mom and I talked about it last night," he says. "About how it might be OCD, maybe. I've heard of OCD. But I guess I thought it was something different."

I know what he means, I think I felt the same way. Maybe I almost forgot it was a real condition, a real problem, and not just something people say. How many times has Oliver teased me for being "so OCD" about how I stack the dishwasher?

"And how are you feeling about...the rest?" I say.

Sam ducks his head.

"I feel bad about what I said to Grandma. But I hate that she lied," he says "I wish she hadn't lied."

"Yeah," I say. "I don't feel great about it either, Sam. But I guess she and your grandpa were probably just doing what they thought was best. Adults do make mistakes, you know. Sometimes big ones."

Sam gives me a look that I interpret as, *you can say that again.*

"I'm kind of angry at Mom too, though," he says. "She made everyone so mad."

I nod.

"I think she was feeling pretty mad, herself."

Sam chews his croissant.

"I know you're my real aunt still and everything. But...it's weird, isn't it?" He looks at me. "I mean, finding out you're kind of not who you thought you were. Like you thought you were one person but it turns out you're not exactly that person. Have you ever had anything like that happen?"

I think about the days I spent believing I was pregnant last time—certain I could feel the cells gathering and taking shape inside me, that I could feel myself becoming softer, more glowing—and then it all turned out to have been a mirage.

"Kind of," I say. "I mean, I think I understand what you're feeling."

"Do you think she'll want me to call her Grandma?" he says. "You know—Mom's...mom?" I can almost feel his brain pulsing at the weirdness of it all.

"She'll probably want you to call her whatever you feel like calling her," I say.

Sam makes a noncommittal sound, then

opens a second croissant and starts dismantling it like the first one.

"Do you think that she regrets it now?" he says. "Giving Mom away?"

I take a long hit of coffee. Sam definitely knows how to ask a tough question.

"It can be very hard to know what other people really feel about their lives, Sam," I say. "And we can't always ask. But I'm going to guess and say she probably has some mixed feelings about it."

Sam makes a face.

"'Mixed feelings.' Adults always say that. Don't you ever just have *feelings*?"

Despite myself I smile a little. This exasperation is an oddly endearing side of him, and there's something so teenage about it. I guess I remember feeling that too at his age: that adults were always equivocating, never committing to something 100 percent.

"I think the older we get the more we have mixed feelings about things. Especially complicated things."

Sam shrugs, and demolishes the last of his croissant.

"Still hungry?" I say.

He nods.

"Hi, you two," a voice says. I turn around to see Abigail walking towards us.

"Hi, Mom," Sam answers as Abigail sits down beside me.

"Sorry I slept late," she says, and glances at me. "I haven't been sleeping so well recently." I can believe it—in the morning light I can see the tiredness etched in her face.

"Oliver's coming today too," Sam reports, and Abigail looks at me, eyebrows raised.

I hope this isn't going to add to our problems.

I explain the situation to her as Sam goes back to the cereal bar, but she just nods.

"That makes sense."

I glance at the clock hanging over the breakfast station.

"When are you leaving to visit Lorna?"

"Soon," she says. "After breakfast." She looks at me, clears her throat. "Do you...would you want to come?"

I feel the hairs on my neck rise.

"I...yes. If that's okay?"

The second I say it I feel a pang of dread.

What am I going to say to this woman? What if the whole thing just feels awkward and dismal?

"How—how is she?" I say, keeping my voice low so that it doesn't travel to the breakfast bar. "I mean, how is she coping with all this?"

Abigail glances at me.

"It's hard to say. She doesn't talk about it a whole lot—not to me, at least. She has friends here, maybe she talks to them. But I think she's a pretty tough nut." She swallows. "You can see sometimes when she's in pain but she says that's just since the surgery and is manageable. I think it's mainly her independence she's afraid of losing. You know," Abigail hesitates. "If things get bad."

She looks at me. "At first she talked about not doing any chemo or radiation at all. She said maybe it would be better to just let her body "go its way naturally". She seems to have changed her mind about that, but I don't know if she'll stick to it, you know, once it all starts..."

Abigail shrugs, her shoulders heavy.

I don't respond, because Sam's already coming back to the table with two chocolate milk cartons and a paper bowl of Rice Krispies.

"I'm beginning to think I wasn't feeding you enough," I say, and he flashes me a half-smile.

"Sam, your aunt is going to come to visit Lorna with us," Abigail tells him, and Sam bobs his head as he lays into the cereal. "What about Grandma?" he says, looking behind us, and I turn to see Mom coming into the room. Looking at her, I can see how she steels herself to walk over to the table.

"I think that might be a little *too* much for today, don't you?" Abigail says, her voice cool as Mom draws up beside us.

"Morning, Mom," I say. "How was your walk?"

"Oh, fine. Fine. Morning, everyone. Morning, Sam."

"Morning, Grandma," he says, a little more warmth in his voice than yesterday.

I fill her in about Oliver too, and she looks faintly surprised, but just nods.

"And then Dad, too," Sam reminds us. "Everybody's coming." He spoons more Rice Krispies into his mouth. "What's Grandma going to do while the rest of us visit Lorna?"

Mom looks around at us, her eyes moving from mine to Abigail's with a flash of surprise that quickly shifts to acceptance. It's the acceptance that makes me feel guilty.

"Perhaps you'll give her my regards," she says quietly. "It's been an awfully long time."

*

The streets are lively—a different kind of lively than when we drove through them yesterday evening—and the morning air is warm. Kids clamor on the sidewalks; old men sit in front of their houses, silent in ones and twos, or talking fast in groups of five or six. Apparently we're just on the outskirts of Little Havana, which is the neighborhood Lorna lives in.

"That's Domino Park," Abigail points as we pass the gated entrance to a plaza with big stone chessboards where white-haired men in shorts sit playing.

"I could have played with Grandpa if he were here," Sam says.

"He'd have liked that," I say.

We weave through some more streets, leaving the busier and more touristy areas behind again, and after a while Abigail stops at the entrance to a nondescript brown building and hits the buzzer for a second-floor apartment.

I think I see a tremor in her hand as she lowers it.

"Hello?" A woman's voice says. It doesn't sound like the voice of anyone I know. I had sort of expected it to sound familiar; like Abigail's voice

"It's us," Abigail says into the intercom, and it clicks and buzzes. My sister leads us inside and up a shabby flight of steps with the automatic movements of someone already familiar with the place. The door on the second floor opens before we reach it and a woman stands there, tall and thin, smiling slightly.

A woman with my sister's eyes.

Chapter Twenty-Three

Lorna's gaze pans across our little trio. Her eyes are bright, her face soft as she takes us in. I think how extraordinary it must be for her to see Sam; probably even more unreal, in a way, than seeing Abigail again.

"Well," she says. "You must be Sam. My goodness." She stares at him a moment longer before turning to me. "And Gillian. You look like Gloria."

"You look like Abigail," I say, and she smiles a wry, eyebrow-raised smile. It's like my sister's, but different. I feel a shivery sense of disjunction, standing here in front of this woman with my sister's eyes. A familiar stranger, strangely familiar.

"Hi," Sam says, radiating curiosity. Both he and Lorna seem pretty relaxed, funnily enough. I'm certainly not, and I can almost feel Abigail's nerves sparking beside me.

"It's all very strange, isn't it, Sam?" Lorna turns towards him. "Well, come on in."

She waves us into an apartment that's modest in size—considerably smaller than my house, and it would probably fit in Abigail's Westchester home eight times over—but vibrantly painted and decorated. We walk through an ochre-colored hallway into a bright living room full of furniture and ornaments, with smoked-glass mirrors and a collection of prints adorning the walls. The art is eclectic, everything from tiny oil paintings the size of an egg carton to framed prints of birds and sea creatures. Sam stares around him as though he's found himself inside of a curiosity cabinet, and I feel a bit the same.

Lorna follows his eyes and smiles.

"Yes, I'm a bit...eccentric, I suppose, in my design choices. I like having the reminders of the places I've seen, you see."

"Have you been everywhere?" Sam says, and she smiles. I get what he means. There are African masks on the wall by the door, and some Tibetan prayer flags in another corner, and it seems like a hundred other things.

"Sometimes it feels that way." Lorna gestures at the couch. "Want to take a seat? I'll get us some drinks."

We sit, and I have the odd feeling of being in a doctor's office or something, the way the three of us are all lined up here on the sofa, waiting.

"Here, let me take that," Abigail says as Lorna emerges from the kitchen with a tray, and I'm reminded of the fact that Lorna is a lot sicker than she looks. She's thin, certainly—too thin— but there's a sort of glamor to it, what with her high cheekbones and her swept-up hair, and I had forgotten for a moment how beneath all that is a person who is not at all well.

"Thank you, Abigail."

It's odd hearing my sister's name on her tongue. Knowing that in some alternate universe, she'd have called that name a million times over the past thirty-odd years. That it would be the most beloved, most familiar series of syllables in the world. But not in this universe.

Lorna folds herself into a large armchair and smiles at me. Looking at her now I start to notice how young she really is—just about twenty years older than me.

"So," she turns. "I suppose this all feels very

startling to you, Sam."

He glances quickly at Abigail and then at me.

"It's pretty weird," he agrees. "I mean, it's good that Mom found you and everything, but…" he shrugs. "It feels weird about Grandma. And Grandpa too, I guess." He glances my way too, including me in his mental list of relatives that aren't exactly who he thought they were. Lorna's eyes flick towards me, following his. I wonder if I remind her of Mom—and if so, what that feels like. She turns back to Sam.

"Yes: your grandma and I…and your grandpa…we probably should all have handled things differently. You're right. But you know, we lived in a very different time."

Sam's quiet for a moment, his eyes traveling around the room.

"Lorna's been to so many countries, Sam," my sister says. "I've been hearing all her stories over the past few days."

Lorna glances at her, a warm look.

"Yes—we had so very much to catch up on." She clears her throat. "And it's true, Sam, I was a bit of a nomad, particularly in my younger days."

I see the way my sister's watching Lorna now—frowning a little as though she's still trying to learn this woman, still trying to absorb her. I wonder if she's had sharp words with Lorna since finding out the truth; if she's confronted her in ways that were angry or resentful. I'm not really getting that impression. I think maybe the resentment is a switch Abigail has chosen not to activate.

"You don't have any kids?" Sam says, then glances at Abigail. "I mean, you know. Besides..."

Lorna shakes her head.

"No, my dear. I didn't really have that sort of a lifestyle."

I don't hear regret in her voice. It's interesting—the way Mom talked about Lorna, I was expecting something of a lost soul, I guess. Someone who never really found a way to get what she wanted from life. But Lorna doesn't strike me that way.

Sam seems mesmerized by the idea of this grandmother who isn't anyone's actual grandmother.

"So...what *do* you do?" he says, apparently

struggling to picture the life of someone of her generation who doesn't seem to crochet, bake, or compare stories of grandkids with her fellow-grandmas.

Lorna laughs and tells him about her world here: the shelter she volunteers at; the reading group and AA group she goes to. Sam asks her what an AA group is, and she explains it to him carefully and without shame.

"But it's like...a hangout?" Sam says.

She smiles.

"Some of those people have become my best friends over the years, Sam. We know each other's demons, so to speak. It's terribly valuable to have friends like that."

"Did Mom meet any of those friends?" Sam casts a look Abigail's way.

"I didn't want to overwhelm your mother," Lorna says gently. "She and I had plenty to talk about just between the two of us. And, well, I haven't been terribly active the last couple of weeks, I'll admit."

Sam nods carefully.

"I'm sorry you were sick," he says. "Mom said you had to get an operation."

"Yes," Lorna says, so that I can tell Abigail has briefed her on what we're not yet saying to Sam.

"I know a kid at school who had to be rushed to hospital in the middle of the night because of her appendix," Sam says.

"That sounds dramatic," Lorna says. "Thankfully, no one had to rush me anywhere in the middle of the night." She sips her glass of water. "Meanwhile, I'd love to hear more about you, Sam. Your mom has told me so much already."

Sam shrugs deeper into his hoodie, glances sidelong at me.

"Well...I like video games a lot. And watching basketball. And I also like movies, and books. Aunt Gillian and I started watching the *Lord of the Rings* movies when I was staying with her, actually. Grandpa used to read me those books, when I was a kid."

"Did he?" I see Lorna's fraction of a smile at that. I bet she finds it as touching as I do to hear Sam say the words, *when I was a kid.*

"I remember how much he liked those books," she says. "You know, they were relatively new when your grandfather was young—like the Harry Potter of its day. He made me read them all once I got to high school; bought me my own box set." She smiles. "He was quite a bit older than me, you know. By then he'd been married for probably a decade; he seemed quite middle-aged to me!"

Sam half-smiles at that. I see him trying and failing to imagine his grandpa as a young man.

"Did you like them?" he says. "The books?"

Lorna smiles at him.

"Oh, I loved them."

Sam smiles back.

"And what about you, Gillian?" Lorna turns to me. "Your sister tells me you're living in Birch Bend still, and that you're a teacher there?"

I find myself flushing, suddenly caught off guard. She doesn't mean it this way but her question makes me feel dowdy somehow. Lorna's life has been so full of travel and adventure, and Abigail's has too in its way. Even Sam wants to be an astronaut. I'm the one who's never lived outside of her home state and whose late-twenties "exploratory" period only brought me a thirty minute drive south to Troy.

Feeling self-conscious, I fill in Lorna on my teaching career; I tell her about Oliver and the brewery start-up.

"Marvelous," Lorna says.

"Their house is awesome," Sam pipes up.

I look at him in surprise, and so does Abigail—which I get, because you probably wouldn't expect a kid who lives in that Westchester mansion to describe Oliver's and my home as "awesome." And enthusiasm isn't exactly what Sam's been known for of late. But Lorna's nodding attentively and, confident of her full focus, he continues.

"It has this garden that's really wild, with tons of birds and squirrels and everything. And there's a tree that goes all the way up past the roof, it must be super old, with two different birds' nests in it."

Lorna smiles past Sam at me.

"That sounds quite magical."

"Yeah, and my room has this, like, slopey ceiling, and in the morning you see the tree shadows moving all over it, and it kind of feels like being in a treehouse."

I almost choke on my coffee. Who *is* this

eager child?

My room, he just said. I feel warm at the words.

I watch from the sidelines again as the conversation moves back to mostly Sam and Lorna talking, with my sister interjecting from time to time. Lorna asks Sam about school, about his favorite subjects, his hobbies, and tells him about some interests of her own, bringing over a fossil on the mantelpiece for him to hold and look at. Mostly I watch Lorna as she talks, noticing all the things that are specific to her and not like anyone in our family: her accent, her clothing, the piled-up way she wears her hair. She seems interesting, and strong-willed, and likable...but she doesn't feel like part of my family. And I realize part of me is waiting for something to click into place and for her to suddenly become someone I *know*, someone I feel connected to. It doesn't really happen, which I guess after all isn't surprising. It occurs to me that this fascinating room with its museum's worth of objects isn't just a collection of souvenirs, it's a monument to Lorna's life— the life she built without a trace of Abigail in it.

A life of adventures and experiences and not looking back. And I wonder if Abigail expected more looking back. If she expected regret.

"How come you never visited?" Sam says then. I can tell he knows it's a potentially dangerous question; he doesn't ask it in the bright-voiced way a younger child might. But he asks it anyway.

"I mean, I can understand that you didn't want a baby back then. And I guess I sort of understand why you all wanted it to be a secret. But how come you didn't ever visit?"

Lorna looks at him.

"Well, you know, Sam...I was terribly fond of your grandfather, he was a very good big brother. But we didn't really grow up being close as a family. I don't think I felt terribly...connected, to the siblings I grew up with. And then, after everything with your mom, I think visiting your grandpa and Gloria would have been harder on everyone. I suppose it just seemed cleaner to stay away." She pauses. "Your grandfather sent me pictures though. He sent one of your mom every year. And then, after you were born, pictures of you."

Sam stares.

"Really? I didn't know about you but...you knew all about me?"

Lorna nods. "It's rather imbalanced, I know. But I was grateful to your father. It gave me pleasure to see those pictures of you. I remember one year there was one of you on a red bike."

"I remember that bike," Sam says, awed.

Lorna takes another sip from her water glass.

"You know, I'm really so glad you could all visit. I realize, Sam, that your mother's trip was quite last-minute and unplanned, and that it's been a disruptive time for you and your family. But it's been a gift for me having those days, so thank you for letting me borrow her for a while. And then, to see you too!...What a treat." She glances at me. "And you, Gillian." She clears her throat. "And I know your visit is very short, Sam, but I'd love to introduce you to a little bit of my neighborhood. I have a favorite restaurant nearby that I think you might like—I asked your mom if we could maybe all go to lunch there today."

"Cool," Sam says, tipping back his Coke and

crunching on an ice cube. "I really like Miami so far. I like those huge chess sets in the park."

Lorna laughs.

"Oh yes, they're very popular."

I excuse myself to use the restroom before we head out, and it's a relief to be away from the conversation for a minute. It all feels a bit intense. I splash water on my face, and in the vanity mirror a flushed, serious-eyed person stares back at me. I have a slight headache and venture to pull back the mirrored door in case there's a bottle of Advil inside—and I guess out of curiosity too. But what I see chastens me instantly. The cabinet's full of pain medications, over-the-counter ones and prescription ones too. I close it, feeling guilty. I guess it's nothing I didn't already know. It's just a reminder, though, of what Lorna's going through and of what Sam doesn't yet know.

Back inside, Sam's saying something about Mom and I see Lorna dart a quick look towards Abigail.

"Gloria's here? She came with you?"

Abigail clears her throat.

"Yes, she flew in with Sam and Gillian."

Lorna frowns down at her glass of water.

"She didn't want to see me?"

"I..." Abigail glances my way. "I didn't know you'd want that."

Sam blinks, sensing the tension in the room, his eyes darting from Lorna to Abigail.

Lorna glances towards the window. "Well, it's been such a long time," she says. "Such a very long time. I would say we're overdue."

"She could come meet us?" Sam says helpfully. "For lunch?"

Abigail swallows, looks helplessly at me.

"I think that's a very good idea, Sam," Lorna says, and looks around at my sister and me. "Maybe one of you can give her a call?"

Chapter Twenty-Four

Calle Ocho, it turns out, is the main artery of Little Havana, and Lorna leads the way unhesitatingly to a little restaurant on a corner that looks no different from the others.

"This is the one," she says, and points to a line at a take-out window. "See? The locals know."

"Sam," she says, after we've taken our seats, "have you tried fresh guava juice before?"

"Guava?" Sam screws up his face.

"Just you wait." Lorna kisses her fingers theatrically and Sam smiles, but I can't help noticing how thin her fingers are, how gaunt her cheeks as she mimes the kiss.

I see Mom coming down the street first, eyes on her phone as she navigates with Google Maps to the address I gave her. When I see her walking towards us I feel a pang. She's coiffed and groomed again, looking much more herself, but amid all the bustle of this vibrant city she looks out of place; older.

Lorna breaks off from what she's saying and follows where I'm looking, and I hear her slow exhale.

"Thirty-six years," she says.

It hits me that when she last saw Mom, Mom was my age. And now she's seeing her age more than three decades in the blink of an eye. And when Mom looks up and finally sees us, I see the same slow, settling shock in her eyes too, as she takes in the woman sitting next to me, no longer the eighteen-year-old Mom knew.

We all fall silent, and Mom's pace seems to slow as she closes the last few feet. Lorna stands from her chair.

"Gloria," she says, and I see the tremor pass over Mom's face.

There's a hesitant, uncertain moment while they both look at each other, and then, carefully, move into a tentative embrace. It doesn't look especially comfortable but it lasts a few seconds, as though they're both trying to find something in that moment that they've been searching for. Whether they do or not, I don't know.

Lorna pulls back.

"I guess you're not looking too bad, Gloria,"

she says. "Considering."

Mom lets out a laugh that's mostly just a release of air.

"I suppose I could say the same," she says, and awareness pulses around the table as everyone but Sam remembers Lorna's diagnosis.

"So many years," Mom says, standing back. She glances around like she's taking in the city for the first time. "This is where you've been?"

Lorna shrugs. "For the last while. You know me, Gloria. Always the nomad."

Mom shakes her head faintly. It's a while before she and Lorna seem ready to break eye contact with each other and sit down at the table with us. A server comes by asking us if we're ready to order and then quickly retreats when she sees our dazed looks.

But after a while, we manage to order, and a faint sense of normalcy starts to creep in. Lorna asks Mom about the flight, and Mom asks Lorna about the Floridian climate. And then, after a while, we start to talk about Dad. I can tell Mom and Lorna both want to, and not just because he's safe ground. It's like together, they can re-create the whole of him. Soon they're telling stories about him, trading them back and forth. The two of them are dry-eyed, but across the table I see Abigail's tearing up. Sam joins in with Mom and Lorna, offering little stories about things Dad said and did during his summer visits.

There's a little respite from the conversation when the food comes out. Sam tucks into his and loudly endorses Lorna's choice of restaurant, and then for a few seconds everyone focuses on their plates.

"He visited you, didn't he?" Mom says then. I look up and so does Abigail, wide-eyed. We all look at Mom, then Lorna.

"Dad?" Abigail says.

Lorna tilts her head yes, and looks embarrassed.

"It wasn't often, you know. Every few years, maybe—in the early days, at least. The last few years I hadn't seen him at all. His back, you know—he didn't much like getting on planes. I think he had this idea that it would hurt you, Gloria—knowing that he was making those trips." She sighs. "I don't know why. I always thought he should tell you."

Mom smiles, bittersweet.

"I thought so. I remember years ago, every now and again there'd be some weekend trip that he'd try to explain away. He never was a very good liar."

I'm startled. It's one thing hearing about Mom's secrets, but it's another hearing about Dad's. Because he was such a soft, guileless person; and because he's gone, and now we can't ask him about them.

"I know he always felt a little guilty about me," Lorna says. "He shouldn't have. I never did want the life he wanted for me."

I think about that. Dad, the family man. It was everything in the world to him, being able to come home to his wife and kids; he was domestic through and through. No wonder he thought Lorna's bohemian life—no partner, no kids—wasn't a happy one. I think again how, while she's clearly so pleased and curious and gratified to have met Abigail and Sam, she doesn't seem consumed by thoughts of what might have been, or like she's aching to get those years of motherhood back. I glance over at my sister, wondering if she sees what I see and how it feels.

"The funeral," Lorna says. "I wanted to be there. It felt wrong to miss it. But then, you know, it would have been unfair to just show up..."

Mom nods. It would have been too risky, I suppose. The secret between them too electric.

"They were beautiful flowers," Mom says. "The ones you sent. The most beautiful of all." There's a long silence.

I wonder, if Dad had known he had only years or months or days to live, what he would have done differently. I wonder, if someone could have told him that Abigail and I would find out the truth, would it have been a secret relief to him?

I can't figure out if the timing of all this is terrible or good. If we found Lorna much too late or just in time. Is it tragic and ironic that we're only meeting her now...or is it a mercy that we're meeting her while she's still around to meet? I look at my sister and I hope this doesn't destroy her. I hope that the mercy outweighs the tragedy.

Because I know perfectly well that sometimes

having just a little—having just enough to dream of more—can be the hardest thing in the world.

*

When both Lorna and Mom have gone inside to use the restroom, the three of us look at each other.

"I don't think they hate each other," Sam says.

"No," I say quietly. "I don't think they do."

Abigail pulls Sam closer to her, kisses the top of his head.

"She's nice," Sam says. "But she doesn't really seem like a grandma, does she?"

"No," Abigail says, her eyes somewhere in the middle distance. "I guess not."

Sam's eyes are on the doorway through which the other two have gone.

"Is Dad going to meet her tomorrow?"

"I think your dad will want to go back early in the morning, Sam," my sister says. "I don't think he feels the need to meet Lorna."

Sam frowns. "Why not?"

"It's complicated."

Sam looks at her. "I think we should stay longer."

"You have to be back for school in a few days," I remind him, and he glances at me, annoyed.

"But Lorna can visit us," he says. "In Westchester. Right?"

Abigail pauses. "I hope so, Sam."

"She wants to," Sam says. "I can tell."

I glance at my sister over his head. *Are you sure you shouldn't just tell him,* I'm thinking. I don't know if she can tell; she blinks at me, looks away.

My phone pings with a message from Oliver.

At the hotel. Room 504. Let me know if I should come meet you somewhere.

"Oliver's arrived," I say. "Should I tell him to come here?"

Abigail hesitates.

"I think maybe we should let Lorna rest," she says. "She seemed to be getting kind of tired, don't you think?"

I'd noticed that too—how towards the end of lunch she seemed to be flagging, and losing a bit of color.

"I'll go settle the check," I say. "And then we can decide."

Inside, a busy server points me to the bar where I wait to pay. I'm right next to the restroom entrance: over the sound of a tap running, two familiar voices drift out from through the saloon doors.

"You did a good job with her, Gloria," Lorna's saying.

Mom scoffs. "Lorna, we've been locking horns since before she was thirteen years old. She spent most of her adult life about as far away from me as she could get."

The tap shuts off.

"You're here with her, aren't you? And so is her sister. That's family." Lorna pauses. "There's something feral in us, Gloria—there was in my mother, there is in me, and perhaps it's the same in Abigail. Maybe she's always just been staying as near as that side of her will allow."

There's what sounds to me like a skeptical pause, and then Mom sighs.

"I thought I'd do it better," she says. "I thought I'd do it so much better."

"Gloria," Lorna says, "don't mourn your failures." I can hear the touch of a smile in her voice. "You've always had high standards, you know. That's why I knew Abigail would be raised well, with you and Greg."

The silence lengthens, and I hear the sound of Mom blowing her nose.

I quietly settle the check and head back outside into the sun.

"They're taking forever, aren't they?" Abigail says.

I look at her. "I think they're making up for lost time."

Mom and Lorna emerge from the restaurant a while later, Lorna looking much the same but Mom distinctly red-eyed.

"Well," Lorna says, "I hate to be the party pooper, but I have to admit I'm feeling a little..." She glances at Sam. "A little tired. But Sam, this has been a real treat. You're going to visit tomorrow morning before you go, right?"

"That's right," Abigail says, her voice tight. I can tell she's already thinking about tomorrow's goodbye; about how much weight it's going to carry. "How about Sam and I walk you home?"

"I'd like that," Lorna says. She looks at Mom and me. "What about you two, will you join us?"

"Certainly." Mom flushes.

Abigail shoots her a look of annoyance; I hesitate.

"My husband's just arrived into town. I think I'd better go back to the hotel."

"Oh, indeed," Lorna says graciously. "Well—I'm so glad to have met you, Gillian. Perhaps you'll swing by tomorrow with Abigail and Sam, if you have time."

I nod.

We part ways on the corner, and I walk back to the hotel in a strange mood, feeling somehow light and heavy at the same time. I can't help thinking of Dad, of what he'd make of all this. I think back to the day of his funeral; to the picture we chose for the front of the memorial card. It was taken on some long-ago Father's Day: Abigail on one side of him, me on the other.

And I think about how now, meeting Lorna, we're not tying up any loose ends, only creating new ones. Adding more questions. Finding more unknowns. But maybe that's just the nature of life.

I go through the sliding doors, and through the over-lit lobby. I hit the button for the elevator and step in. I think about the unknowns still spreading out before me in my own life. About how Lorna is nearing the end of her time here yet shows no regret, and how I've probably never gone a day of my life *without* regret. I think about Oliver and me, and what lies ahead for us. The impasse we seem to have reached, and his impulse trip here, which I guess is a kind of apology for that. But I'm not sure that an apology can give me what I need right now.

I knock on the door.

"Gillian." He swings it open, his smile faint and tentative. Nervous, almost.

And suddenly I can't help the feeling that he's not just here to see me.

He's here to tell me something.

Chapter Twenty-Five

I wonder if I've imagined it, then, because once I step inside the doorway the nervous look seems to vanish from Oliver's face and suddenly he's back to his usual self—if anything, just more energetic, as though he, too, is running on adrenalin right now.

He pulls me in towards him. It seems longer than a day since I've seen him, and the familiarity of him, those wiry curls and the soft, savory smell of his skin—it feels like home.

"I'm glad you're here," I say into his chest.

"I'm glad I'm here too." He pulls back. "So how has it been? Is everyone okay? What's this Lorna person like?"

"She's...nice," I say. "Interesting. I like her. But..." I hesitate. "She's still a stranger. And I guess maybe she always would have been."

It's true; it's inevitable. Because true intimacy is built over time: it's built *on* time, like a house is built over stone. It's built through shared pain, shared joy, and the more mundane things, too:

shared boredom and irritation and even, sometimes, disillusionment.

That's real family.

I notice Oliver's gaze shift from mine then, and once again I catch a flash of something in there.

"Is everything okay?" I say.

"I was just thinking about it all," he says. "About how wild it is, you know—after all these years. What it must have felt like for Lorna, to have Abigail just turn up like that, out of the blue."

"Yeah," I say.

"Would you have wanted that, do you think?" he says. "If you had been Lorna, I mean. Would you have wanted to meet Abigail?"

"I...I don't know," I say. I hadn't thought about it that much. "I think so." But I can also appreciate how risky this has been for both my sister and Lorna. Seeing what can't be un-seen; knowing what can't be un-known.

Oliver nods, but distantly. He's drifted away from me again just now. I think again about how unlike him this was—the impulse trip to Miami, this why-the-hell-not attitude. Despite myself I feel a nervous quiver, and quickly push away any thoughts of strange messages on his laptop. He came here for me, I remind myself sternly. For *us.*

He sits, abruptly, on the side of the bed, and pats the space beside him.

"Sit down, will you, Gill?"

I suppress the little flicker of nerves, and sit beside him. Side by side like this, knees touching, on this unfamiliar bed in this unfamiliar room, it's like we're two teenagers.

"I've been thinking," he says. "I wanted you to know. I think we should do it. The fertility clinic. The IVF thing. I'm sorry I've been dragging my feet. When we go back...we should do it."

I stare at him, half-waiting for him to take back the words, but he doesn't. *This* is it? I could cry with relief. This is what he's been looking nervous about?

"Really?" I say.

"Yes. Really. I've just been...my head hasn't been in the right place. But if this is what we need, then..." He shrugs, his eyes steady on mine. "It's what we need."

I feel goosebumps spread along my arms— prickles of relief and disbelief, feelings I didn't even know I'd been storing, leaving my body like a giant exhale.

"Thank you, Oliver," I say.

He smiles.

"I had this kind of crazy idea, Gillian," he says. "I know the others will be going home tomorrow...but we don't have to. What if we stayed? You don't have to be in school for another three days." He smiles at me. "What do you think? Cocktails on Ocean Drive?"

I have to laugh—his enthusiasm's infectious, and it's so long since I've seen him like this.

"Well...it *is* kind of a crazy idea," I say. "But...why not?" *A new chapter,* I think. This is a good place to begin it.

"Maybe tomorrow we can go to the beach," he says. "It's a long time since I've seen you in a bikini."

"A bikini?" I laugh. "I'm afraid I didn't pack one."

He raises an eyebrow. "Uh oh. It'll have to be skinny dipping, then."

I laugh, and he grins as he lays me down

across the bed.

*

Some time later, we're half-dozing when raised voices outside pull me back to reality. It's Abigail: Mom's room is just across the hallway, and they're arguing with the door open.

"—think I can just snap my fingers and forgive you and then things would be okay?" my sister is saying, her voice getting louder. "But that's not how it works! Nothing can just *go back*. So I don't have room to deal with your emotions, Mom, and whatever it is you want from me right now!"

I hear a door slam and angry footsteps—Abigail's, no doubt—in the corridor outside. I lie still for a few moments, wondering if I should just let them be, but then I sigh and lever myself out of bed, glancing behind me to where Oliver's still dozing. I place his arm back around a pillow and slip on my shoes, then go knock on Mom's door.

She opens it looking apprehensive.

"Oh," she says, and glances along the corridor.

"Just me," I say.

She shakes her head.

"Can you talk to her, Gillian? I don't know what to do. She's...she's just so unhappy right now."

I hesitate. "I'll talk to her," I say. "But I don't know that it'll help."

Soon I'm knocking on the door at the end of the hall. Sam opens it, the television on loud behind him.

"They were arguing, weren't they?" he says. "Mom's in the bathroom."

"Gillian, is that you?" Abigail's voice sounds muffled; the tap runs for a few moments and she comes out, red-eyed. "What is it?"

"I...do you want to talk?" I say, and gesture outside her room. *Not in front of Sam.*

She sighs, doesn't answer right away.

"Sam, are you okay watching TV for a bit?"

He nods, his eyes panning from me to his mom.

"Just for a few minutes," I reassure him.

Abigail closes the door, and the two of us find a space nearby on an empty stairwell, sitting on the thinly carpeted steps with our backs against the wall.

"Abigail...what's happening? Are you okay?"

"No," she says shortly.

"It's...a lot to take in, isn't it?"

She leans her head back against the wall and closes her eyes.

"You know, Gillian... when I found out the truth about Lorna, and Mom, and everything... I can't explain it. It felt like I was one of those wasps you see at the end of summer, you know? The ones that look mostly dead but then, if you poke them, it's like they suddenly realize they're still alive, still angry, they've still got a sting in them."

She looks at me.

"I think I was just so tired, you know, from things with Dennis and then the anxiety I'd been getting... and not having Dad around. I felt like I was disappearing, and then this just—it shocked me back into myself, I guess.

I don't really mean in a good way. But it did *something.*"

Makes sense, I think. Maybe if I'm honest I've even felt a little of the same thing myself. That feeling of growing fainter, less colorful, as though some little piece of you is in danger of fading away.

"And then..." She shrugs. "I wasn't expecting Lorna to feel like my mother, Gillian. But I think... I think I was expecting more, somehow." She stops. "It's not *her.* It's not Lorna's fault, I mean. I like her. I even feel connected to her, in some ways. But I don't... I don't feel *better.* I don't feel better about anything the way I thought I would."

"I'm sorry," I say.

She sighs, tilts her head back against the wall again.

"What do you think it would have been like, Gillian—if Mom and Dad had told us the truth? If we'd grown up just *knowing*?"

I look away. I've been wondering that too: what other shape our family might have grown into if there hadn't been this secret in our home, pushing Mom and Dad to act in the ways they did. If Mom hadn't been so anxious. If Dad hadn't felt guilty. If he hadn't always been Abigail's protector and I hadn't become Mom's ally.

I wonder what it would have meant to me growing up, knowing that my older sister was adopted. Would I have used it to torture her when she and I got into childish arguments? Would I have bragged about it in school, thinking it made our family exotic?

Who knows.

I look at my sister across the stairwell.

"Why *did* you leave like that?" I say. "After high school. You didn't even say goodbye."

She shrugs.

"I don't know. Mom always seemed to think I was just one step from disaster, you know? Maybe I just felt it was time to call her bluff. Find out if I really *was* a mess, or if I was going to be able to hold it all together and make a life for myself." She looks at me. "And you know, after all, I was *good* at being an adult, Gillian. I figured things out. I never had to ask them for money once I left home, not once. I didn't have to come back with my tail between my legs. Sometimes I think Mom wishes I had. That she's mad that I proved her wrong, by *not* being a disaster."

I look at her.

"I don't think she wishes that, Abigail. I don't think so at all."

My sister looks away, chin jutting out.

"Does it...change anything for you, about Dad?" I say finally. "Finding out all this."

She sighs.

"I just wish I'd gotten to tell him that it was okay, Gillian. That he was really my dad, that he'd always be my dad."

I swallow.

"I think he knew," I say.

The fact that Abigail was Dad's favorite...I guess it feels like something I always knew, and that always hurt a little. But even that feels different now. It hurts in a different way, if I'm honest, and I feel ashamed of myself for that— as though Abigail has less right to be his favorite now, just because she wasn't his biological child. It seems wrong that I should be jealous over something like that, given what she's going through.

Abigail slides her eyes towards me.

"I think it's different," she says, thinking aloud. "Because I never doubted how Dad felt about me. Never. But Mom...I was never quite so sure. And now that I know the truth, it's like I see our whole relationship in double vision." She closes her eyes again. "It doesn't seem like over a year since Dad died, does it?"

"No."

I picture my father leaving Westchester that morning: the early fall weather, Abigail waving from the doorway.

"I just can't believe that Sam's been dealing with...with all this stuff, since then," Abigail says. "I feel like such a terrible parent."

I look at her tired face.

"It probably happened very slowly," I say. "And besides, he was *trying* to hide it. I think it probably needed someone with more distance to see it," I add, remembering Dinah, and Josie.

Abigail sighs.

"I guess I knew he was an anxious kind of kid, Gillian. Maybe a little more anxious than most. But I didn't want to think anything was wrong." She pauses. "He's great at school, you know— focused, doesn't interrupt, doesn't make trouble. I was just relieved, Gillian, that he didn't seem to have any of the stuff going on that I did."

That makes sense, I think.

"At least it's on the table now," I say. "At least you can talk to him about it." I hesitate, then say the thing that's been on my mind. "But don't you think you should tell him, though, Abigail? About Lorna?"

She looks at me.

"Seriously, Gillian? After how triggering Dad's death was?" She sighs. "I've got a specialist lined up for when we go back to Westchester. We're going to deal with this—this OCD thing or whatever it is—one day at a time."

I chew my lip.

"I know what you mean but...it might be better telling him now rather than later."

She looks at me.

"I know you want the best for him, Gillian. So do I. So can you please leave this to me?"

I hold my tongue. She's right. It's not my place.

"How's Oliver?" she pivots.

I hesitate, glancing back down the corridor to our room.

"Fine."

"It's nice that he came."

"Yeah." I pause, the mention of one husband making us both think of the other.

"So...Dennis is arriving in the morning?"

Abigail looks away.

"I don't think I can have that kind of talk with him before we all get in that car tomorrow."

Abigail's car is already down here of course, so I guess they have to drive it home. But that's going to be a hell of a ride back.

She swallows. "We'll just...we'll do the drive up to Westchester, and then once we're back home I'll—we'll talk it through."

I raise my eyebrows.

"Ending the marriage," she clarifies. "I'm going to do it, Gillian. I am."

I hope I believe her.

"You deserve better, Abigail. You deserve so much better."

She sighs.

"Life is short, right?" she says, and I know we're both thinking of Lorna. "The time we have is precious."

*

Back in our room Oliver's sitting up in bed doing something on his phone.

"Been pouring oil on troubled waters?" he says. I fill him in on Mom and Abigail, and on Dennis and just how bad things have gotten there.

"Wow," he says. "And you always thought he was such a hot-shot."

I flush.

"No I didn't."

"You did," he says. "You really did."

"I'm sorry." I kiss his cheek. "You're a good guy, Oliver McCrae."

Something flickers across his face again for a moment, then disappears.

"I'm just going to hop in the shower," I say. "And then maybe we can think about dinner?"

I take a short, bracing shower, but for once I take the time to actually do my hair and put on a little makeup. This is the beginning, I tell myself. This is the start of a new chapter. If I've learned anything from the past few days, it's that life is short and you don't get do-overs. So now it's time to make the most of things.

I open the bathroom door and go back into the bedroom, wrapped in my towel, glancing up at Oliver to see if he has any playful remarks to make about me being all dolled up with no clothes on. But when I look at his face it's not playful at all. He has his head half-cupped in his hands, hiding the lower half of his face but not the expression in his eyes. It's the expression I've been afraid of, except now it's writ large and unmistakable. My mouth goes dry.

"Oliver?" I say. "Oliver, what is it?"

He clears his throat.

"I...Gillian, there's something I need to tell you."

Chapter Twenty-Six

Something I need to tell you.

The human body is amazing, isn't it? The fact that those six little words can ricochet from my ear to my brain to my heart so that it's pounding before he's even finished the sentence.

"I...I've been trying to figure out how to say it."

So it's true, I think with a dull horror. *Hannah Feldman.*

I'm just another blind-wife cliché. I just thought...I thought Oliver was *different.* Now his eyes scan the room, looking everywhere but me.

"Gillian...you know how I asked you what you'd have done—if you were in Lorna's shoes?"

My brain feels fuzzy. Why is he saying this? What do I care about Lorna now?

He clears his throat.

"I asked because, well, because I'm kind of in her position, you could say."

I blink. Everything's a fog. Is he *not* having an affair?

"I don't understand," I say, my voice sounding high and sharp, not like my own.

"I got some news last week," he says. "I mean: Jeff got some news. That night I came home. You asked me why he'd called...I was so shell-shocked, Gill, I didn't know what to say. I didn't know how to tell you."

"Tell me what?" I say faintly.

"Gillian, you know how Jeff and Dinah did those tests? The DNA tests?"

I stare at him. *Obviously* I know. The stupid voucher they gave us was what led to all this upheaval.

"Somebody," Oliver says, "contacted Jeff on the platform."

I wait, not getting it. Jeff found some distant relative? What's the big deal; why is Oliver almost shaking right now?

He clears his throat. "Gillian...Back when I was in college, I...I saw an ad on campus. It seemed like okay money for something so...simple." He looks at me, his anxious face on mine like he's waiting for the penny to drop.

"It didn't seem like a bad thing," he goes on. "Helping people who wanted a baby. I didn't really think that much about it, to be honest. I was just a student. It was all anonymous. We were promised that. It never occurred to me that it would change."

And boom, there it is, the penny. Dropping like a bomb.

"You donated sperm," I say.

He looks at me and nods. His face has turned pink, which for some reason infuriates me.

"*Now* you're blushing?" I say. I'm sure he wasn't blushing back when he made his "donation"...or *donations*; how many times? And he's never once blushed during those awful, painful conversations I've put us both through about IVF and fertility and the future. But *now* he's all pink and flushed like the very idea makes him bashful?

He swallows.

"Everything was so different, then, Gillian—this was back when paternity tests were only something that happened on the *Jerry Springer Show*. It never occurred to me—I never thought anyone would come looking for me."

"That's the real reason why you didn't want to do the DNA test," I say, and my voice sounds flat and cold. "Isn't it?"

He shakes his head. "I wasn't even thinking of that. I should have been, but honestly, Gillian, it was so long ago. I had pretty much forgotten I ever"—he flushes again—"donated. To be honest, I sort of just thought it would sit in a sperm bank somewhere forever. I didn't really imagine someone would *choose* me. That this would happen."

"Her name's Hannah, isn't it?" I manage to say, and he stares at me.

"I saw an email," I say. "I saw you writing to her. You wanted to meet her."

He opens his mouth, closes it.

"She told Jeff she'd like to meet me. And I'd like to. But I...well..."

"You have a *daughter*," I say, and as I say them the words slice me open.

He flinches.

"Biologically, yes. But Gillian, I'm just her donor. I'm not her *father.* She already has two parents. I'm just..."

"You *gave her life*," I say, fury suddenly

breaking open in me, and right now, weirdly, it's Hannah I'm furious for. "Stop *denying* her, Oliver. Stop trying to make it sound like she's no big deal. She's a *person.* You helped *make a person.*" I close my eyes. Oh, the irony. Here I was just days ago, wondering if Oliver had fertility issues.

"Listen to yourself, Oliver," I rage on. "*'I'm just her donor.'* You didn't donate a used car! You didn't donate a...a pizza! You donated the building blocks of *life*, and then that life *happened.*"

He looks down at the floor.

"I know."

We're silent for a moment.

"I'm sorry," he says. "I never meant for it to be like this. I understand how it must feel for you, Gillian. Especially the...the timing..."

And now all the indignation I've felt on Hannah's behalf, any urge to defend her, it all falls away. And in its wake all I feel is bitterness: a hard, closed feeling in my chest, as if this bitterness is the only thing I'll ever feel again.

"You know for sure?" I say quietly. "For sure she's yours?"

CLAIRE AMARTI

He nods without looking at me. "The DNA percentages are really accurate. And besides, when Jeff told me about her—told me what she'd told him, her date of birth, the way she'd been conceived...there's no doubt."

From the little I know about these tests, I know he's right. He's Jeff's only sibling. If the test says Jeff is this girl's uncle, there's only one way that can be true.

"Does she want something?" I say.

Oliver looks blankly at me.

"I mean does she *want* something," I snap. "I don't know, Oliver—money or something. What does she *want?*"

"She doesn't want anything, Gillian."

"She wants to meet you," I point out, which isn't nothing.

"She's curious," Oliver says. "Wouldn't you be? Her moms said she could do the whole DNA thing when she turned eighteen, but to be prepared that I might not welcome it. She's been very respectful. She understands I might not want to have contact, and that it's up to me."

"But you do want to have contact," I point out.

"You've *been* contacting her."

Oliver closes his eyes.

"Gillian...she seems like a nice kid. She really does. I owed her more than silence, didn't I?"

"You owed *me* more than silence," I rage. "You owed me the truth about what was going on, Oliver!"

He looks away.

"I know. I should have told you when Jeff told me. I'm sorry, Gill. I freaked out."

I sit there, silent. I know he's sorry. I see that. But it doesn't help: this hurts like hell.

Hannah.

"She's smart, Gillian. She's going to Princeton, early decision. Can you believe that?"

I see the flicker of wonder on his face. More than wonder: Pride. Pride at what his genes have achieved. And the pride, I can't handle.

"Gillian, where are you going?" He looks at me, worried, as I wipe my eyes and yank my purse from the floor.

"Out," I say. "Don't follow me."

*

I walk without thinking, on the streets we walked earlier today and other streets I haven't been down. Streets that are dark and streets that are bright with life, and they all feel dead to me.

Hannah.

A pretty name. I've thought plenty of times about what I'd call my daughter—our daughter—if we had one. Hannah was on the list.

But not anymore.

She probably *is* a nice kid. And smart. She probably graduated high school with flying colors, beloved by all. She's probably perfect.

It's just so transparent how invested he already is in her, just the concept of her. How some part of him already wants to take some of that credit. And she's invested too, isn't she— why else would she reach out?

Hannah Feldman. What's she even like? Does she look like him? Smile like him? Does she close one eye like he does when he's concentrating, and sneeze when the light's too bright? Does she hate asparagus too; does her hair have red highlights in the sun? Is she the kind of person you can't help but love?

I know Oliver will meet her—of course he will.

And when he meets her, will he love her?

I picture a new version of the years ahead. The small snippets of Hannah Feldman's life. Will she email him every year at the holidays and tell him about her latest triumphs, and will his eyes shine like they did just now at the hotel? Will he walk a little taller that day, reminding himself: *Hannah made captain of the soccer team; Hannah graduated Princeton cum laude; Hannah was valedictorian; Hannah performed her first brain surgery...*

And what if she's *it?* The only child Oliver will ever have? What if we never have one of our own? And meanwhile, all the time: Hannah Feldman.

Chatter, English and Spanish, spills out of an ice cream parlor on the street. I walk around the entwined young couples, and the giggling kids up past their bedtimes. All that happiness and I feel poisoned; poisonous, like there's nothing and no one in the world that I care about right now.

I hate that I feel this way. I hate this dead, dark feeling in my heart that I did nothing to earn. I feel like Oliver just *put* it there with his news and there's nothing I can do about it. No way to lift this bitterness off of me.

Maybe I'll just stay numb like this forever, stale and dried-up and sharp-edged.

*

Back in the hotel lobby, jelly-legged from all my walking on an empty stomach, I end up going to the bar. I don't want to go back to my room. I don't want to go back there ever.

A Miami vacation! A fresh start! I'm seething when I think about it. How dare he play these charades with me.

I think back to New Year's Eve, the way he acted like he was too tired to deal with what I'd told him I needed. About how cranky he's been lately. I was just the one he was taking it out on.

I sip my glass of bourbon—neat, though I never drink it neat—and feel a fiery burn down my throat. It feels right, the way holding my hand to a flame right now would feel right. I'm not numb anymore; I'm angry.

Then someone calls my name. A man's voice. Not Oliver.

I turn, frowning, and see a handsome, furious

man striding across the lobby in my direction.

    I   guess   Dennis's   flight   landed   early.

Chapter Twenty-Seven

He's almost the Dennis I'm used to seeing. Almost. The suit is still top-notch, but a little rumpled now, the neckline of the shirt a little yellowed. His face is still chiseled and handsome, but there's patchy growth—quite the opposite of designer stubble—across that sharp jaw. And his eyes—his eyes just look harder to me now than they did before.

"Gillian!" It's like the sight of me is a trigger, and he's getting angrier as he walks towards me. "Where is he? Where's my son?"

I put down my drink, carefully.

"He's upstairs," I say, doing my best to keep my voice cool and firm. "He's in his room. He's fine. Everything's fine."

"Everything is *not* fine," he snaps. "My son was supposed to be at your house, under your supervision, in the...in the *countryside*. Not in some crime-ridden city being told his real grandmother is some washed-up alcoholic."

Where does he get off with this "*real*

grandmother" thing?

And for someone who tends to make a fuss about all his philanthropic donations, he really doesn't seem to have gotten the memo that alcoholism is an actual disease.

"Dennis."

Oliver's voice. He's by the elevator bank, walking towards us.

"Oh, *you're* here too," Dennis says. "Quite the little reunion."

"I just texted the others," Oliver says pleasantly. "To let them know you're here."

Dennis's eyes narrow. Oliver's cheerful tone makes it impossible for him to sound threatening but there's a clear undertone of *I'm watching you*.

Sure enough, soon the elevator doors open again and Mom and Abigail emerge, Mom frowning, Abigail looking like she's holding her breath.

"Where's Sam?" Dennis raises his voice, and people across the lobby are turning our way; the clerk looks up uncertainly from the welcome desk.

Mom steps closer to Abigail, looking suddenly

taller.

Abigail's voice is steady. "He's upstairs. I didn't want him coming down to a scene."

"A scene? I could call the police on you, Abigail. Taking him across state lines without my consent..."

"Actually," Mom steps in, "It was Gillian and I who did that, if you're going to read the riot act about it."

Thanks a bunch, Mom. But at least she's standing up for Abigail.

"No one asked you, Gloria," Dennis says grimly.

He turns back to Abigail. "You're one to accuse me of making a scene. *I'm* not the one who went AWOL; who *abandoned my family*. What do you think a judge will say to that, hm? You think they'd call you a fit mother?"

My sister's expression flattens instantly. I feel the tension in the room take a beat, a sort of heat-shimmer around us.

"Now hold on a minute," Mom says, but Abigail holds up her hand.

"Mom. Not now, please." She fixes her eyes on Dennis. "Come upstairs, Dennis. Sam's upstairs. You can talk to him there. And you and I can talk too."

She gives Mom a *please stay out of this* look, and I put a hand on Mom's arm as Abigail bangs the elevator call-button, and she and Dennis step in. They don't say a word to each other, not looking at each other as the doors close. The elevator hums and the numerals start lighting up, and Mom lets out an angry sound.

"To think!" she says. "That man!"

"Abigail will be okay, Mom," I say. "She'll stand up for herself."

Mom takes some breaths, still shooting furious looks at the elevator doors.

I glance back around at Oliver. He's looking at me, and the look has so many layers. What I read there most of all is an appeal: *Let's not ever be them.*

"I'm sure Gillian's right, Gloria," he says. "Abigail is a very strong woman."

I flash back for some reason to a long-ago day in a neighborhood playground: high summer, I'm five or six. Abigail on the monkey bars, crowing as she makes it all the way across. Me trying to follow, getting stuck halfway, clinging with both hands to the bar, refusing to let go. Abigail, the strong one, watching in bewilderment as Dad detaches me from the bars.

"Mouse," he'd laughed, unclamping my fingers and setting me down. "Oh, Mouse!"

Oliver's seeking my gaze, trying to connect.

"Maybe we all need to take a minute after that," he says. "Gloria, have you eaten? Gillian...?"

"I'm not hungry," I say, turning my eyes away.

"Gillian—" he appeals.

"Oliver, *I'm not hungry*, okay?"

He looks down, nods.

"Well, there's a diner two doors down, and I guess I'm going to go there. And"—he meets my eyes again—"I would love it, Gill, if you wanted to join me, when you're ready, if you change your mind."

When he's gone, Mom looks at me.

"Gillian?"

I sigh.

"It's complicated, Mom."

"Yes," she says. "It looks that way."

Back over at the bar, the young bartender is

wiping down the counter, throwing curious glances our way. He was there when Dennis came striding over, calling my name.

"Want to sit?" Mom points to the bar and I shake my head.

"Well then, you're coming upstairs," she says, in a no-nonsense voice that takes me right back to my teens, "and then you're going to tell me what on earth is going on."

*

Mom just listens as I tell her the story. Her eyes widen a little, but that's all. Even when I'm finished she just sits there, nodding slightly, her mouth neither tight nor agape, but neutral.

"Well?" I say, feeling suddenly impatient.

"What should I say, Gillian?" She shakes her head. "It's terribly startling for you, of course. I'm certainly sympathetic. But I'm not sure it matters as much as you think it does."

"How can you say that?" I feel outraged for the second time tonight. "After everything with Abigail?"

"It *is* extraordinary, isn't it?" Mom says. "How one little thing...an anniversary present, you said? How one little thing could have set off such a chain reaction."

It's not the DNA tests that are the problem, I think bitterly. The problem is that no one's been telling the truth. No one's been facing up to the past. And then the past came back to bite us all.

"But maybe," Mom goes on, "maybe it's *because* of everything with Abigail, Gillian, that I can suggest that this...development...of Oliver's, doesn't matter so much."

"Gillian," Mom pauses. "Oliver is a very nice man—very nice—but perhaps he's not in quite as much demand as you think he is." She looks at me. "You're acting as though this young woman has asked him to be her father—but what I'm hearing is that she simply wants to *meet* him. Which, if you ask me, sounds perfectly normal." She pauses. "The thing is, Gillian...well, blood isn't family. *Family* is family."

It would be easy, and probably cruel, to retort right now with a comment about Abigail, and ask whether my sister would agree. But then Mom's right. It's not questions of blood that have rocked our family this past week. It's questions of trust.

It's not that blood doesn't matter. But it's up

to us to choose *how* it matters.

"But..." I take a breath, and come out with it. "But what if she's all the family we get?" I look up at Mom. "What if I never get pregnant and she—Hannah—she's *it?*"

Mom gives me a long, unreadable look. Another mother might take my hands in hers right now, or wrap her arms around me. But that's not Mom's way.

"In that case, Gillian, you'll have a lot to navigate. You'll have a lot of pain to get through. But the pain won't be about this Hannah person. The pain would be there either way. Although if I may, darling, that's a rather gloomy cart you're putting before the horse."

I swallow. My mother's never been the person to come to for a wallow. But she's quite good at being right.

"Can I still sleep in this room tonight?" I say.

"Well, of course," Mom says. "If that's what you want."

She stands then, and goes to the corner of the room, opens the minibar, and pulls out two small whiskeys. She cracks them open neatly, one after the other, and brings over two plastic glasses.

"I've always liked the name Hannah," she says.

*

We should be talking about this, Gillian, Oliver texts back when I tell him I'm sleeping in Mom's room again tonight.

I think of all the times I've tried to get us to talk about hard things, when he always found a way to kick that ball down the road. How he never seemed to think we needed to talk when *I* felt we needed to talk. And now he's the one on uncertain footing, and he finds he doesn't like it. Well, let him not like it.

When a knock comes on Mom's door, she and I look at each other. I assume it's Oliver, and I open the door stiffly, ready to give him a piece of my mind. But it's not Oliver.

"Abigail? What's going on? Are you okay?"

She looks a little shaky.

"Abigail!" Mom echoes, and stands up from the bed.

"Can I come in?"

All that anger she was emitting towards Mom earlier, something else seems to have overpowered it. And looking at her, it seems to me like the something else is fear.

"Abigail..." I say again, sharper now, "what's going   on?"

Chapter Twenty-Eight

My sister's shoulders, her jaw, all stiffen, and for a moment I think she's not going to answer. Then she shakes her head, and I can almost feel the composure drain away from her.

"He told me...he said if I divorce him he'll sue for sole custody. And that the judge would be bound to grant it." She takes a huge breath. "Based on my unfit parenting." She looks at me. "How I'm 'unstable.' The anxiety that was *getting in the way of my parental duties*...And then 'abandoning our family.'" She stops. "When he puts it all together, Gillian...." She shakes her head. "Dennis is always so impressive. He could turn a judge against me, I'm sure he could."

I glance at Mom.

"Abigail," Mom says, "sit down."

Abigail sits on one of the beds, her face pale.

"He doesn't want to be married to me," she says. "He just doesn't want to fail." She swallows. "Do you think he'd win?" She knits her hands together. "He *might* win."

"Abigail," Mom says. "No matter what he says about custody, no matter what he tries to hold over you...you can't live like that."

Abigail shrugs off the words. "It's easy for you to say, you don't get it. Sam—"

"It's for Sam I'm saying this," Mom insists. "Sam *and* you. Think what it'll do to him, Abigail, to watch you in a marriage that's destroying you. You think you can hide that from him? He already senses it—can't you see that?" She looks at me. "You see it, don't you, Gillian? You're just going to mess with that boy's mind if you're acting like everything's fine when he knows it's not. Thinking he's supposed to pretend he's part of a happy family when he knows he isn't. Don't make him live inside some performance where he can't tell up from down."

Abigail glares at Mom.

"And who are you to talk about performance? *Don't mind my daughter, Mrs. Brandt, she's just a little tired today.* Growing up with you was nothing *but* performance, Mom," she snaps. "I was the naughty puppet in the puppet theater. A theater full of all sorts of fiction. So don't talk to me about performance!"

Mom just stands there, letting the words come at her.

"I'm sorry, Abigail," she says steadily. "I'm very sorry you felt all those things. But I want you to be happy, and I always have. And I don't want you to make the mistakes I made, by pretending things were all right that weren't all right. I understand why it's so tempting—but in the end, you don't help the people you think you're helping."

Abigail blinks at her. And suddenly it's like all the fight goes out of her.

"I...Can I sleep here tonight?" She looks away. "I asked Dennis if he could rent a different room for tonight but he says why would he, *we're a family*." She swallows. "He doesn't even *like* being married to me."

"Of course. Gillian's sleeping here too," Mom says, with a glance my way. "There's room for you both."

Abigail frowns at me.

"You? Why?"

I glance over at Mom.

"How well-stocked is that minibar?" I say.

*

Abigail's eyes widen as I tell the story.

"Extraordinary," she says when I finish. "I suppose he put it out of his mind," she goes on. "It should have occurred to him, that these days, somehow—but I suppose it was easier to forget."

I think of Oliver's historical dislike for Dennis, which I'd always partly put down to wealth; to how Oliver had to work nights all the way through his college years to support himself. It's not hard to see how a quick trip to a sperm bank seemed like a smart choice.

And I can't even say it was a *bad* choice. Because who understands more than I do what a miracle it is to be able to give someone a baby? To be able to make that possible for them?

I just wish it hadn't been him.

Abigail shakes her head again, swirls the last of the whiskey in her plastic glass.

"But you, Abigail," I say finally. "You're not going to go back to that marriage, are you? You can't."

She looks at me.

"I...I have a lot to think about, Gillian," she says. "I think I need some legal advice."

"But Abigail—" I look at her. "If you go back with him tomorrow; if you let that whole world become your routine again..."

"I know," she says. "I know, Gill."

Wordlessly, Mom tops up our glasses, and Abigail sighs.

"You know, *The Bridges of Madison County* is on pay-per-view," Mom says.

It's such a non sequitur, such an outlandish suggestion, that I can't help but laugh.

But Abigail swigs her drink and shrugs. "I've always liked Robert Redford in that."

And soon, with our minibar whiskey in our plastic glasses, the three of us are lined up on one queen bed as *The Bridges of Madison County* runs its opening credits.

*

I go back to my room before breakfast. Oliver stirs as I come in.

"Gillian...can you sit down? Can we talk about this?"

"I'm not staying," I say, keeping my eyes averted as I comb through my suitcase. "I just need a change of clothes. I'm going out with Abigail and Sam for a couple of hours."

Abigail told me she'd like it if I came with them, when she and Sam go to say goodbye. I'm her moral support, I guess. I haven't been that in decades.

"But when are we going to talk?" Oliver says. "Gillian, we need to talk."

"You know," I turn around. "You had no problems shutting down the conversation whenever I was trying to talk to *you* about our future. Anytime I brought IVF up you acted like I was some kind of masochist who couldn't just leave the conversation alone. But now you think I have some kind of moral responsibility to sit here and talk about all this with you?"

Oliver sets his jaw.

"I just...it's in both of our interests, Gillian. In the interests of us as a couple—"

"Right," I say. "Just like all the times I tried to talk to *you* about what would be in our interests as a family."

Oliver's gaze snaps to mine. Alongside the exhaustion, I see the spark of a challenge.

"Okay, just answer me this, Gillian," he says. "What happens if we do it and it doesn't work? What then?" His voice is steady in a way that unnerves me. "What happens to us? You and me. Adoption? Divorce? What?"

I pull my eyes away, focus on pulling a fresh T-shirt from my bag.

"You don't know," he says quietly.

He's right. I don't. And I hate that he's making me think about all that.

"Those are hypotheticals, Oliver," I say.

"Well, they're hypotheticals that matter to me!"

"Well, what matters to *me* is that you lied to me."

Oliver makes an exasperated sound.

I pull on a shirt and jeans, my hands trembling, looking anywhere but at him.

"Should I book our return flights for later today?" he says.

I close my eyes. I picture sitting next to him on the plane, beside happy holidaymakers returning home from their holiday vacation. I picture going back to my bathroom cabinet full of pregnancy tests, and my kitchen counter arrayed with prenatal vitamins. I picture the days we were supposed to have here: the new beginning, the cocktails on Ocean Drive.

"I don't know, Oliver. Whatever. Do what you think best."

And with that I leave the room, and jog downstairs to find my sister.

*

I find them in the breakfast room—Abigail, Sam, and Dennis. Dennis is clean-shaven again, immaculate as ever, and with my sister's striking looks and simple linen clothes they look like the kind of family you might envy: elegant, good-looking, perfectly harmonious. I wonder if that's what the other hotel guests see.

But when I look closer I can see how Sam is more subdued this morning; how when he looks up from his food he glances from one parent to the other and says nothing. And I see the stiffness in my sister's back, and the stubborn, determined look in Dennis's eye.

"Hey, Aunt G," Sam greets me in a quiet voice.

"Hello, Samwise," I say, but he doesn't crack a smile.

"Are you done, Sam?" my sister says, and he nods, pushing away his breakfast plate. Dennis looks between the two of them, and with a glance acknowledges me for the first time.

"I'm expecting you back by eleven, remember."

Sam nods. Abigail says nothing, just gets out of her seat.

"Abigail."

She looks at him, eyes cold.

"I heard you. Come on, Sam."

I glance at her once we're outside in the fresh air. The sun feels almost startling in its gentleness; how perfect the day is. But the stiffness doesn't leave Abigail's shoulders.

We walk down the same streets we walked down yesterday. The men in Domino Park are out again, and someone has a radio on. Two kids on skateboards course by us.

"Are you okay, Mom?" Sam says.

She looks at him.

"I'm glad we got to do this, Sam."

He frowns. She's not answering his question.

"It feels kind of rushed though, doesn't it?" he says.

Abigail says nothing.

"I mean, even if I *do* have school...I don't see why we can't have another couple of days," he says. "Do you think Lorna will visit us next, or will we come visit her—like in the summer?"

Abigail shakes her head.

"Maybe. I don't know. We have a lot to talk about, Sam."

Sam's frown deepens, and he glances at me quickly before looking away.

Abigail actually asked Mom this morning—not altogether graciously, but still—if she wanted to come with us, but Mom shook her head. She said she and Lorna had said what they needed to say to each other. I think she didn't want to intrude.

Soon we're back outside the squat brown apartment building. Abigail just stands for a moment, not ringing the bell.

"Abigail," I say gently, and she nods and takes a breath.

It only takes a few seconds for Lorna to buzz us in. Sam's first to the stairs; I walk behind with my sister.

"It's not a last goodbye," I murmur to her. We don't yet know how Lorna's body will respond to chemo or radiation therapy. And nothing's going to happen overnight. There will be time for real goodbyes.

But Abigail glances at me. It's what this goodbye stands for: the other, final goodbye, which may be in a year or two or may be as soon as a few months from now. And how the next time she sees Lorna, Lorna may be in very different shape.

Upstairs, Lorna welcomes us with an easy smile. She doesn't seem to be feeling the heaviness of the moment the way my sister is—the way I am, too, if I'm honest—but maybe that's what dying does to some people. Maybe Lorna is one of those rare people who's mastered the art of letting go.

"We, um, can't stay very long." Abigail swallows. "Dennis wants us to hit the road early."

"Of course," Lorna nods. She puts a light hand on Abigail's arm, then looks at Sam.

"Well, what a pleasure it's been, Sam." She shakes her head. "I'd heard all about you over the years—your grandfather was so terribly proud of you, you know—but I never really thought I'd get to meet you. I'm so glad I did."

Sam nods.

"So will you come see us in Westchester next time?"

Lorna hesitates. I feel some slight question in the half-glance she casts at Abigail then, as if to say, *just tell the child.* Or maybe that's just me.

"I...I don't think that's likely to work out, Sam. But perhaps you'll be able to come back here one of these days."

"Okay." Sam frowns.

"Meanwhile, I thought you might like to have these," Lorna says, and takes a small stack of books from the coffee table where she's obviously left them ready for him. They're a gold-embossed hardcover set. Handsome-looking books.

"It's the Lord of the Rings trilogy," she says, handing him a bag to put them in. "My old set that your grandfather gave me. Maybe you'll enjoy them."

Sam looks flustered but his eyes spark with pleasure.

"Thank you."

Lorna turns her eyes on me then.

"And you too, Gillian, it's been a pleasure meeting you. I always wanted a sister, growing up. I'm so glad Abigail has you."

I glance at Abigail. I wonder if Lorna understands what it's been like for me and Abigail; that we've probably never been the kind of sisters to each other that people dream of having. But I suppose, even so, we *are* sisters. We may not be a model of sisterhood, but we made it this far.

"Thank you," I say—like Sam, it seems like I'm a bit lost for words right now. I have a flash of what Abigail means, and how it must feel for her, trying to square this circle: how the woman in front of us is still basically a stranger, and yet the most important stranger she'll ever meet. Of course my sister's week of visits hasn't made Lorna feel like a second mother, how could it?

You can't fill in a past you didn't have, you can only imagine it. And what is imagining but a question that can't be answered?

I think about how my family will never look clear or simple to me again. We've lost simplicity; we've gained truth. I guess the world is always showing us that it's more complicated than we thought.

"I—I'd like a little time alone with Lorna,

Sam," Abigail says then, turning around. "To say my own goodbyes. Is that okay?"

Sam frowns, glancing between the two of them, then at me.

"Sure…"

"I'll walk back with you to the hotel," I say. "Your mom can see us back there. We can make a detour for some guava juice if you want."

He lifts one side of his mouth at that, but the smile doesn't reach his eyes. I get the sense he's trying to make me feel better, instead of vice versa.

"Okay, well…goodbye," he says to Lorna.

Lorna smiles at him, then at me.

"Goodbye, you two," she says, her voice steady, giving nothing away. I put my hand on Sam's shoulder as I steer us towards the stairs, and feel the hairs on my neck prickle—the prickle of uncertainty, of a future we can't see coming.

Chapter Twenty-Nine

Outside Lorna's apartment the sun is shining, the city is bright and thriving and suddenly loud. I realize how tired I am, and now this farewell with Lorna seems to have used up whatever emotional energy I had left after Hannah Feldman.

"I could use a coffee." I look over at Sam. "Want to get something?"

Sam shakes his head, not looking at me.

"Want me to carry those books for you?"

"It's okay."

We walk on through the streets, and I'm thinking again how much life there is here, how small a city can make you feel, surrounded by so much energy that's not yours. I wonder if Hannah Feldman lives in a city. Oliver didn't say, but I imagine her living in New York: a sharp, slick eighteen-year-old, fluent in cultural references that are too witty for me to ever understand, with a confidence I'll never possess.

I wish she'd never emailed him. I wish he'd

never known.

I don't like to think of myself as ungenerous—she's just an eighteen-year-old girl. And maybe it's a cop-out but I feel so sure that if we had kids of our own, I could bear it better. I'm almost certain I could.

She hasn't stolen anything from you, Gillian.

It's true, I know it is. But my heart and my head feel different things.

Sam slows his pace as we walk on, and at a certain point he looks at me. I can see there's something on his mind. He takes a breath.

"Aunt G?"

I look at him.

"Is there something wrong with Lorna?"

I blink. "What do you mean, wrong?"

He drops his eyes to his shoes. "I don't know...You and mom, everyone's treating her kind of weird. Yesterday you kept talking about if she was tired, and...you just all acted like she was sick."

He looks at me, clear-eyed, expecting a clear answer.

I take a breath. "Yes, Sam. She's sick."

He says nothing for a moment.

"How sick?" he says, seemingly determined not to blink. "Bad sick?"

I think of all the lies that have been told in this family over the years, the lies and the "withholdings of truth." And I'm just not going to do it, I decide. No matter what my sister thinks.

"Yes," I say. "Bad sick."

Sam looks away.

"Is she going to die?"

I draw down another breath. *In for a penny...*

"We don't know, Sam. We don't know how long she has. It could be years. But...probably not."

Sam is quiet, but he nods, not meeting my eyes.

"I'm sorry, Sam," I say.

He nods again. He's deflated, but he's absorbing it, not falling apart. He's taking it in in his slow, careful way. Abigail underestimated him, I think; probably parents often do. In the end, I suspect I'll have done her a favor—I've been worried about how Sam might hate her when he finally learned the truth and realized she'd kept it from him. Abigail knows what that feels like, after all.

On the curb a few paces away there's a coffee cart, and I suddenly feel exhausted in the most profound way.

"I need a coffee," I say aloud. "I—I'm sorry, Sam," I add, looking again at the dejected figure beside me. "I'm so sorry that she's sick. It's not fair, I know that."

Sam shrugs, morose, and follows without looking up at me as I move us over to the coffee cart line.

"Can I get you a drink?" I say, and he shakes his head.

I put my hand on his shoulder. "I know this is bad news," I say. "But it's so good you got to meet her, you know. Whatever happens next."

Sam says nothing and a man's voice says loudly, "Can I help you, ma'am?"

The coffee cart line is all gone.

"Oh," I look at him. "Black, two sugars, please." I feel in need of the extra hit right now.

I root around in my purse for change. He asks if I need a lid and holder and I say no to the lid and yes to the holder. I take my change, blow on the coffee, and drop some coins in the tip jar. Then I turn to Sam—

And he's not there.

"Sam?" I feel like I'm going crazy. He must be here. He was right here a second ago. "Sam?!"

I turn back to the man at the cart. "Did you see the kid who was with me? He was right here..."

He cranes out of the little to-go window, scanning the scene and looking back to me like I'm crazy.

"You had a kid with you?"

I raise my voice, and a few people near us look around: "Has anyone seen a ten-year-old boy?" I say.

Some just look confused or annoyed. A twenty-something looks up from her phone and shrugs helplessly. A middle-aged woman stares at me, stricken, her mind clearly racing to the dark places mine's determined not to go. Which way did he go—right, back the way we came? Or left, towards the hotel?

He might not remember the way to the hotel that well. And besides, he was in a temper: he'll have wanted to go the way we weren't going. So, right, I decide. Back the way we came.

I push the coffee cup back into the man's

hands and take off, scanning the streets, telling my heart to stay calm.

He has a phone, I remind myself, and pull mine from my pocket and scroll to his number. No answer.

Maybe I should have gone left at the cart instead of right.

I keep going, but the fact that I can't see him on this street, and knowing he didn't get much of a head-start...he must have gone up one of the side streets. I hang right on the next one, calling Sam's name now, making strangers stare. At the next avenue I scan both ways and turn left, continuing in the direction I'd been going. I'm trying not to overthink the route. He was upset, he wanted to get away. I follow what seems most intuitive.

How could you have let this happen? How could you, Gillian?

Of course I couldn't be a mother! Look at me. How could I take care of an infant when I can't take care of a ten-year-old boy? I swipe my phone for my sister's number and hit Call, thinking I might be sick. I don't know how I'm going to say these words to her. But she doesn't pick up and the phone just rings out. I feel the tears of frustration pricking at my eyes as I call Oliver's number.

"Gillian?"

"Oliver"—my voice trembles—"I've lost Sam. I told him Lorna was sick; he was upset. I guess I looked away for a minute. I don't know where he went."

There's a beat, and Oliver speaks in his calm, steady voice.

"Okay. Remember, Gillian, Sam is a smart kid. He's ten years old. He has a phone with GPS. He knows the name of the hotel. Let's remember that." Then he takes a breath. "Where are you right now?"

I scan the street for signs, read him the name of the intersection.

"I'm not sure if I'm going the right way," I say. "I thought I was but I don't know."

"I'm getting in a cab right now," Oliver says. He swallows. "He'll be fine, Gillian. Seriously, he'll be fine."

But it's my fault, I think. *I'm to blame.*

"You're not to blame," Oliver says, as though he can hear me. "And this is all going to be fine."

My phone beeps with an incoming call.

"I've got to go," I say. It's Abigail. I hang up on Oliver, feeling the blood drain from my face. I ask the universe for forgiveness before I make this day into every mother's nightmare, and pick up the phone.

"Sam ran off," I say. "And I can't find him."

Chapter Thirty

I tried to stay calm for Abigail so that she would, but I could hear in her voice that she was just inches from losing every last shred of composure. I remind myself that Oliver is right: Sam is a responsible, resourceful ten-year-old. He has a phone, and he's only a few minutes from home. But it's not like that was Abigail's view of the matter.

I pause on the next big junction and glance down either side of the intersection. Maybe I should go to a police station, maybe that's what I should do...

A car pulls up behind me and I spin around as Oliver gets out.

"Gillie." He puts his hands on my shoulders. "I told your mom, she's waiting in reception for him. He's bound to go back there, you know."

"Yeah." I breathe. "Yeah, I guess so..."

"Come on," Oliver says. "Get in the car. We'll go around the block. We'll keep looking for him."

He guides me into the cab and the driver greets me with sympathetic confusion.

"Around?" he motions. "Just...around?"

"Yes," Oliver says.

At the top of the street we turn right, then climb a few more blocks. Suddenly on 15th Ave and 8th, I put my hand on Oliver's elbow.

"Wait, let me out here for a minute."

We're at Domino Park.

The driver glances in the rearview, pulls over.

I see Oliver push some bills on him, asking him to wait.

I dash through the arch, taking in the chatter, the groups of men leaning over their games. And then over in the corner on a wooden bench under a mural, a smaller figure with blond, matted hair. He's not surprised to see me.

"*Sam.*"

He looks at me as I stand in front of the bench. Not surprised and not repentant. Now that we've found him I can feel some of the adrenalin go still inside me, all too ready to tip towards anger. Instead I sit.

"You ran off," I say. "You can't just do that— you know that, right?"

Sam looks away, jaw out.

"Sam?" I say.

I wait.

"You lied," he says. "And it isn't fair."

I sigh.

"No," I agree. "This isn't fair. Life often isn't."

He turns then, and glares at me.

"You know, no one ever even talks about Grandad dying. They act like he just was living and then stopped living, as if the *dying* part didn't even happen. But it did! And he was *alone.*"

I swallow.

"Well... he was and he wasn't, Sam. I think we were with him, you know. Even though we weren't there physically."

Sam's glare deepens.

"Don't say stupid stuff like that to me. You know it's just *words.*"

Are they just words? It's a scene I've pictured too, more than I'll admit. Dad in the car, pulling over: his eyes darting to the passenger seat from habit, as though Mom's there beside him. The rearview mirror, as though his girls are in the back, like when we were kids we always used to be.

"Sam..." I say cautiously, "He wasn't a young man. Death was definitely something that had crossed his mind. He was probably very aware of the fact that when it happened, we might not all be there with him, for whatever reason. But that's a different kind of alone to the really bad kind of alone, and I'm pretty sure Dad knew the difference." I hesitate, trying to find the word—not just for Sam, but for myself.

"You know," I say, "how babies freak out when someone leaves the room? How they think that, the second they can't see you, you don't exist any more?"

Sam doesn't respond.

"Well," I say, "that changes as we get older, right? And I think," I swallow. "I think the older you get, the more strongly people exist even when they're not there. By the time you get to Dad's age, Sam, you carry everyone with you. You carry everyone all of the time. So you were with him, Sam. I really think you were with him."

Sam's silent for a while, and then turns back to me.

"You're hypocrites," he says. "All of you. You're all just hypocrites." His voice wavers. "You're always pretending. Always acting like everything's okay, like life is just *fine*. But it's not! People die—all the time! I mean, just look at the news. It's full of *terrible things happening,* all of the time. And you all just pretend that they're not!" He says the last sentence in a burst of rekindled anger and when he's done he looks away again, as though even my face is too offensive for him to bear.

I sit back on the bench. Over by the entrance I see Oliver, talking on the phone. He looks at me and mouths, *Abigail.*

"You think we're just ignoring it," I say to Sam. "Is that it? You think we're ignoring all the terrible things going on in the world?"

Sam scoffs.

"I don't just *think* it. You *are*, you all are."

There's a breeze coming through the gate, and for a moment I close my eyes and feel it.

"No, Sam," I say. "We're not."

I look at him; at the side of his face, which he refuses to turn my way.

"Sam..." I say. "You know how you hate those

'mixed feelings' adults are always talking about?" I swallow. "Well, this is where they start. This is where they come from. Because you're right, Sam, we live in a world full of terrible things." I look at him. "I agree with you. I'd have to be in denial not to see those things. And you're right. They're bad. And they're scary." *They scare me every day,* I don't say. I'm scared of the floods and the wildfires, of the destruction being wreaked on our planet; of wars and terrorism and illness, and man's inhumanity to man. "You're right to be scared. And angry. It's good to be angry sometimes; it's how we remember to change the things that need changing." I pause.

"I feel all those things, Sam. But—I *also* feel joy. And wonder and curiosity. And I've had so many years to stop feeling those things, Sam. So many more years than you for those feelings to get old and tired and go away, but they never quite do—although it can seem that way for a while.

"You're right that we're supposed to feel the bad things, Sam," I say. "Fear, pain, even dread. But...we're allowed to feel the other things too."

I look over at him. "There are so many feelings, Sam, and so many things to have feelings about. It's just how life is. It's a whole lot of trains on a whole lot of tracks, and the trains are all running, all of the time. We don't get a break. We feel them all."

I look at my nephew, his blue eyes staring out into the distance—not angry now, but something else. His chin trembles.

"But it's supposed to get easier," he says finally. He says it like I've taken something from him—like I've stolen something he was once promised.

"I'm not sure that it does," I say gently. "Not really."

He looks at me, those blue eyes all indignant and angry and afraid.

"But you get stronger," I say. "You do, Sam. You will."

He turns away from me again and I see an angry hand reach up to swipe at his eyes. I give him a minute, then reach my arm around his shoulder. He shrugs it off sharply but then, face still turned away, he leans his body into mine and starts to cry. I put a hand against his warm hair.

It won't be the last time he feels this way. It won't be the last time something inside him cries out, *it was supposed to be easier, this isn't what I was promised.* And yet, life will continue to offer him its gifts.

I hold my nephew against me, as he cries the tears of a brave child. And maybe it's me but I could almost swear I feel a shift in the air, like a changing of the seasons. I have the sense that Sam is saying goodbye to something as he cries—to the last pieces of his childhood, maybe; of its protective shell. And when he's done he will be different somehow: he'll be out with us, here in the adult world, in all its icy beauty.

And something will be lost, and something gained.

I keep my hand against his warm head.

"Brave boy," I whisper. "Brave boy."

*

Oliver called Mom to let her know everything was fine, but she's still waiting in the lobby for us as our bedraggled group of four troops in. Dennis is waiting too, springing from his seat as we walk in. Abigail called him in the cab on our way back, letting him know what had happened. I figured she'd be hardly speaking to me, but in fact she doesn't really seem angry at me at all. She's been so focused on Sam, chiding him and apologizing in almost equal measure.

"What the hell?" Dennis says as he reaches our little group. "Sam, what were you thinking? What kind of behavior do you call that? In a strange city, Sam!"

Sam clears his throat.

"I'm sorry," he says.

"It's not acceptable behavior, Sam," Dennis insists. "And now we're going to be hitting the road way later than we were supposed to. The traffic's going to be abysmal." He looks at Sam, then Abigail. "Are you packed? Ready to go?"

"Dennis."

My sister's voice cuts in, quiet but firm. I think there's something in her tone that makes us all turn.

"I need to talk to you. Can you step outside with me for a bit?"

Dennis looks incredulous.

"This is not the time, Abigail. You need to get a move on. My bag is downstairs already. "

She clears her throat.

"No, Dennis...We need to talk."

Mom glances around.

"What about if I take Sam over to the diner? He could probably do with something to eat."

"I'm okay," Sam says, but I see what Mom means. He does look a bit peaky.

Dennis glares at Mom.

"I think that's a good idea," Abigail says. "Dennis?" She looks at him. "We can talk right here in the lobby if you prefer?"

He looks at her like it's a trick question, which maybe it is.

"Fine," he says irritably. "Fine. If you must."

We watch them leave. Sam looks at Mom, and Oliver looks at me. Mom sighs.

"Come on, dear," she says to Sam. "Let's get you a sandwich." She looks at Oliver and me. "Coming?

"Um." I glance at my husband, his wiry curls all askew from driving around in the cab with the windows down, helping me scour the streets.

Suddenly I have a glimpse of his face from back when I first met him: before he had those vertical lines creasing his forehead; before he had those flecks of grey through his curly hair.

"Actually, we need to talk, too," I say. "Right, Oliver?" I glance at Mom and Sam. "We'll see you in a little bit."

*

The seats in the lobby are squeaky and not the most comfortable, but we find a spot away from the elevators and sit down. As if by mutual agreement we've decided not to go back upstairs, avoiding our bedroom like the scene of a crime. I don't want to be reminded of last night; of that moment of coming out of the shower, bright-eyed and all made up, and seeing that look of terrible knowing on his face.

I look at Oliver's eyes across from mine. Nervous but steady. Ready to listen.

I take a deep breath.

"I'm not ready to forgive you yet. Maybe that's unfair, maybe it's not. But I don't want to be stuck in this place, Oliver. The place I've been in since yesterday—it's not a good one. This is..." I sigh. "This is just how things are now, and I need to deal with that."

Oliver nods. "So...what can I do?"

I look over at him, and those steady eyes. I picture a girl with that same bright stare, and take a breath.

"Tell me about her," I say.

"Tell   me   about   Hannah."

Chapter Thirty-One

When Mom and Sam come back into the lobby a half hour later we're still there.

"Are Mom and Dad back yet?" Sam casts a glance out towards the sliding doors. The rest of us look at each other.

"No, Sam," I say. "They haven't come in. I guess they're still talking."

Sam frowns, glancing at Mom.

"Am I still supposed to be driving back today?"

Mom looks at Oliver and me.

"I don't think you will be, dear."

"Then can I go to my room?"

"I'll bring you up," Mom says.

Sam looks sheepish.

"I'm just going to my room, I'm not going to run off or anything."

"Let him go, Mom," I say, and Sam throws me a sidelong, grateful look. Mom sighs in acquiescence.

I watch Sam go over and call the elevator as

Mom sinks into the lounge chair beside Oliver. A skinny little boy in an oversize hoodie. He doesn't remind me of my sister in this moment, even though he's reminded me of her so much these past few days. But looking at him now, I don't see my sister, I see just Sam, his own person; the teenager within him coming into being.

"What a day," Mom says.

Oliver's eyes fix on something over my shoulder and I turn around. It's Abigail. She's alone.

Oliver clears his throat.

"I think I'll leave you ladies alone," he says, standing up. "It looks like you might all have some things to talk about."

Abigail reaches us, hesitant. I don't know if she really wants to talk to Mom and me right now, but I don't think she has much hope of getting away from us.

"I'll check on Sam," Oliver says, and excuses himself. I feel a wave of gratitude for him as he turns and makes his way to the elevator bank. Abigail swallows, and sits down in the seat he's vacated. There's something brittle about the way she does it, like she's afraid something in her might break.

There's a moment of silence.

"We're not going home today," she says. "It's too late." She swallows. "He's getting a different hotel for tonight."

I glance at Mom. Abigail takes a breath.

"I told him," she says finally. "I told him that I wanted a divorce." She corrects herself. "No: I told him that I was divorcing him. That it was happening. It was—it was horrible."

"What did he say?" I ask quietly. "Is he really going to try and get sole custody?"

Abigail meets my eyes. Hers seem dazed, a little glassy.

"I don't know. We didn't come to any conclusions about anything. It wasn't really what you might call a *talk.* He mainly just raged about how selfish I was and always had been; how I was destroying our family." She draws in a breath. "How Sam would never forgive me for this."

"Oh, Abigail."

I reach out and put a hand on her arm.

"You're brave, Abigail," Mom says quietly

from her chair. "That was very brave."

Abigail exhales.

"Well, I thought...it's true what you were saying the other night. No custody situation is going to destroy my relationship with Sam. But staying in this marriage would destroy *me*. And what can I possibly give to my son if I have nothing left of myself?" She swallows.

"I had this moment, earlier—" She looks at me. "This flash of realizing what it would be like to lose Sam, to *really* lose him." Her voice hitches. "And it was unbearable. But then it kind of made me realize, well...everything else was bearable. Bad, maybe, but bearable. Even if"—she takes a deep breath—"even if Dennis does carry on with this sole custody thing, and even if he does win...people can appeal those decisions." She looks at me. "After you two were asleep last night I spent a lot of time on Google. You can appeal for custody decisions to be revised whenever there's a 'meaningful change' in circumstances. Often judges will look at the same case again every couple of years. Two years...that's bearable." She blinks. "That's just how I'll have to think about it. I'll fight tooth and nail, but if the worst happens, the very worst...I'll hang in there, and I'll wait out those two years. I can bear it, you know? Now I know that I can bear it."

I squeeze her arm.

"They won't give him sole custody, Abigail. I really think they won't. Besides," I say. "It might be just bluster. Once he realizes this divorce is really happening and he can't stop it, Dennis might see sense and let this drop. He loves Sam, too. Maybe he'll see that fighting over him isn't the best thing for him."

Abigail sighs.

"Maybe," she says, clearly not too convinced.

There's a pause.

"It's just," she says, "this isn't the end, you know? It's the beginning." She swallows. "This conversation might be over for me, but it's not over for Dennis. I'm going to have to have it again and again. I'm going to have to try so hard, Gillian, for it not to wear me down."

I know what she means. She's said her piece, and now she'll have to hold her ground. Every day she'll have to fight the fight again—if not with Dennis, then with herself. She'll have to deal with the nagging voice in her head asking her if she really did the right thing; if she just should have tried harder, done more, stayed longer. But I believe in her. If she could stand her ground today, she can stand it tomorrow. Even amid the stress of lawyers and money worries, and of making an independent life for herself again after so long.

"We're proud of you, Abigail," Mom says.

Abigail says nothing. Her eyes well up with tears.

"Thank you," she says, voice trembling. "But...I wish Dad were here."

Mom swallows.

"Of course you do."

"I miss him," Abigail says. There's just a hint of defiance mixed with the grief—as if she's daring us to contradict her.

"Of course you do," Mom says again.

Abigail looks at her.

"Do *you*?"

Mom makes a little noise in her throat. I don't think Abigail was trying to offend her. It's true that Mom has never really talked about Dad's absence much.

"Of course I do," she says, a quiver in her voice. "Of course I miss him."

We sit in silence for a moment, then Mom shifts in her seat and clears her throat.

"Your father was easy to love," she says. "I'm not as easy. I know that. I always understood why he was your favorite."

Abigail looks up, eyes wide. And I stare too. Favoritism, favorite: they're ugly words, not the kind we say aloud in this family. We've only ever skirted around them. But what's startling me is that Mom wasn't just looking at Abigail when she said that. She was looking at both of us. She was speaking to me, too. And I feel an intense wave of guilt—because she's not wrong.

"I resented it, you know, when you were younger," Mom says. "How he was always the 'good cop.'"

I see Abigail's frown deepening. Mom glances between us, absorbing the looks on our faces. Her eyebrows knit together.

"You never saw it, I suppose? I loved him tremendously, you know, but I used to feel he let me down on that front. The way he courted you girls, both of you. I always had to be the bad guy."

I mean...again, she's not wrong. Dad was the soft touch in our home, Mom was the tough one. The one who set the rules, doled out punishments; the one who got angry. But I never thought of it as "good cop, bad cop." I never thought of it as a parenting style at all. I thought it was just who they were.

I see the angry look on Abigail's face as she opens her mouth then closes it again. I know what she's feeling because I'm feeling it too. I have to struggle not to jump to Dad's defense. It's new to hear Mom say something critical about him, and I don't like it. It's new to blame Dad for any of these cracks in our family, but Mom's right about the *good cop bad cop* thing: he loved us so much but I guess he didn't really do the hard parts.

"Of course he never saw it that way," Mom says. "He was just being himself. He adored you both—it came naturally. He would want to be here for you," she says to Abigail. "He really would."

Abigail nods, wipes her face.

Somewhere inside, a voice tells me that one

of these days I will have to release Dad from his obligation he has in death to be perfect. That he and I will both be a little freer once I do. And I guess Abigail's going to have to do the same thing.

"I didn't know you felt that way," Abigail says to Mom. I hear the guilt in her voice too, and a sulky, wounded note. "But it was the same for us, you know." She glances over. "For Gillian and me. You and Dad, you split us down the middle."

Mom winces.

"I... I understand why you would say that—"

"It's pretty true, Mom," I say quietly. I don't want to rub salt in the wound. But it seems like this is our day for honest talk.

Abigail nods.

"Gillian was yours; I was Dad's."

I feel the old fault-lines shudder as my sister speaks. There's plenty I would have changed, too, about our childhood, but I've never wanted to hold it against my parents. Not because I'm a kinder person than my sister, but because it feels too uncomfortable for me to criticize. If anyone asks, I say my childhood was happy.

And it was—some days.

Mom looks at her lap. "It's a terrible thing to admit, Abigail, but sometimes I think...I think maybe I was jealous. When you were very little."

Abigail looks at her, disbelieving.

"Of *me?*"

Mom frowns. "Not of you. Of your father. Or maybe of both of you. He had such a bond with you right from the start. He'd always had such a soft spot for Lorna, you know; he'd treated her more like a daughter than a sister. All of that devotion, all of that instinct to protect, he brought it straight over to you, but times a hundred. You were so small, but so strong. The grip your tiny fingers had. Lungs of steel." She shakes her head. "You responded to him so differently than you did to me. Right from the start. He was the one that could always get you to sleep. Who could get you to calm down when you cried."

"*Mom*. Are you serious?" Abigail stares at her. "I was a *baby*. Babies don't pick favorites. I probably just liked the way his chest rumbled or something."

Mom blinks at that. I can see it's all but impossible for her to reconfigure those memories: to view it the way Abigail's suggesting.

She sighs.

"Then, when Gillian came along, you see...I was worried that he was so appalled at the thought of you being displaced, Abigail, that he *over*compensated. That he didn't fuss over Gillian as much as he'd fussed over you." She looks from one to the other of us. "I'm sorry for how it all got to be. Your father and I should have realized. I think we were just both so afraid of one of you feeling neglected."

She pauses.

"Your father adored you." She looks at me fiercely. "*Both* of you. And so do I." She clears her throat. "I don't really know how to say this, but...this favoritism stuff, I don't think it was ever really about love. I mean, I don't think it was about being loved more or loved less. We just...we knew how to play to our strengths, I suppose. And we kept doing that, and told ourselves that that was enough."

Abigail frowns, but I think some small part of

me might be starting to understand what Mom means.

Because even if Dad was the favorite, I realize that my love for Mom has always been as bone-deep, as inescapable, as my love for Dad was. But Dad was just...*easy*. It's like Mom said.

He was easy to love.

Maybe that's all that favoritism really is in the end. Not about being loved more or loved less, but about what comes easy.

Dad would have stepped in front of a bus for me just as fast as he would have for Abigail, but it was Abigail's wildness that made him feel carefree. And, maybe because that carefree feeling was what had been denied him as a child, that was the feeling he needed the most.

Meanwhile, for Mom, I was the kid who made her feel relaxed and assured, and like she had it in her to be a good mother—and I guess that was what *she* needed the most.

She's right: they should have tried harder. They should have tried harder at the parts that didn't come so easy. But they *were* trying. I think I can say that now: they at least were trying.

Chapter Thirty-Two

Upstairs, Oliver turns off the TV.

"So?" He looks at me.

I flop onto the bed.

"Well, she's divorcing him," I say. "It's definitely happening. And we all had a talk. A pretty big one."

He looks at me, wondering if I'm okay. Am I? I don't know.

I look at my husband.

"Are you happy, Ollie?" I blurt. "I mean...in life? In our marriage? All of that?"

He looks at me dubiously at first, like it might be a trick. When he sees it's not, he's silent for a while.

"I think," he says at last, "I think maybe there's too much pressure to be happy, Gillian. People make it sound like we're supposed to feel that way all the time, unless there's something wrong. But I don't think happiness is a default setting. I think it's a gift. I think most of the time we're just...normal."

"Normal?"

It sounds so...underwhelming. But maybe, in a way, also liberating. Not to be chasing happiness. Not to think there's something wrong with me if more of my days feel ordinary, unpunctuated by magic, than not.

I wonder if he's right. Or if his standards are just too low. If this is his way of saying that he's not that happy in his life with me but he'll settle for it anyway.

"Ask me something else instead," Oliver says then, and his eyes meet mine, unflinching. "Ask me," he says, "if I feel alone."

I swallow.

But I do it.

"Do you feel alone?" I say, and saying the words is like standing on a tightrope over a deep valley.

Oliver keeps his eyes on mine.

"Never, Gillian" he says.

*

We go out to the diner nearby and talk for a long time, and come back to our room and talk some more. We talk about the future, and the past. We talk about Hannah Feldman. Oliver has told me that he still hasn't managed to email her. He's been trying to find the words but doesn't know what he should say. At some point I look up and make a spur of the moment suggestion.

"You should write it now," I say. "You should just write it."

"Gillian...it's late."

I look at him. "You've been procrastinating about it for a week already. You might as well just write it." I take a breath. "You should invite her to the house. If you want to. If she wants to meet me too, I mean. Maybe we could even invite Jeff—he's her biological uncle, after all. And Dinah, and Josie."

Oliver swallows.

"Are you sure?"

I nod.

I wonder how hard it's going to be for me to control my face when I see hers. If the resemblance will be too much.

Oliver sits down at the small hotel desk, pulls out his laptop. I pour us both a drink. I hear the keys tapping, slowly. When he's done he turns the screen around to me.

"Will you read it?"

"I don't need to see it, Oliver," I say.

"Gillie. I need a second opinion. Read it?"

I read it.

Is it a good letter? Does it say the right things—enough and not too much; does it set the right boundaries? I have no idea.

"It's perfect," I say, and kiss his temple. "Hit Send."

He glances at the time.

"Maybe it's too late."

"Oliver," I say. "Come on. Hit Send."

He swallows, and hits the button. When he looks back at me, his eyes are afraid and glassy.

"Ol..."

He swallows.

"What if—what if she doesn't like me?" He looks at me. "What if I...don't like *her*?"

I look at him.

"I don't know," I admit, then clear my throat, thinking of the line Mom used on me. "But that's a rather gloomy cart you're putting before the horse."

Oliver shakes his head at me.

"I suppose you're right. Come here, Gill." I do, and he taps his plastic beaker of wine next to mine.

"To horses and carts," he says. "In their proper places."

I'm thinking about what Lorna said earlier about the movies we play in our heads. She meant books, but you could say the same thing about our whole lives: how we're all playing a movie in our head the whole time, and everyone's movie is different. I think about Lorna, and how in a while her movie might not be playing anymore. How even the boring parts of the movie are worth being grateful for. And how all our movies tell the same story differently. What would I learn if I could sit in the seat beside Mom's movie projector, and watch how it all looks to her eyes? What would I learn if I'd been able to watch the movie inside Dad's head? What would I see in Abigail's; what would I see in Oliver's?

By the time we're all talked out I feel a sudden wall of exhaustion hit me, as though my brain's been sending me small reminders for hours and now suddenly, like a petulant child, has had enough.

I lie back down on the bed, still in my clothes.

"Gill?" Oliver's voice drifts towards me like a sound through fog. "Are you going to brush your teeth? And take off your clothes?"

"Nope," I grunt. "None of the above."

I hear the slight laugh in his voice.

"Good to know. Hey—move over a little."

I hear the creak and feel the weight of Oliver moving onto the bed beside me. There's the sound of bedding rustling. Oliver's body spoons against mine, his arm around my stomach. The clunk of a heavy men's shoe falling to the floor, and then the other.

Somewhere from deep in my sleepy brain, laughter bubbles up.

"Gill?" Oliver says, bewildered.

"Waiting for the other shoe to drop," I murmur, and wonder how long I've been feeling that way. Weeks, certainly. But months? Years?

I don't think Oliver's heard me, but then he squeezes the arm around my belly. And we lie there a little longer, until a final wave of grateful exhaustion comes over me like a tide, and without a chance to say another word, I'm pulled under.

*

We see them off the next day. Dennis has said he's driving Sam back in the car and Abigail can be in that car or not; her call. She's going, but I know from her face she's going to hold the line. I have faith in her. She's not going to let this relationship claim her again, and sink under.

Sam looks tired. I saw him for breakfast today and he blurted out something about a kid at his school whose parents just got divorced and her mom took her to Disneyland for a week. I didn't say anything or ask him why he'd brought that up. I guess I shouldn't have been surprised. Sam can tell which way the wind's blowing, of course he can. He's smart. And he's strong, too, if you ask me. He and Abigail are going to be okay. They're going to have a hard time but they're going to be okay.

Oliver and I are dropping Mom off at the airport later.

He and I are going to stay, though. I still have a few days before I have to be back at school, and we're going to make the most of it. Those cocktails on Ocean Drive. Time on the beach. Seeing some art museums. Why not? Life is short and full of curve balls, and here we are bang in the middle of it.

I don't know if there's really such a thing as fresh starts. We pretend there is, but you can't go back in time. You can't un-know, you can't undo. But I guess you could also say that starting fresh isn't about innocence; that actually it's about the opposite.

We're flying back in two days' time, on the sixth of January. The Epiphany, I remember. I smile at that.

Epiphany. Well, may it be so.

Chapter Thirty-Three
Six weeks later

The apartment is small, bright, and smells of fresh paint. The second bedroom is big enough for a twin bed and a wardrobe.

"Nice view, isn't it?" The realtor turns to Abigail. They're right, it is a nice view, a few blocks back from the Saw Mill River, looking out towards the Pace University Pleasantville campus. "I'll step outside for a minute," the realtor adds. "And let you ladies talk amongst yourselves."

They go back out into the corridor and Abigail turns from the window and looks at me.

"What do you think, Gill?"

"It's nice," I say, looking out towards the campus green space—not so green right now, but come next month there'll be signs of spring. Meanwhile it has a quiet, austere feeling on this February morning. January turned out to be a beautiful month, all clear skies and air so cold it tickles your lungs. Now in mid-February, it's been getting a little dreary.

"I like it," Abigail says. "It's...different. But I think it could work for me. For us." She took about a million photos as we toured the unit—a pretty short tour, given the cozy size of the place—with the intention of showing Sam later. The second bedroom, of course, is for him. The rent's about right and I guess February isn't a hot time for the rental market so hopefully the odds are in her favor. Her motion for interim alimony is going through the court now, but I guess things have been pretty rough for her the past few weeks. I can see from Abigail's face how much of a toll all this is taking on her, but there's something about her these days that's reminding me more and more of the sister of my early youth. I can see the determination in her, the sheer grit that she's relying on to get through the days.

"That, and caffeine," she joked in the car on our way here.

She drums her fingers on the windowsill. Ringless fingers. The last apartment we went to see, I noticed how the agent quickly glanced down at her hands when Abigail mentioned needing a second bedroom for her son. I didn't mention it but something in Abigail's eyes let me know she'd noticed it too. Maybe it was naive of me to be surprised; I guess I didn't think people still cared so much in this day and age.

Sam's been doing okay, Abigail says. He knows about the divorce and has been upset but not devastated, according to her. Privately, I wonder if he's a bit relieved. She says his main concerns were whether he'd be moving schools and where he'd spend Christmas, but that overall he's doing okay with the news. He's going to a therapist who's working with him on something called "exposure therapy" to treat the OCD; as far as I can make it out it seems to be a fancier clinical term for "feel the fear and do it anyway." The therapist has told Abigail that the job right now is twofold: to treat the compulsion, and also the shame around it, and that treating the shame is actually the more important issue right now. But she says even in a few weeks, Sam seems to have come quite a way. Dennis has taken him to basketball practice this morning, but we're going to pick him up for lunch after the apartment viewings.

Abigail and I talked about Hannah, too: how Oliver Skyped with her for the first time two weeks ago, and how we've agreed that she and her moms will come visit us over February break. How I keep trying to tell myself I'm not nervous, but unfortunately I'm a terrible liar, even to myself.

I'm planning to start a round of IVF treatment over February break too, but oddly I'm not jittery about that. Oliver is, though. But he's feeling the fear and doing it anyway.

"It's supposed to be a pretty good university, you know," Abigail says, her eyes still fixed out the window at the bare trees and lawns of the college campus.

I glance out at the view again, then back at my sister. It occurs to me this isn't just a random observation.

"Have you been looking into it?" I say.

She colors a little and nods.

"I have a bunch of brochures in my tote," she says. "I'll show you later. I have to do *something,* Gillian. I think it's go back to school, or work at a temp agency or something, and that was fine in my twenties but..." Abigail clears her throat. "I was thinking...maybe it would be interesting to study something in genetics. I thought, maybe genetic counseling..."

I look at her.

"That sounds really great," I say, and Abigail nods.

She told me earlier today that Lorna's just started chemo this week. Apparently the first session was okay, but it's supposed to get worse with time, which seems so unfair. Unlike other things in life, this isn't something that your body gets better at the more you do it.

"And you think she's going to stick with it?" I asked.

Abigail shrugged.

"I really hope so, Gill. But in the end it's up to her."

They email now, Abigail and Lorna, and Abigail told me they've talked on the phone since she came back from Florida. Meanwhile, Sam isn't the only one who's started therapy: Abigail's going for the first time too. She told me she feels like there's still this mom-shaped hole inside her, or at least something that's not quite a hole but not quite full, and that she's slowly realizing that neither Lorna nor Mom are going to be able to fix that. That the only person who can really fill it is Abigail.

I glance back out at the university campus, and think of the brochures in my sister's bag. The New Year really is looking to be a year of new beginnings.

"It's true, you know," I say. "You always were the brave one."

She raises her eyebrows at me.

"And you're what, a coward?"

I shrug.

"'Mouse,'" I remind her.

She glances at me, wincing.

"You always hated that name, didn't you?"

I give her a look. Who wouldn't?

"You know I was the one who started it, Gillian? I knew you hated it, but I called you it anyway. Dad didn't mean anything by it. He just called you that because I did; he thought it was sweet."

Sweet?

I stare. Is that true? It's certainly not how I remember it.

"You're very like him, Gillian, you know that?"

I blink.

"Me?" I say. "Like Dad?"

She nods.

"Thoughtful. More on the introvert side. A peacemaker." She looks out the window. Two birds are hopping around in the crook of a branch nearby. It seems way too early for them to be starting on a nest, but I suppose you never know. We've had a little stretch of milder days lately. I just hope they won't get caught out and have to start over. It's painful to watch a creature try so hard.

"You know," Abigail goes on. "The more I think about it lately, the more I think Dad liked how much I *wasn't* like him. I think he got a kick out of people who were really different from him." She weighs her words, and looks at me.

"You're the same way, Gill."

"I am?" I'm so surprised by the whole direction of this conversation. I've never thought about Dad in that way. I've never thought about myself in that way either—drawn to people who were unlike me. But Abigail raises an eyebrow.

"Hello? Oliver? You two are like chalk and cheese."

As far as that goes, actually, I don't think she's wrong.

I'm always looking forward, always planning ahead, whereas Oliver's always mellow, content with the status quo. I'm detail-oriented, he's big picture. I crave quiet nights in front of the television, he loves to go out. I'm fast where he's slow, and slow where he's fast. The more I think about it, the truer it seems. We *are* opposites.

"Right?" Abigail says, eyeing me. "Seriously, Gillian, even back in elementary school. Who was that wild little kid you used to hang around with, the one whose hair I threatened to cut off that time?"

I roll my eyes.

"Melanie."

"That's right." Abigail suppresses a smile. "You couldn't have been more different."

I think back to the people I've gravitated towards in my school days; in college; in the years since. I think of my best friend Dinah, who's so much more outspoken than I am, and of the colleagues I choose to spend time with in the staff room.

Abigail watches me like she sees something dawning on my face.

"Some people want to be around people who are just like them," she says. "I think you've always liked being around people who are different than you."

I think about that

"I guess it's...refreshing?" I say. "Being around people that are different from me."

Maybe it's about contrast. Because contrast helps me see more clearly the traits I value in myself—being careful, say, or a good listener— and it also reminds me that I don't always *have* to be that person. That there are other ways to be. It reminds me that we all have freedom. And that different as we are, we can all belong.

"See?" Abigail says. "I'm right, aren't I?" She looks at me, her face thoughtful. "Do you get it, now? With Dad?"

The funny thing is, I kind of do.

It's like an old wound that has been slowly suturing over these past weeks—not all the way and not all at once, but it does feel different than it used to. Talking about him with my sister, I still feel the old, painful tug, but I'm understanding things a little differently these days. Something new comes into view for me now: how Abigail's personality opened a door for him, a door that only she could be the one to open.

What they had *was* special. But he loved me; he loved me fiercely. I do know that.

"He thought the world of you, you know." Abigail readjusts her tote bag on her shoulder, and turns away from the window. "We all did." She looks at me. "Still do."

I swallow.

She gestures around us at the white-painted walls. "So, Gillian, be honest with me. What do you think?"

I turn my gaze back to it all, and in the small galley kitchen the mica counter glitters briefly as a ray of February sun comes and goes.

"Put in an offer," I say.

She looks at me and smiles.

"I think I will, Gillian. I think I will."

Chapter Thirty-Four
Two weeks later

"*Wow*, Gillian."

Dinah puts her can of "goji berry" seltzer, as Jeff likes to call it—it's just raspberry but he insists we're fancy hipsters—back on the kitchen table.

"I didn't think you were..." she says. "I didn't think that was something you were interested in doing."

I meet her eyes. "I know."

Josie and Sam are in the living room; he's teaching her origami, and the house is already littered with wonky paper cranes.

"I wasn't," I say. "I wasn't interested in adoption at all, before. I think...I think it felt too much like failure."

I clear my throat.

This has been kind of a surprise development for Oliver and me: it's something we've spent a lot of late nights talking about, questioning our feelings, examining them. Checking if we're coming at this from the right angle. If we're being too impulsive, or irresponsible.

"But, I mean..." Dinah says carefully. "If the IVF works out...are you still—?"

"Yes," I say quickly.

Here's the plan: we're starting IVF, *and* we've scheduled to meet with an adoption caseworker who's going to help get us started with filling out an application. This isn't an either/or thing. It's one of the reasons we want to start the adoption process now, before we know what results the IVF might or might not bring. We don't want it to seem—to ourselves or anyone else—that the adoption is dependent on whether we become pregnant or not.

Everyone says the adoption process moves at glacial speeds, but given how spaced out the IVF is going to be, given my teaching schedule and how I basically need to stick to school holidays for while I'm being monitored at the clinic, that's going to move pretty slow too. It's perfectly possible that we might get selected by a birth parent before we have a verdict on the IVF situation.

In short, who knows how the cards will play out, but what our ideal is, is to have both at some point. And maybe it'll happen and maybe it won't, but what a dream it would be to become a family of four this way. I'm not saying it's all the same to us, by the way, pregnancy versus adoption: I know they're different things. Two experiences of gratitude and wonder: the same emotions, different nuances.

What a dream to experience both.

I can't pinpoint when this began exactly. It didn't start as an idea, but literally as a dream. After we came back from Florida, about a week into the new school term, I started having this odd dream. I'd wake up in the middle of the night and realize the doorbell had just rung. In the dream I got out of bed, walked downstairs to the front door. And then, when I opened it, there was a child there.

They'd be standing on the front step, facing away from me, looking out at the sky where the first threads of dawn were showing.

I never saw their face. Every time before they turned around, I woke up. I never even saw if it was a boy or a girl. All I saw was that small, intent body turned towards the horizon.

I think it was after about a week of that dream that I sat Oliver down and asked him what he thought about adoption.

Not as backup. A different kind of gift.

Slowly, something sparked in his eyes that surprised me.

"And what if you end up with both at the same time?" Dinah says, eyes wide. "Gillian! What if you've, like, *just* given birth and then you're going to the hospital to collect this other kid?"

There's an appalled look on her face which she's trying so badly to conceal that we both laugh a little.

I clear my throat.

"I don't know," I say. "I hear you, it probably *is* crazy. But people have twins and survive it. I think we're just...going to do this, and what happens...happens."

I don't discount I'm being a little naive here. In fact I'm almost sure that I am. But isn't that kind of how we survive life in the first place—by staying naive when we need to be?

If we knew how hard things would be, there

would probably be no such thing as marriage, no such thing as parenthood; none of life's big risks. That's life, right?—you have to live it to know it.

And obviously it's full of pitfalls, trying to create a blended family like this. It's rife for jealousy and rivalry and all the rest. I should know, right? But on the other hand, who better than me to do it? I've seen the pitfalls, I get it.

I can't say we'll get it right, Oliver and I. But I'm confident we'll do our best.

Dinah exhales.

"I don't know, Gillian. Rather you than me."

I smile—I don't blame her. I'd play devil's advocate to anyone who suggested such a thing to me, and I can understand that it might seem a bit reckless, but that's why I feel confident about it. Oliver and I aren't reckless people. If we're doing this it means we mean it.

"Well, well," Dinah says, and smiles at me. "It's only February still, and what an interesting year."

Her words jolt me back and I clear my throat, glance out the window.

It's almost two o'clock.

Dinah follows my glance, and looks back at me: supportive; expectant. There's a reason she's here today; and that Jeff's here, and Abigail, watching TV in the next room with Oliver and trying to help him to pretend he's not terrified. A reason why Mom's on her way here too right now. Why I've washed and readied pretty much all the glassware in the house and bought in a ton of finger food—it's a long time since we hosted for nine. It was Mom's idea. At first I thought it would be overkill, but as the time draws near I'm glad there's a little crowd.

"Is my hair okay?" I say to Dinah, feeling another roll of butterflies coming on.

She gives me a soft smile.

"Perfect."

I kind of wish I were drinking again right now. I'm not because of the IVF, but today would be a great day to take a little of the nerves off.

In the living room I hear the television go off mid–ad break, and Dinah and I look at each other as a car door slams outside.

"They're here," I murmur, feeling queasy.

Oliver, Jeff, Abigail, Sam, and Josie file out of the living room into the hallway. Oliver's face is mirroring mine except so much worse.

Two sets of footsteps crunch outside on the driveway. Behind Oliver, out the living room window, I see the unfamiliar car and a woman in the driver's seat who's slowly getting out. The other footsteps sound like they're nearing the house but this woman's hanging onto the car door like it's a life raft, refusing to let go.

"Mom! Come *on!*" a voice calls outside, and I see the woman's face turn. It's an illusion I'm sure—she can't see me from out there—but it's as if for a second our eyes meet.

She's mid-fifties, I guess, around Lorna's age. She's petite; grey-blonde hair trimmed neatly; carefully dressed. And as her gaze locks on our living room window, I see the courage in her eyes, the courage and the fear. It's so transparent that I know it instantly: the universal parent's fear of not being enough. The fear of being in some way supplanted; of finding out after so many years of trying so hard, that somehow you haven't really gotten it right. In this wrung-out moment I sense in her the same prayer I've sent up myself in preparation for this day: *Let them be lovable, God, but not too much.*

My heart squeezes. The woman lets go of the car door at last and pushes it closed, the sound damp and clear in the February air. She steps towards the driveway and out of view of the window frame, and I come back to earth.

"Gillie?" Oliver looks at me.

I nod, and he opens the door.

A girl stands on our doorstep.

I couldn't even say if she's pretty. Perhaps she is, perhaps she isn't, perhaps she's beautiful simply in the way that youth is beautiful. But to me, right now, she drowns out the world. Though I'm dimly aware of the two women standing behind her it's as if they're in shadow; it's as if the girl is shining, almost. Radiant.

Or is it just me with this feeling, as though I'm looking straight into the sun?

Her eyes rove over us, this little group assembled in the hallway. Her gaze finds me, then Oliver. And she holds out her hand and smiles.

It's my husband's smile.

The most beautiful smile in the world.

"Hello," she says. "I'm Hannah."

THE END

A letter from the author

Thank you so much for reading *After She Left*. I'm pretty sure that our most valuable resource these days is time, so it means a lot that you would choose to spend some of your hours with Gillian, Oliver, and their friends.

If you can, I'd be very grateful if you could leave a quick review on Amazon or wherever you purchased your book. For less established authors, it's incredibly helpful as a way of letting other readers know that this is something they might enjoy.

Meanwhile, I thought I'd share a few words with you about this new novel, and what it means to me.

At its core, I believe *After She Left* is a novel about parenthood. Gillian longs for parenthood, to the extent that her yearning to be a mother is even interfering with her daily life (for example, changing pharmacies because of the greeting card rack in her nearby store). When she is initially stuck taking care of her ten-year-old nephew, it only serves to drive home the sense of pain and loss she feels at having to care for someone else's child instead of her own. But soon, she's finding that Sam's presence is opening a door for her, and allowing her to connect with thoughts and feelings she wouldn't otherwise have given voice to. She's reconnecting with parts of herself that she's lost touch with—particularly in a marriage that has lost some of its shine of late. That experience, combined with news of her best friend's pregnancy, is what drives her to confront Oliver with a kind of ultimatum: despite his reservations, she is set on trying IVF.

IVF has become such a huge industry these days, and while it's wonderful to see it giving hope to so many individuals and families, there are admittedly negative sides, too—the huge financial strain it often puts on people, for example, and the rollercoaster of high stakes and stress that can ensue. Sadly it's an opportunity that a lot of people struggle to afford, and at tens of thousands of dollars a pop, it's all too easy to drive hopeful would-be-parents towards debt. In my view, another issue around IVF in our society is how it can focus a lot of blame on women's bodies. As Dr Tremaine in this book points out, the social messaging is not quite in keeping with the medical reality.

I wanted to try to offer a fair portrait of a couple struggling with this problem—not just with infertility itself, but of this fundamental disagreement of how to address it. While I have huge sympathy for Gillian, I can also see Oliver's position. Things that require major medical intervention tend to scare us, usually with good reason. Oliver also feels that Gillian has been 'disappearing' somewhat from their marriage already, and he's afraid that starting into IVF will carry her further down that obsessive road, and that he'll somehow end up losing the woman he married.

The irony, of course, is that Oliver has already participated in IVF, without ever consciously thinking about it in that way. As a sperm donor, he is already someone else's biological father, a revelation that has blindsided him and that he hasn't known how to break to Gillian.

What's interesting to me here is what it makes us ask ourselves about family, bloodlines, and identity. I wholeheartedly sympathize with Gillian's desire to have a biological child, and her (at least initial) strong preference for this over adoption—I don't think this desire is anything to be ashamed of. And yet as we see elsewhere in the book, blood often doesn't mean as much as we think it does. Oliver's biological child—his "donor daughter"—may over time become someone special in her life, but he's not her father and never will be. Meanwhile, Abigail experiences some disillusionment of her own that her biological mother, Lorna, doesn't fill the hole she feels after discovering the truth about her birth. And yet that blood connection can feel threatening to others—Oliver's blood connection with a biological daughter is deeply threatening to Gillian, and the truth about Abigail's birth was kept secret expressly to avoid exactly these kinds of jealous comparisons and moments of self-doubt.

Hopefully what all of the characters in the story come to see is that while blood is often a good starting-point for family, it's not necessary and nor does it define us. Family, after all, is built upon love, and as Gillian points out, upon "time—the way a house is built upon stone". The way I see it, a family that defines itself by blood defines itself by exclusion—by putting up a barrier between it and the rest of the world—whereas a family that defines itself by love, is opening itself to the world, and defining itself by inclusion. That feels like an important message to me, as someone from a binuclear family whose family members are not all blood relatives.

Finally, a word on OCD and mental health in general. I hope I have done justice to Sam's situation here; it's important to note that it is obviously not a comprehensive representation of OCD, which can manifest in such a huge variety of ways and, like many conditions, can range from very acute to "sub-clinical" (meaning, in the case of mental health issues, symptoms are so mild and non-disruptive that we simply see them as aspects of personality).

In the end, everybody's different, and labels and diagnoses can be useful for some people and less so for others, so this book isn't meant to offer any "instructions" on how a parent should proceed if their child is behaving in a some atypical way. But I do believe that when problems have patterns, understanding the patterns helps us address the problems. With that in mind, if this story does help some people, parents or otherwise, to be more attuned to the challenges of OCD, then I'll be so glad to have been able to offer that help. If you would like to learn more about OCD, here are some resources that might be useful to you:

☐The Child Mind Institute's guide to OCD in children: http://childmind.org/guide/parents-guide-to-ocd

☐NAMI, the National Alliance on Mental Illness: https://www.nami.org

☐The International OCD Foundation: http://iocdf.org

Thank you again for spending time with Sam, Gillian, and their families, I hope you enjoyed it.

All my best wishes,

Claire

Acknowledgements

How wonderful to be on Book Number Three...and with every book, I realize with increasing gratitude how many people are to be thanked for enabling me to get this far.

First of all I just have to thank you, the reader. I am, of course, beyond grateful to the many readers who've bought a book or two of mine, or who've recommended it to a friend, or shared mention of it on Facebook. Word of mouth is still the most important and meaningful advertisement a writer can hope for, and it makes me so happy that readers have found things in these pages they want to share.

More than that, though, it has been such an eye-opening experience to have readers actually reach out and write back to me on occasion, giving me little tidbits and stories about their worlds, from how the weather is in Colorado, to how many grandkids they have and whether they, too, have dreamed of being writers. Sometimes I find myself opening an email that feels like it's been written to a friend instead of a stranger. How lovely it is that through reading my books, without ever meeting, we have in some sense managed to become friends. I continue to feel quite humbled by the warmth and generosity that people show. Thank you so very much. Particular thanks to the small group of advance readers who read pre-release copies. Your enthusiasm makes me feel like a million dollars and your feedback is so valuable.

Thank you, then, to all my beloved friends and family who have been so generous with your good wishes, your crossed fingers, your time and your energy. I continue to be particularly grateful to Natalie Butlin for our ongoing conversations about the publishing world and everything besides, and I won't forget in a hurry helping Réachbha Fitzgerald unpack the boxes in her new home only to discover not one, but a full trove of copies of The First Wife's Secret. Thanks again to Maggie Gales, first proofreader and as ever one of my chief sanity officers. Thanks to Halle and Stephanie Amore-Bauer, Sarah Dickman, Jack Paterson, Henna Silvennoinen, and everyone else who helped give this book a little nudge out of the gate.

I'm grateful to my first ever Zoom bookclub, the Women's Institute group of Darbyshire led by Stella Shoesmith, and arranged by Caroline Shoesmith; and indeed to Maureen Mitchell for her event organizing also! To all my family in Dublin and London, I'm so chuffed and appreciative of the interest and pride you take in the new releases, thank you so much for that. Thanks as well to the extended Lowe family, and to the Massachusetts branch of my Irish clan--Janet, Barb, Glenn and their families--who have really been generous with their support. It is all appreciated!

Finally, thanks to Mum, Dad, Frank, and Manuel. You are a tremendous bunch of people, and I'm so very lucky. Thanks for promoting my books so shamelessly to all your friends and no doubt various unfortunate strangers! Thanks for the love, pride, and happiness shared, and most of all, thanks for celebrating with me.

Love,
Claire

Made in the USA
Middletown, DE
24 June 2022

67625282R00246